It Was an Awful Shame and Other Stories

It Was an Awful Shame and Other Stories

Charlotte MacLeod

Five Star • Waterville, Maine

Five Star First Edition Mystery Series.

Published in 2002 in conjunction with
Tekno-Books and Ed Gorman.

Set in 11 pt. Plantin by Rick Gundberg.

Printed in the United States on permanent paper.

Library of Congress Cataloging-in-Publication Data

MacLeod, Charlotte.
   It was an awful shame and other stories / Charlotte MacLeod.
     p. cm.—(Five Star first edition mystery series)
    ISBN 0-7862-4174-8 (hc : alk. paper)
    1. Detective and mystery stories, American. I. Title.
  II. Series.
  PS3563.A31865 I85 2002
    813'.54—dc21   2002023274

Contents

Foreword
by Elizabeth Peters

How wonderful to have Charlotte's stories back in print! And what a pleasure to discover that the stories are as fresh and charming as I remember.

Charlotte MacLeod is best known for her comic mystery novels, which are so hilariously funny some readers fail to observe their other strengths: skillful plotting and character development and unobtrusive erudition. This collection shows her range: from wicked satire ("Homecoming") to eeriness ("Force of Habit"), from the brilliant goofiness of "The Mysterious Affair of the Beaird-Wynnington Dirigible Airship" to . . . But I will say no more, for fear of spoiling the surprises in store.

Some readers labor under the delusion that short stories are easier to write than full-length novels. After all, they are shorter. A delusion it is. A short story is not a chunk cut out of a longer book; it is, or should be, a complete work in itself. The form has its own challenges and not all writers can handle them.

Some short stories can be turned into novels. If I had to select my favorite of all Charlotte's shorter works, it would probably be "Rest You Merry"—one of those tales one reads with a broad grin and frequent guffaws of laughter. It is perfectly constructed and complete in itself. But it later became the first chapter of the novel of the same name, and in Charlotte's skilled hands it worked just as well.

Charlotte took another story in the present collection, "It Was an Awful Shame," twisted it around, shook it up, added and subtracted and multiplied, and developed it into *The Convivial Codfish*, one of the most delightful volumes in her Sarah Kelling series. For those who are interested in the craft of writing, a comparison of the short story and the novel is a lesson in how to do both, and do them right.

But the primary function of fiction, as Charlotte herself has always maintained, is to entertain. This collection is entertainment of the highest quality.

Go for it.

It Was an Awful Shame

"The Coddies gave a party just about a week ago.
Everything was plentiful, the Coddies they're not slow."

With an ever-so-knowing wink, Exalted Chowderhead
Jeremy Kelling of the Beacon Hill Kellings raised his foaming
flagon and quaffed. In accordance with time-honoured ritual,
the other Comrades of the Convivial Codfish gulped in
unison, then slapped their own tankards down on the emerald green tablecloth with one great, unarduous thwack.

"They treated us like gentlemen, we tried to act the same,
And only for what happened, sure it was an awful
    shame."

Again the tankards were raised, this time in gallant toast to
the plump and pleasing person in kelly green who sailed into
the room bearing the Ceremonial Cauldron. Behind her in
single file marched the Highmost, Midmost, and Leastmost
Hod-carriers.

As Mrs. Coddie, for such was her title, set the Cauldron in
front of Jeremy Kelling, the three Hod-carriers clicked the
poles of their hods smartly together, then stepped back in
order of precedence to form a guard of honour behind their
Exalted Chowderhead. Jem tied an oversize green linen

9

napkin under his bottom chin, then went on with the incantation:

"When Mistress Coddie dished the chowder out, she
   fainted on the spot.
She found a pair of overalls in the bottom of the pot."

The Comrades had engaged many Mistress Coddies in their long and sometimes glorious history, but never one who swooned with more elan or finesse. As they rose in admiration of their recumbent hostess of the day, Comrade Bardwell voiced the consensus.

"By gad, this Mistress Coddie is a ring-tailed doozy with a snood on."

"Any objections or abstentions?" said the Exalted Chowderhead.

There being none, he raised the Ancient and Timeworn Overalls which had occasioned Mrs. Coddie's well-feigned swoon slowly from the cauldron.

"Fluke Flounder he got fighting mad, his eyes were
   bulging out.
He jumped upon the pi-an-o and loudly he did shout."

This year, Comrade Archer of the real estate Archers was Fluke Flounder. Despite his fourscore years and then some, despite the fact that he had to be boosted to the top of the Steinway by a dozen comradely hands, right loudly did Comrade Archer in good sooth manage to shout:

"Who threw the overalls in Mistress Coddie's
   chowder?
Nobody spoke, so he hollered all the louder."

★ ★ ★ ★ ★

And, by George, he did. So did they all. In reasonably close harmony, making up in volume for what they lacked in tone, the Comrades bellowed their way through the ballad composed in 1899 by George Geifer and bastardized in 1923 by Jeremy's late uncle Serapis Kelling.

At the end of the first chorus, Mistress Coddie (actually Mistress Cholmondely of the Perkins Square Cholmondelys) recovered her senses with fine dramatic effect and rose to take away the Ceremonial Cauldron, into which the Exalted Chowderhead had again lowered the Ancient and Timeworn Overalls with due ceremony and pomp. Escorted by the Highmost, Midmost, and Leastmost carriers, she bore away the sacred relics and returned with a tureen full of genuine codfish chowder.

Excellent chowder it was, and full justice did the Comrades do it. Not until the tureen was bone dry did they quit baling. And not until Jeremy Kelling had untied his green napkin from beneath his nethermost jowl did he realize he was no longer wearing his insignia of office.

"The Codfish," he gasped. "It's gone!"

"It fell into the Cauldron, you jackass," said Comrade Archer, who'd got his wind back after a bellyful of chowder and several more restorative flagons.

"I didn't hear it clink."

"Of course you didn't. You're deaf as a haddock and drunk as a skunk."

This was the kind of after-dinner speaking in which the Comrades delighted. They kept it up with variations and embellishments while their leader commanded the Keeper of the Cauldron to go get the goddamn thing and bring it back. This done, the Exalted Chowderhead personally shook out the overalls, fished in the pockets and down the mortar-

11

crusted legs to the accompaniment of ribaldries most uncouth, and finally stuck his head into the empty pot.

"It's not there," he wailed.

"Then it's under the table, where you generally wind up, you old souse," shouted Archer the wit.

It was not. It wasn't anywhere. That cumbrous chain of heavy silver with its dependent silver codfish, so recently ornamenting Jeremy Kelling's neat little paunch, was now vanished like the chowders of yesteryear.

"You forgot to put it on," sneered the Highmost Hodcarrier. "Softening of the brain, that's all. Nothing to worry about. Let's have our Codly coffee."

All hailed this sage counsel except the Exalted Chowderhead. A relative infant among the Comrades of the Convivial Codfish, being yet on the sunny side of seventy, Jeremy Kelling had labored long to achieve high office. He'd worked his way up from Journeyman Bouncer to Leastmost Hodcarrier. He'd been Fluke Flounder for one halcyon term, during which he'd pulled a calf muscle leaping to the piano and strained a tonsil putting too much fortissimo into his shouts.

At every meeting and frequently in between, he'd dreamed of the day when he would wear the Great Chain, sit behind the Ceremonial Cauldron, and show these clods how to run a meeting. His installation had taken place only last month. This was the first time he'd got to officiate. How breathtaking had been the moment when the Great Chain was withdrawn from its secret hiding place by the Opener of the Shell and hung around his palpitating neck. At the end of the meeting, the Chain was supposed to be returned to its hiding place with the Secret Valedictory Chant. How the hell could he conduct the concluding ceremonies without the blasted Codfish?

12

Where, Jeremy asked himself as he sipped with less than usual relish at his whiskey-laden coffee under its cargo of whipped cream, had the damn thing got to? The Great Chain couldn't have fallen off. Its overlapping links had been clinched together forever and aye by an old-time artisan, there was no clasp to come undone. The only way to get it away from him would have been to lift it over his head.

Quod erat absurdem. An experienced toper like Jeremy Kelling could never have got drunk enough on a paltry few schooners of special dark to be oblivious to any such trick as that. Furthermore, he'd been in full view of all the Comrades ever since he'd donned the Chain, and there was not such unanimity of spirit among them that somebody wouldn't have ratted on anybody else who made so free with the revered relic.

As the Codly coffee mugs were replenished, speculation about the Chain's disappearance grew more imaginative. Everybody naturally accused everybody else of codnapping. They took to visiting the men's room in squads to make sure nobody was trying to sneak the Codfish off in his codpiece.

Mrs. Coddie, of course, was exonerated, firstly because she'd been under escort by the three Hod-carriers all the time, secondly because she'd been in her swoon during the time when the fell deed was most likely to have befallen, and thirdly because she proved to be somebody's mother.

At last a thorough search of the room was conducted, with all the members crawling around the floor on hands and knees, barking like a pack of foxhounds, but finding nothing. For the first time in the club's history, they had to close the meeting without the Valedictory Chant, though a few Comrades gave it anyway either because they were too befuddled not to or because they always had before and they damn well would now if they damn well felt like it.

Most appeared to regard the Great Chain's disappearance as a jolly jape and to be confident it would turn up at the April meeting pinned to the seat of the Ancient and Timeworn Overalls. Jeremy Kelling was not so sanguine. His first act on returning to his Beacon Hill apartment was to fight off the ministrations of his faithful henchman Egbert, who took it for granted Mr. Jem must be sick because he'd come home sober and perturbed instead of sloshed and merry. His second was to put in an emergency call to his nephew-in-law, Max Bittersohn.

"Max, I've lost the Codfish!"

"I knew a man once who lost a stuffed muskellunge," Max replied helpfully.

"Dash it, man, cease your persiflage. The Great Chain of the Convivial Codfish is a sacred relic. Like the grasshopper on top of Faneuil Hall," he added to emphasize the gravity of the situation. "It disappeared while I was removing the Ancient and Timeworn Overalls from the Ceremonial Cauldron."

"That was probably as good a time as any," said Max. "The Chain didn't fall into the pot, by any chance?"

"How the hell could it? I looked. Anyway, the thing was around my neck. I'd have had to fall in, too. Which," Jem added, "I did not. I'd have remembered. I'm not drunk. Egbert can testify to that."

"Put him on," said Bittersohn.

Egbert, to their mutual amazement, was able to vouch for his employer's unprecedented sobriety.

"It's very worrisome, Mr. Max. I've never seen him like this before. Except sometimes on the morning after," he qualified, for Egbert was a truthful man when circumstances didn't require him to be otherwise. "I think he might be described as shaken to the core."

"To the core, eh? Okay, let me talk to him again."

14

Max Bittersohn was a professional tracker-down of valuables that been stolen, pawned by spouses faced with private financial emergencies, or otherwise detached from their rightful owners. Thanks to his expertise, he was able to extract from Jem a complete and perhaps even reasonably accurate account of what had happened. He offered words of cheer and comfort, then went back to his Sarah, who did not want to hear about her uncle's missing Codfish, she being a recent bride with other things on her mind.

In truth, Bittersohn himself gave little thought to Jeremy Kelling's dilemma until the following evening when Egbert dropped by to break the tidings that Mr. Jem had fallen downstairs and broken his hip. Sarah was horrified. Max was intrigued.

"Fell downstairs? How the hell did he manage that? Jem hates stairs."

"The elevator appears to have been stuck on the top floor, Mr. Max."

That was credible enough. The building where Jem and Egbert lived had an antique elevator about the size of a telephone booth, that wouldn't work unless it had been tightly latched by the last person who got out of it, which frequently didn't happen.

Jem's usual procedure in such cases was to bellow up the elevator shaft until somebody was goaded into going out and shutting the door properly. In desperate circumstances, however, such as when it was Egbert's day off and he'd run out of gin, Jem had been known to walk down the one flight of stairs from his second-floor apartment. This had been one of those times. Now he was over at Phillips House with a brand new stainless steel ball where the hip end of his left femur used to be. Egbert thought Mrs. Sarah and Mr. Max would want to know.

"Of course we do," cried Sarah. "How ghastly! Bad enough for Uncle Jem, of course, but think of those poor nurses. What happened, do you know?"

"All I know is, I got home about five o'clock and found him sprawled on the floor of the vestibule, yowling his head off. He said Fuzzly's had called to say his whiskers were ready and they'd be closing soon, so he'd rushed out, found the elevator stuck, and gone cavorting down the stairs. There was no darn need of it, you know. I could perfectly well have gone and got them tomorrow morning but, you know Mr. Jem. He wanted those whiskers."

"What for?" asked Max.

"The Tooters' railroad party," Sarah told him. "Uncle Jem was going to dress up in Dundreary whiskers and Grandfather Kelling's old frock coat, and impersonate Jay Gould."

"Did Jay Gould have Dundrearies?"

"Who knows? Anyway, Uncle Jem was all in a dither about the party. He's an old railroad buff like Tom Tooter."

"Do you mean model trains?"

"No, that's Tom's brother Wouter. Tom collects real trains. He has his own steam locomotive and a parlor car with velvet-covered settees and fringed lampshades. Also a dining car and a caboose."

"Any particular reason?"

Sarah shrugged. "I suppose he got them cheap. The Tooters have always been in railroads. Anyway, Tom and his wife are having an anniversary and Tom's rented the B&M tracks for the evening. They're going to have a string ensemble playing Strauss waltzes and a fountain spouting champagne."

"My God," said Bittersohn. "Jem will have apoplexy at missing a bash like that."

"He was in a highly aggravated state of profanity when I

16

left him," Egbert agreed. "They were about to administer a sedative."

"I don't wonder." Sarah poured Egbert a tot of their best brandy, for he was an old and beloved friend. "Here, have one yourself, then Max will walk you home. Go to bed early, you're going to need your rest."

"Truer words were never spoken, Mrs. Sarah."

"At least a broken hip ought to take his mind off that silly Codfish for a while. He's been phoning every hour on the hour to see whether Max has found it yet."

"As a matter of fact, his parting bellow was that I—er—call the matter to Mr. Max's attention."

Max grinned. "In precisely those words?"

"Not precisely, Mr. Max."

"Tell him I'm hot on the trail. More brandy?"

"Thanks, but I ought to be getting along."

"Come on, then."

The two men set out to walk the short distance from Tulip Street to Pinckney. "Who else is going to the party?" Max asked. "The whole Codfish crowd?"

"No, I believe Mr. Jem was the only Comrade invited, except for the Tooters, themselves, of course, and Mr. Wripp, who's recently had a cataract operation. Mrs. Tooter felt the outing would do Mr. Wripp good."

"No doubt," said Bittersohn. "What office does Mr. Wripp hold?"

"Mr. Wripp is a Formerly Grand-Exalted Chowderhead. Being by now ninety-two years of age, he appears content to rest on past laurels. Oh yes, and Mr. Obed Ogham will be among those present. So maybe it's all for the best that Mr. Jem won't."

"Why? Don't he and Ogham get along?"

"None of the Kellings get along with Obed Ogham, Mr.

Max. He's the bird who sued Mr. Percy Kelling for two dollars and forty-seven cents he claimed Mr. Percy overcharged him. That was after Mr. Percy's accounting firm had helped Ogham recover the five and a half million dollars Ogham's comptroller had been swindling him out of."

"Oh yes, the King of the Crumbs. How come he and Jem both belong to the same club?"

"There have always been Kellings and Oghams among the Codfish," Egbert explained. "Neither is willing to cede his ancestral right. Noblesse oblige, as you might say."

"But don't the Tooters know Jem and Ogham are feuding?"

"They're not exactly feuding, Mr. Max. I believe it's more a matter of maintaining a haughty silence in each other's presence."

Max found his mind boggling at the notion of Jem's maintaining a haughty silence in anybody's presence, but he was kind enough not to say so.

"Besides," Egbert went on, "Mr. Ogham and Mr. Wouter Tooter are this year's Highmost and Leastmost Hod-carriers respectively. It's not the done thing for one Hod-carrier to exclude a Comrade of the Hod from any of his routs and junkets, personal feelings notwithstanding. Comrade White, the Midmost Hod-carrier, would normally have been included, too, but he's just left for Nairobi on a business trip. Mr. Jem was to have escorted Mrs. White."

"Mrs. White's a good-looking, well-dressed woman somewhat on the buxom side and fond of a good time in a nonthreatening sort of way, right?"

"You know the lady, Mr. Max?"

"No, but I know Jem. And the rest, I suppose would be friends of the Tooters?"

"I expect they'll be mostly railroad buffs and members of

Mr. Wouter Tooter's model railroad club. It won't be a large party, since the parlor car can't accommodate more than thirty or forty people comfortably."

"That sounds like a lot of money to spend on a relatively small affair, wouldn't you say?"

"Between you and me, Mr. Max, I think it's partly what they call public relations. Somebody's been spreading a rumor that the Tooter enterprises are in financial difficulties. I shouldn't be surprised if making a splash now is their way of squashing the rumor before their stock starts to drop."

"Very interesting. Well, here's the old homestead. Mind if I come up with you?"

"Thanks, Mr. Max, but you mustn't feel obliged."

"I want to see where it happened."

"Just a second till I find my key. Ah, here we are. There's the staircase, you see, and Mr. Jem was on the floor at the foot."

"Marble floor, I see. Damn good thing he didn't go down headfirst. Who uses the stairs as a rule?"

"Nobody, unless the elevator gets stuck. I used to, I have to say I find them more of a climb than I like nowadays."

"Did Jem say how he happened to use them today?"

"He said there was a power outage just as he received the phone call from the shop. The lights were out and the radio went off. That meant the elevator wouldn't be working either, of course. A very unfortunate coincidence. My mother always claimed bad luck came in threes. First the Codfish, and now this. What next, is what I'm wondering. Do you think we can count Mr. Jem's having to miss the party as the third piece of bad luck, Mr. Max?"

"I'm not sure we should count any of it as just luck. What happened to the clothes he was wearing when he fell?"

"I brought them home from the hospital and dropped

19

them off before going on to your place."

"Good. Let's have a look."

The tiny elevator was sitting in the lobby, its folding brass gates meticulously fastened. Word of Jem's accident must have got around. Max and Egbert squeezed in together and rode to the second floor. Egbert fetched the clothes and Max pulled out a magnifying glass.

"Aha! See that, Egbert?"

"A grease spot on his pantleg? Mr. Max, you don't think I'd have let Mr. Jem go around looking like that? He must have done it when he fell."

"My thought exactly. There's grease on his shoe sole, too. Got a good flashlight?"

"Oh yes, I always keep one handy."

"Come on then, let's see which stair got buttered."

It was Egbert who first noticed the brownish glob under the fifth tread from the landing. "Would this be what you're looking for, Mr. Max?"

Bittersohn rubbed a little on his finger and sniffed. "It sure as hell would. Bowling alley wax, I'd say. It's been cleaned off the step with some kind of solvent, but whoever did it forgot to wipe underneath, probably because he was in a hurry to get away. I'll bet he was hiding in the cellar while they were lugging Jem off. Let's go call on the neighbors."

The first-floor people were away. On the third floor lived an elderly lady, her cook and her maid. The lady was out playing bridge with her maid in attendance because Herself didn't like going out alone at night, the cook explained. "Can I give you a cup of tea in the kitchen, now?"

The two men were happy to accept. "I see your electric clock's right on the dot," Max remarked as they sat down.

"Has to be," said the cook. "Herself likes her meals prompt to the second."

"You haven't had to reset it lately?"

"No, I haven't touched it in ages, except to dust it now and then when the spirit moves me."

Cook was plainly glad of company and ready to talk, but she didn't have much to tell. The first-floor people were in Palm Beach, and had been for the past two months. Her own household hadn't known about Jeremy Kelling's fall until they heard him being taken away in the ambulance. Herself considered him to have been struck down by a Mighty Hand in retribution for his ungodly and riotous ways. Cook personally thought Mr. Kelling was a lovely man, always so kind-spoken when they happened to meet, which wasn't often because Herself was of the old school and believed in servants using the back stairway. This very night, Mary the maid had been required to go down the back way, around the alley, and walk back up to the front door while Herself used the elevator in lone elegance. Mary might get to ride up after Herself when they got back, it being so late and good maids hard to come by.

"That's nice," said Max. "Thanks for the pleasure of your company. The cake was delicious."

"Would you be wanting a piece to take to Mr. Kelling, now?"

Egbert expressed the opinion that Mr. Jem would prefer a cake that had a bottle of Old Grandad baked into it, and they parted on a merry note.

Going back to Jem's flat, Max asked, "Egbert, would you have a recent picture of that Codfish crowd?"

"Scads of them, Mr. Max. Mr. Jem keeps an album of all the doings since he joined the club."

"Great. Where is it?"

New Englanders love to look at photograph albums, for some reason. They spent quite a while over this one. Jem had each photograph neatly labeled. He himself appeared in most of them wearing various appurtenances of office. The latest showed the Great Chain of the Convivial Codfish adorning his well-padded front.

"I'll take this," said Max.

Egbert was alarmed. "Mr. Max, if anything should happen to that album, Mr. Jem would have a stroke."

"I'll guard it with my life. Where's his invitation to that ungodly revel he was supposed to go on?"

"It's a ticket. Mr. Tooter had them printed up special. Can't ride the train without a ticket, you know." Egbert produced the precious oblong. "Is it a clue, do you think?"

"Who knows? Anyway, Jem won't be needing it now. Sleep tight, Egbert. Sarah will be over to the hospital at crack of dawn, I expect, so take your time in the morning."

Max took his leave, pondering deeply. The next day, leaving Sarah to comfort the afflicted, he first collected Jem's whiskers from Fuzzly's, dropped in on some pals at the Fraud Squad, lunched with a prominent member of the Securities and Exchange Commission who owed him a favor, had a chat with his Uncle Jake the lawyer, paid a call on a fair and buxom matron who was mystified, gratified, and eager to cooperate; and finally went home to placate his wife.

"Sorry I can't have dinner with you tonight, sweetie-pumpkin."

"And where are you off to, pray tell? What are you getting all dressed up for?"

"A train ride," he replied from the depths of a starched shirt. "Seen my studs lately?"

"You might try your stud box. Uncle Jem wants to know when in blazes you're going to catch his Codfish."

"Anon, I hope. One kiss, my bonny sweetheart, I'm off for a prize tonight. With the voluptuous Mrs. White, in case some kind friend thinks you ought to know."

"In that disgusting clawhammer coat? Where on earth did you get it?"

"Same place I got these." He put on Jem's Dundreary whiskers. "How do I look?"

"Don't ask. I'm going next door and cry on Cousin Theonia's shoulder. Mrs. White, indeed! I hope she singes your whiskers."

Mrs. White was ready and waiting when he went to pick her up. They had some trouble stowing her into the taxi on account of her bustle, feather boa, and a hat freighted with a whole stuffed pheasant; but at last they were able to proceed.

On Track Four at North Station, business was booming. A conductor in a stiff cap and brass-buttoned uniform was joyfully clipping tickets. Max recognized him from Jem's album as Tom Tooter, their host. Up ahead in the engine cab, a melancholy individual wearing a high-rise cap of striped ticking, greasy striped overalls, and a tremendous scrubbing-brush mustache leaned out to survey the throng flocking aboard. This could be none other than Wouter Tooter, throwing himself into his role.

Max himself received some puzzled glances as Mrs. White introduced him right and left as her dear, dear friend Mr. Jay Gould. People must either be putting him down as somebody they'd met before but couldn't place, or else making mental notes to have a quiet chat with Mr. White when he got back from Nairobi.

Mrs. Tom Tooter was doing the honours inside the parlor car, wearing silver lace over a straight-front corset, with white gloves up to her armpits and strings of pearls down to her knees. She looked a trifle nonplussed when Max made his bow, but pleased to have such a good-looking man aboard even if his ginger side whiskers did clash rather ferociously with his wavy dark hair. Luckily, Mr. Wripp tottered in just behind him and had to be fussed over, so Max escaped without a grilling.

The lights were dim enough to make all the ladies look charming and all the men distinguished. There was no fountain splashing champagne, but they did have a swan carved out of ice to chill the caviar, and a bartender wearing red arm garters and a black toupee neatly parted down the middle. Max got Mrs. White a white lady, which seemed appropriate, then turned her over to her friends and went prospecting.

Tom Tooter was in his glory. He'd changed his conductor's cap and coat for a Prince Albert. He bagged at the knees and bulged at the shoulders, but what did he care? Kings might be blest, but Tom was glorious, o'er all the ills of life victorious. He couldn't possibly be the man Max was looking for.

Mrs. Tooter kept glancing at her husband with fond wifely indulgence and brushing imaginary specks off his lapels as women do in public places where decorum forbids more overt displays of affection. Max indulged himself for a moment in thinking that if Sarah were here, she might be brushing specks off his lapels, then got on with his job.

Obed Ogham was easy to spot and would no doubt be a pleasure to dislike. He was one of those loud, beefy men who trap people in corners and tell them a lot of stuff they don't want to hear. Max stayed well clear of him. He'd be the sort to ask personal questions of strangers.

Wouter Tooter was not in the parlour car. Various guests were asking for him; no doubt cronies from his model railroad club as they wore trainmen's caps with their false whiskers and old-fashioned clothes. Tom said he was around somewhere and why didn't they come into the dining car?

This was an excellent suggestion, Max found. Rows of tables with snowy napery and genuine old railroad cutlery were set out around a long center buffet laden with hams, roasts of beef, whole turkeys, hot dishes under metal covers the size of igloos, cold platters of every description, and epergnes dripping with fruits, sweets, and exotic flowers. Edward VII would have found it adequate.

Waiters hovered ready to fetch and carry. A wine steward wearing a silver corkscrew on a heavy silver sommelier's chain circulated among the tables murmuring recommendations through a well-trimmed but all-covering beard. He sounded as if he had a marble in his mouth. Max took one long, earnest look at the wine steward, then slipped out into the vestibule. When the man came through, Max tackled him.

"Mr. Wouter Tooter, I believe? Changed your overalls, I see."

"Who the hell are you?" mumbled the man.

"You'd better take that marble out of your mouth, Mr. Tooter. You might swallow it. To respond to your question, my name's Bittersohn and I'm a private detective sent by the Securities and Exchange Commission to guard Mr. Obed Ogham. They don't want anything to happen to him before he's indicted."

"Indicted? What for?"

"You don't really have to ask, do you? You know damn well Ogham's trying by highly illegal methods to scuttle your brother's firm so he can make a killing on the stock market. That's why you're playing wine steward tonight with the Great Chain of the Convivial Codfish."

Wouter looked down at his chest as if he thought it might possibly belong to someone else, and said nothing.

"That's why you deliberately disabled Jeremy Kelling, so that he couldn't come tonight and catch you wearing the chain. Your brother's too busy with the guests to notice, and old Mr. Wripp's too bleary-eyed from his cataract operation. Ogham might catch on, but he's not supposed to live long enough to rat on you, is he?"

"I don't know what you're talking about."

"Like hell you don't. You cut off the electricity in Jem's apartment yesterday afternoon and waxed the stairs. Then you put in a fake phone call from Fuzzly's, knowing that would send Jem charging out to get his whiskers. He'd find the elevator inoperative, gallop down the stairs, and take a toss, which he did. And you've got some kind of muck in your pocket right now that you're planning to drop into Ogham's wine as soon as he's drunk enough not to notice. You needn't bother. He's on his way to jail, though he doesn't know it yet. Your brother's business is safe and so are you, on two conditions."

"What conditions?" said Wouter sulkily.

"You leave Ogham alone and you show me how the hell you got that chain off Jem's neck."

"Oh." Light dawned on what little Max could see of Wouter's lavishly disguised countenance. "I know you now. You're the bird who married Jem's niece. The pretty one who's always getting murdered."

"Right. And you're the wise guy who landed your buddy in the hospital with a broken hip."

"Well, hell, what was a man to do? I couldn't make Tom listen to reason. He simply refused to believe even that reptile Ogham would scuttle a Comrade. Jem won't mind once he knows I did it for Tom. I knew the old sculpin would land on his feet, he always does. This time he bounced on his backside first. Too bad, but it was in a good cause. Surely you must realize that."

"Couldn't you just have asked Jem to stay away from the party?"

"Jem Kelling miss a bash like this? You must be out of your mind. I'd have had to explain why, then all Jem would have done was swagger in here, waltz up to Obed, and paste him straight in the mouth. He'd have to stand on a chair to reach that high, I expect, but he'd do it. You know Jem."

Max did know Jem, and he could not dispute Wouter's logic. "Okay, if you can make that sound sane to Jem, more power to you. What were you planning to fix Ogham's wagon with?"

"Just a Mickey Finn. I thought I'd make believe he'd passed out from too much booze, drag him to the observation platform supposedly to sober up, and shove him overboard. Then I'd take off my disguise and go back to being me."

"While Ogham was found suffering from minor contusions and rushed to the nearest hospital, where the doctors would start wondering how he got bunged full of chloral hydrate and your nice family train ride would turn into a major scandal. Nice going, Tooter."

"Well, damn it, I never committed a murder before. This seemed like a good idea."

"Take it from me, it stinks. Hand me the chloral and show me how you worked the Chain."

"Oh well, there's nothing to that." Wouter gave Max the little bottle, then took off the Chain. "You see, last year I was Opener of the Shell, which meant I had custody of the Great Chain. Just for fun, I split one of the links and inserted a tiny magnetic coupling to hold it together. You'd need a magnifying glass to see it."

"No problem." Max had one, of course. Wouter's craftsmanship was indeed masterful.

"It's worked by a remote-control switch. I meant to open it as a joke sometime, but when this foul business with Ogham came up, I got the idea of wearing the Chain and posing as a wine steward. No sense in going out and buying one when I'd never use it again, was there?"

"Hardly," said Max. He was feeling a trifle dizzy by now.

"You see, I'm Leastmost Hod-carrier this year. That means I get to stand behind Jem when he pulls the Ancient and Timeworm Overalls out of the Cauldron. This is all highly confidential, topsecret stuff, of course, so don't breathe a word to a soul. So anyway, then Mrs. Coddie swoons. I knew they'd all be watching her, so I released the Chain, grabbed it as it fell, and slid it down inside my own overalls. As soon as I could, I slipped into the men's room, put the Chain around my own neck under my clothes, and wore it home."

"Not bad," said Max. "How were you planning to get it back?"

"Frankly, I hadn't thought that far ahead. Maybe I could write old Jem a ransom note and deliver it myself. I could slink in wearing all this face fungus."

Wouter started peeling off false eyebrows and chin-whiskers. "Might as well get my money's worth out of it. Fuzzly's aren't expecting it back till tomorrow afternoon. In the meantime, I can put the Codfish back on the Chain. Had to switch it for a corkscrew, you know. I mean, without the Codfish, the Chain's just a chain."

"That did occur to me," said Max. "Also, since you fiddle around with model railroads, I thought you might be pretty good at midget switches and convenient power failures. If I may make a suggestion, you'd do better to send Jem the corkscrew and a bottle of something by way of penance."

"Damn good idea. I'll make it a case of burgundy. Speaking of which, now that I've resigned as wine steward, let's you and I go put on the feedbag. Then we can go up to the engine. Maybe the fireman will let us shovel some coal."

A Cozy for Christmas

"So Max has gone off with another woman?" Cousin Brooks Kelling appeared to find the circumstance highly entertaining.

"Wearing false whiskers and great-uncle Nathan's Prince Albert coat." Sarah Kelling Bittersohn didn't think it was funny at all. "He looked so handsome it made me sick."

"Men are all brutes," Cousin Theonia Kelling, wife to Brooks, gave her own particular brute a smile of total adoration. "Whatever possessed Max to do a thing like that?"

"He alleges it's in aid of that insane business about our somewhat beloved relative and the Great Chain of the Comrades of the Convivial Codfish," Sarah told her. "I suppose it's all my own fault for having helped Uncle Jem nag him into tracking it down, which doesn't make me feel any better about being left to pine alone and desolate." Sarah, like all the Kellings except Cousin Mabel, was a Gilbert and Sullivan aficionado. "You don't mind my inviting myself over?"

This time, Theonia's smile was for Sarah. "My dear, how could we?"

Aside from the fact that both Brooks and Theonia would have welcomed Sarah's company under any circumstances, there was the added point in her favor that she owned the house. During the lean years after the death of her first husband, the Tulip Street brownstone on Boston's historic Beacon Hill had been virtually Sarah's only asset, and a heavily mortgaged one at that. To keep herself afloat, she'd turned it into an ever-so-elite boarding house.

Now she was married to one of her former boarders, the handsome and affluent Max Bittersohn, a private detective who'd been a specialist in recovering vanished art objects when she met him but had lately developed a sideline in dragging beleaguered Kellings back from the brink. The newlyweds were living next door in a small apartment while their new house on the North Shore was being built. Brooks and Theonia had taken over the running of the boarding house, an arrangement that suited them all just fine.

"You'll stay to dinner?" Brooks was urging.

"Of course she'll stay," said Theonia. "It's quite all right, Sarah. Our top floor back has gone to Denver for the holidays."

Numbers were always a consideration at the boarding house, its lovely antique dining table could only seat eight in the elegant comfort the Kelling establishment demanded. Elegance had been Sarah's watchword from the start. Right now they were getting an early start on the customary predinner ritual by being served elegant little glasses of rather inelegant sherry from an extremely elegant Waterford decanter by a white-gloved butler who was the absolute epitome of elegance now that he'd had his missing tooth bridged in.

So as not to lower the tone, Sarah had come over in a full-skirted green velvet dinner gown and her second-best diamonds. Theonia was in deep crimson and pearls. The two were sitting together on the library sofa, against a backdrop of greens obtained at no expense from the North Shore property. Flickering lights from the open fire and soft gleams from the red candles on the mantelpiece fell benignly on Sarah's soft brown hair and Theonia's piled-high raven tresses, highlighting the one's delicate youthful beauty and flattering the other's middle-aged opulence.

"Well, if you two ladies aren't the very spirit of Christmas!"

Mrs. Gates, their all-time favorite boarder, had emerged from her first-floor suite and was making her careful way into the library. She herself made a charming picture in a long black gown set off by a fleecy white woolen shawl and an old-fashioned parure of gold and garnets. Charles the butler hastened to pull the old lady's favorite Queen Anne chair a little closer to the fire while Brooks gallantly escorted her to it.

"Thank you, dear boy."

She smiled up at Brooks, the firelight doing wonderful things to her spun-silver hair. "Just hang my work bag on the arm of the chair here, where I can get at it easily. You'll all forgive me if I go on with my sewing, won't you? I promised last February to make some tea cozies for this year's Holly Fair at St. Eusapia's. Now here it is the night before the fair and I'm still trying to finish the last one."

"Oh, it's exquisite!" Sarah exclaimed as Mrs. Gates drew out the cozy cover she was working on. This was a confection of blue moiré taffeta, embellished in the more-is-better Victorian mode with garlands of creamy satin ribbon, ruchings of lace, flirtings of fringe, plus a scattering of sewn-on pearls and an occasional sprig of embroidery to reassure the purchaser that no avenue had been left unexplored. "You must have spent ages. How many have you done?"

"Six counting this one and I must say I'm glad it's the last. If you'll thread my needle for me, my dear, I'll let you tidy my work bag. When my granddaughters were small, they used to think that was the greatest treat in the world."

"And so shall I."

As Theonia went to make sure everything was under control in the kitchen, Sarah perched on a footstool beside Mrs.

Gates's chair, taking a childlike pleasure in sorting out the bits and pieces. "There's enough of the blue taffeta left to do another," she remarked. "Do you think you will, sometime? They must be great fun."

Mrs. Gates sighed. "I thought so when I started last spring. By now I'm so sick of them that I recoil at the mere thought. Take the taffeta and trimmings if you'd like to try one yourself."

"Do you mean it? May I really?"

Sarah had been wondering about a tea cozy for Max's mother. Herself a Wasp of the Waspiest, she was having a hard time reconciling this year's holiday observances between what she'd been brought up to and what might be acceptable to her recently acquired Jewish in-laws. Max thought they ought just to forget the whole thing, but Sarah was far too thoroughly schooled in how easy it was to start family feuds among the multitudinous Kellings to risk one with the Bittersohns. Family relations were desperately important, even if they did add to the agonies of holiday shopping.

Only that afternoon, she'd bought her new sister-in-law a soufflé dish and been rather badly mauled in the process. It would be lovely if she could manage to concoct an acceptable tea cozy rather than having to shop for one, though Sarah knew she'd never in the world come up with anything that compared to Mrs. Gates's. It would, of course, be possible to go over to St. Eusapia's tomorrow and buy this lovely thing if somebody else didn't beat her to it and if she could bring herself to pay the small fortune the church folk would undoubtedly be asking. And why shouldn't they? It would be criminal to let workmanship like this go for a pittance. St. Eusapia's was a wealthy parish, they'd find customers enough.

Sarah folded the oddments of fringe and ribbon inside the

32

remnant of taffeta and stowed the small packet in the capacious side pocket, which was one reason why she'd chosen this particular gown. The other boarders were beginning to trickle in now, it was time to sit up and be a credit to the establishment.

Naturally the boarding house had seen some turnover in its clientele since Sarah had turned the keys over to Brooks and Theonia. The basement room that had for a while been Max Bittersohn's was now occupied by a flautist who looked melancholy and Byronesque but was in fact a jolly soul when he didn't have a concert to play. Since Mr. Snowfjord was performing tonight, he was saving his breath to swell his arpeggios. As far as the conversation was concerned, his silence wouldn't matter a bit; Mr. Porter-Smith could always be counted on to talk enough for two. One of Sarah's original six, Eugene Porter-Smith was a certified public accountant who worked for Cousin Percy Kelling. Tonight he'd given his familiar maroon dinner jacket a Christmassy touch with a bright green tie and a cummerbund to match.

Miss Jennifer Lavalliere, another of Sarah's holdovers, showed up wearing a brand-new two-carat diamond on her fourth finger left hand and little else worth mentioning. She was delighted to show off the ring to her former landlady and to tell her all about the young man who'd bestowed it, plus a few catty tidbits about the one who'd gone to Denver for the holidays days.

Ms. Carboy, who shared the third floor with Miss Lavalliere, was a relative newcomer to Tulip Street: a long-boned, long-faced woman of forty-odd who reminded Sarah of Virginia Woolf. She had some sort of extremely high-powered job over at Government Center about which she tended to be inscrutable, possibly because the job was not in truth all that high-powered. She admired Mrs. Gates's handiwork at some length and made the gaffe of asking whether she might buy it then and there.

"I'm so sorry," Mrs. Gates replied a shade too sweetly. "I've committed myself to supplying six of these for my church fair, and that's all I've managed to do, assuming I get this done tonight. If you really want one, I'm afraid you'll have to buy it over at St. Eusapia's between ten and four tomorrow."

Ms. Carboy sighed. "Then I'm afraid I'll have to do without it. I'll be tied to my desk all day and possibly far into the night. There's always so much paperwork to get through at the end of year."

The sherry-sipping wound to its stately close, the butler announced dinner, Mrs. Brooks Kelling seated her guests. The flautist finished his soup, took two mouthfuls of the main course, excused himself, and rushed out into the night. The rest of the party partook of the excellent meal at their leisure and went back to the library for coffee.

Mrs. Gates picked up her work again and asked Sarah to rethread her needle. "I've just this last little bit to do. Then I'm finished, praise be!"

"What are the others like?" Sarah asked her. "Did you make them all the same?"

"Oh, no, each one is different, otherwise I'd surely have gone mad. I'd show you but they're all wrapped up and stowed away in a shopping bag for Charles to take to the church tomorrow morning."

Sarah would have been quite willing to repack them, but she knew better than to ask. She drank her coffee, said her good nights, and went home to try her hand with the left-overs.

She'd had no high hopes to start with; after a couple of hours she was quite ready to call a halt. The cozy cover she'd achieved looked only superficially like the one she'd tried to copy; it might do as a stage prop, but wouldn't do much to cement her somewhat tenuous diplomatic relations with Mother Bittersohn. Sarah was wondering whether to go to bed or sit and have a good pout when Max telephoned. The party had ended in catastrophe, he was stranded in the hinterlands, and would she drive out to pick him up?

They got to bed late, which meant a delayed start the next morning. Sarah got Max off on his detectival rounds, then set off herself in quest of Mother Bittersohn's tea cozy. On a previous safari, she'd seen some attractive ones at reasonable prices in the shop she still thought of as the Women's Educational. By the time she got there today, though, the only cozies left were striped red and green and appliquéd with saucy elves. Sarah didn't think Santa's elves would achieve their purpose in this particular instance.

The shop held lots of other delights, though. She wandered around for quite a while choosing trinkets for this one and that of her myriad relatives and buying herself a tote bag to carry them home in. After that, she popped into Bailey's to recruit her flagging energies with a hot fudge sundae and sat longer than she'd meant to, scooping up driblets of fudge sauce and trying to remember which of the Back Bay's many churches was St. Eusapia's.

Once reasonably sure of her goal, Sarah was faced with the problem of getting there. A taxi would be out of the question, traffic wasn't budging an inch. Outside Berkeley Street subway entrance she heard dire talk of a tie-up down below. They'd had snow earlier in the week, the sidewalks had been imperfectly cleared, drifts which the plows had piled up at the curbs were trodden into a lumpy mess. The wind had come up since morning, the skies were by now as muddy a gray as the frozen slush through which Sarah had to pick her way, along with far too many other gift-laden strugglers.

A Bostonian born and bred, Sarah accepted all this as a matter of course though she could hardly take it in stride, for striding under such conditions would have been dangerous if not impossible. Dressed for the weather in boots and a windproof storm coat with the hood pulled up, she didn't particularly mind the walk, but she did feel relieved when at last she reached the right church and entered the gaily bedecked parish hall.

What with one thing and another, she'd got here much later than she'd meant to. The fair must have been a great success, the merchandise was pretty well picked over and the volunteer clerks looked ready to drop. Sarah found a fancywork table without any trouble, but only one of Mrs. Gates's tea cozies was left on display, and that one a bedizenment of red and green that featured a charming but hardly ecumenical Christmas tree worked in multicolored glass beads.

"Oh, dear," she moaned to the presiding angel, a Miss Waltham whom she remembered from one of her former late mother-in-law's civic committees, "is this the only cozy you have left? I watched Mrs. Gates finish up a heavenly blue one last night and was praying it might still be here."

"As a matter of fact, it still is."

Miss Waltham was a majestic lady with a determined chin and at the moment an even more determined set to her mouth. "The blue taffeta came with a note pinned to it saying 'Hold for W. J. Ronely' so naturally we set it aside. Needless to say, W. J. Ronely has failed to appear. People will do that, you know, make a great to-do about having merchandise put on reserve, then not show up, so we're stuck with a no sale and the church is out the money. I think we've been quite patient enough with W. J. Ronely, Mrs. Kelling. If you're willing to part with eighty dollars for a tea cozy, I'm more than willing to take it."

Sarah forbore to remind Miss Waltham that she was no longer Mrs. Kelling. However, she paid with a check that had her new name printed at the top, partly as a hint that she was no longer as she once had been and partly because she'd somehow managed to get through most of the generous sum Max had given her before he'd left. Miss Waltham accepted the check, took obvious pleasure in removing the "Hold for W. J. Ronely" note, and wrapped the cozy in many swaddlings of tissue paper.

"Thank you so much," said Sarah. "Don't bother about a bag, I have one."

She stowed her hard-won treasure carefully down inside her tote bag and made a quick tour of the depleted tables. The White Elephants were by now a sick-looking herd, but she did find a charming little Staffordshire cat with a chipped but mendable tail that the bargain hunters had overlooked. The bakery table yielded a box of fudge and a bag of ginger cookies at closeout prices. At last Sarah wound up back at the fancywork table where Mrs. Gates's Christmas tree cozy was still displayed in lonely splendor. What could she do except stifle her Yankee conscience and say, "I'll take it."

By this time her tote bag was crammed. Miss Waltham wrapped the sumptuous gaud in all the tissue paper she had left, then slipped it into a crumpled brown grocery bag she fished out from under the counter.

"There's your cozy, Mrs. Bittersohn," she said in a good loud voice to let Sarah know she'd seen the error of her ways, "if that doesn't give somebody a Merry Christmas, I don't know what will."

Sarah thanked her and tucked the bag under her arm. As she turned to go, she was almost bowled over by a tall man in a dark overcoat who looked a bit like Virginia Woolf's brother.

"My name is Ronely," Sarah heard him bark at Miss Waltham. "You have a tea cozy put away for me."

"I'm sorry," Miss Waltham replied, "but we don't. You shouldn't have left it so late. We gave you up and sold the cozy to somebody else."

"But I got stuck on the subway!"

Sarah decided it would be rude to hang around and eavesdrop. She slipped out of the hall as fast as she could, buttoning her coat up to her chin and pulling her hood down over her forehead. The snow that had been threatening on her way over was coming down now; a mean, driving, sleety fall that obviously meant business. Sarah hoped Max didn't get snowbound in the exurbs, she herself would prefer not to be out in this storm much longer. She hurried up toward Arlington Street and was standing in front of the Ritz Carlton waiting for a break in the traffic so she could cross over and walk home through the Public Garden when she was whopped from behind and fell sprawling in the gutter.

The Ritz doorman was with her in an instant. He'd recognized her, of course; Max's clients were the sort of people who'd automatically put up at the Ritz.

"Mrs. Bittersohn, are you okay? That guy shoved you on purpose, I saw him. Did he get your pocketbook? Let me take that shopping bag. Do you want to come in the lobby for a while? Shall I call you a cab?"

"What did the man look like?" was all Sarah could think of to say.

"Tall, skinny guy in a dark overcoat. No use trying to catch him, he ran down the subway. He sure didn't look like a mugger. You just never can tell, can you? Here's your fudge."

"Thank you."

Sarah ought to know the doorman's name, but she was too flustered to recall it at the moment. At least the fudge was all right, the maker had packed it inside a plastic bag. Her handbag was safely hooked over her arm, its excellent clasp still closed. The only thing missing was the brown paper bag that held the tea cozy, the Christmas tree that had not been set aside for W. J. Ronely.

Eighty dollars down the subway. While she rubbed her bruises and straightened her coat, the doorman hunted between the ruts and under the nearest parked cars but didn't find her parcel. Sarah was not at all surprised. In a way she could even sympathize with W. J. Ronely. Christmas shopping was a desperate business; perhaps he, too, had a mother-in-law.

She tipped the doorman lavishly over his halfhearted protest, told him not to bother about a cab because she could make it to Tulip Street faster on foot, a statement he could hardly gainsay since the snow was snarling the traffic even worse than before, though that had hardly seemed possible, and set off across the Gardens.

She wasn't worried about being pursued again by W. J. Ronely. He'd got what he wanted, or thought he had. Even if he found out he'd snatched the wrong bag, he wouldn't know where to look for the right one. Unless he'd happened to overhear Miss Waltham or the doorman call her Mrs. Bittersohn. Bittersohn was not a common name. Max's was the only one in the Boston phone book.

Sarah tried not to look over her shoulder, but she did wish the walking weren't so beastly treacherous. She was astonishingly relieved to reach Beacon Street and cross over to the Hill. Tulip Street was only a matter of minutes now, and she'd be in the lee of the storm most of the way.

Still, when she reached the purple-paned townhouse

where great-uncle Frederick's old army buddy General Purslane and his wife still lived, she decided to pop in and say
hello. She'd give them the fudge, they both loved sweets.

The Purslanes were delighted to see her and the fudge.
"Weren't you a dear to think of us!" Mrs. Purslane exclaimed. "Leave your coat and boots right here by the door,
you're just in time for a cup of tea. What else did you buy at
the fair?"

"One of Mrs. Gates's lovely tea cozies. Let me show
you."

No use lamenting the cozy she'd loved and lost, Sarah was
happy enough to show off the one she had. "Can you imagine
how much work she put into this? You can barely see the
stitches."

Mrs. Gates had constructed her cozies on the usual
pillow-pillowcase principle: a decorated cover and a padded
double semicircle of plain muslin underneath that did the
actual work of retaining the heat in the teapot. Sarah slipped
off the cover so that Mrs. Purslane could appreciate the
perfection of the stitchery even on the underside. As she did
so, she noticed a small incongruity.

Mrs. Gates had formed the padded underpart the natural
way, by stitching the four pieces that made up the double
semicircle together on the wrong side, then turning them
right side out so that the seams would be hidden after the
stuffing was in. The bottom seams were then slipstitched together so meticulously that the joining could barely be dis-
cerned without a jeweler's loupe. For some reason, however,
about an inch and a half of the seam at the top had been
ripped out, then sewn up from the outside with apparent care
but little expertise.

"Mrs. Gates never did that!" Sarah squeezed gently below
the stitches. "I think I feel something. Mrs. Purslane, do you

have a pair of manicure scissors?"

"Here, use this."

Mrs. Purslane fished in her sewing box and handed Sarah a dainty but efficient seam ripper. Sarah picked gingerly at the clumsy stitches, then poked the slender tool through the opening she'd made.

"It's there, all right. I felt it. Can you find me some tweezers?"

"Certainly, just a second."

Tweezers in hand, Sarah fished around a bit and drew out a tiny transparent envelope. The general took one look and sprang from his easy chair.

"Microfilm, by gad! The woman must be a spy!"

"Mrs. Gates is eighty-nine years old and a bishop's widow," said Sarah. "She'd have had no reason to rip out the seam, she could have put the film inside while she was making the cozy. If she did rip the seam, she'd have sewn it up so you'd never have known. I could have done a better job than that myself. What are they of? I wonder."

"We'll soon find out," said the general. "Come into my study, I have a microfilm viewer there. For my book, you know."

The general was, needless to say, engaged in writing his memoirs. He'd been at them for the past twenty-five years or so, to the best of Sarah's knowledge. She and Mrs. Purslane watched with what patience they could muster while he tweezered the mysterious strip of blackness into place and switched on the light.

"What is it, George?" his wife asked impatiently.

"Wait till I adjust the—great Scott! Ladies, I shall have to ask you both to leave this room immediately. And please close the door behind you. I must get on the phone to the secretary of defense immediately. Sarah, you've done your country a service today. Now go straight home and forget all about it. That's an order."

"Yes, General," said Sarah. "But I'm taking my tea cozy with me."

She thanked Mrs. Purslane for the tea, wished her a Merry Christmas, was assured that she'd just given the general one, and faced what was by now a fairly convincing blizzard. Luckily she didn't have far to go. She entered her apartment with somewhat exaggerated circumspection.

Once inside, Sarah told herself not to be silly and started making a business of hanging up her wet storm coat and unpacking her tote bag. Her purchases might as well stay on the kitchen table, she could gift wrap them there once she'd decided which was for whom. As for the blue tea cozy, she got a needle and thread and mended the place she'd ripped out, exploring first with a thin-bladed knife to make sure nothing else was concealed in the stuffing and wondering who'd been at it before her.

The microfilm couldn't possibly have been inserted before Mrs. Gates finished her work. An expert like her couldn't have missed seeing those clumsy stitches while she was putting the cover over the padding. The job must have been done after she'd gone to bed, leaving the packed bag outside her door for Charles to pick up in the morning.

Brooks would have locked the house up tighter than Fort Knox as soon as Mr. Snowfjord got back from his concert and everybody else was safely inside. Nobody would have dared tamper with the bag while others were still about. Assuming that it would have been possible for an outsider to secrete himself anywhere in the house, it would have been impossible for the intruder to depart in the early hours without leaving some chain, bolt, or bar unfastened to give the fact away. Whoever did this thing had to be somebody who'd come in,

42

stayed in, or gone out, if at all, in the accustomed way; confident that Charles would deliver the altered package to the place where it was supposed to go and that church folk would honor the message pinned to the doctored cozy.

There was, Sarah realized, the outside chance that Charles himself had stopped somewhere on the way to St. Eusapia's and waited while someone else did the dirty work. Charles was an actor when he got the chance; like some other actors, he might not always distinguish between what was good theater and what was bad business. If he'd entered knowingly into any such plot, though, Charles must have been involved in some advance planning. Sarah couldn't imagine his not spilling the secret to Mariposa, the housekeeper, with whom he was on what Cousin Theonia sedately described as close terms. And there was no way Mariposa would have let him go through with such a caper.

Theonia could sew as well as Mrs. Gates. Brooks probably could, too, if he tried; he was incredibly deft with his hands. Assuming they could have stooped to treason, which was unthinkable, neither of them would have made so clumsy a faux pas.

Sarah wished General Purslane hadn't been so desperately hush-hush about those films. If they had something to do with figures, such as a proposal for a defense contract, Sarah supposed Eugene Porter-Smith might conceivably be the culprit, assuming Cousin Percy had the sort of client who could get into this kind of trouble. If he did, Percy would probably do their books himself, though, rather than expose an employee to temptation.

If she'd had any idea what that important job at Government Center was, Sarah wouldn't have minded suspecting Ms. Carboy. As she didn't, the question would have to remain moot for now. That anybody would entrust a featherhead like Jennifer Lavalliere with a subversive microfilm seemed insane, but she did have that new fiancé and, as the doorman at the Ritz had so pertinently observed, you just never knew.

Mr. Snowfjord seemed an unlikely prospect but again, you never knew. A musician much in demand must get to meet a great many diverse people; and flautists were of necessity nimblefingered.

Sarah nipped off her thread, slipped the enchanting blue cover back over the mended padding, and supposed she might as well get Mother Bittersohn's present wrapped before it caused any more trouble. On second thought, she wrapped it in aluminum foil and stuck it in the freezer compartment of the refrigerator.

The cover she'd tried to fashion out of Mrs. Gates's leftovers was still lying where she'd left it last night. Sarah found the padding out of an old tea cozy that she'd been meaning to recover sometime, ripped a couple of inches along the top, and picked up a snapshot Cousin Mabel had sent in lieu of a Christmas card. It showed Mabel standing beside an alligator on a Florida key. Mabel always went away for Christmas so that she'd have an excuse not to buy anyone a present. The alligator had the pleasanter smile, Sarah thought as she stuffed the photo inside the padding. She sewed up where she'd ripped, slipped the padding inside her improvised cover, and dropped the finished cozy back on the table.

These were the shortest days of the year. It should have been pitch-dark by now but the fast-piling snow and the old-fashioned streetlights were keeping the cityscape a ghostly, shimmering charcoal gray. As a rule, Sarah would have been happy to stand looking out at the street, enjoying the play of light and shadow, the eerie beauty of car headlights approaching at a crawl, small as blurry flashlight bulbs, then looming bigger and brighter and blurrier, changing to ruby aureoles as the cars passed by and the taillights came into view, shrinking and shrinking and fading away into the blur. Tonight she pulled down the window blinds and shivered a little as she went back to the kitchen.

Brooks would be here in exactly fourteen minutes to put up the last of the curtain rods. Brooks was always punctual to the dot, but fourteen minutes seemed a long time to be waiting by herself. The upstairs neighbor was at home, Sarah had heard the dragging footsteps and the tap of the cane. Mrs. Levits would have been housebound all day, like the Purslanes. She put some of her bargain cookies on a little plate and ran upstairs, too impatient to wait for the antique elevator, which was the size of a phone booth and slow as molasses running uphill in January.

Mrs. Levits was pleased with the cookies and avid for a long winter's chat; Sarah had to explain that she couldn't linger because she was expecting her cousin. Not being a fool, she used Mrs. Levits's phone to make sure Brooks was on his way before she went back downstairs, and waited for him on the landing. When they went in together, she was not much surprised to feel the draft from a broken pane in the door that led to the fire escape, to discover melting snow on her clean kitchen floor, and to notice that her faked-up blue tea cozy was gone.

"Good Lord, you've had a burglar," Brooks exclaimed. "Check your valuables, Sarah, while I call the police."

"No, don't call them," said Sarah. "I know what he took."

She told Brooks her story. He wasted no time on questions, but whipped out his tape and measured the broken pane.

"I have window glass at home. It will take me roughly eight minutes to nip over, cut a piece to size, and bring it back. Do you want to come with me?"

Sarah shook her head. "I ought to be all right here for a little while, surely, now that Ronely thinks he's got what he's after. I'd better stay and report to General Purslane."

She stuck a folded newspaper over the broken pane to shut out some of the cold air and picked up the phone. She was still talking to the general when the doorbell rang. Assuming it was Brooks with the glass, she said good-bye and went to punch the button that released the downstairs catch. Somebody thumped up the stairs—certainly not Brooks, he walked like a cat—and pounded on the door.

"United Parcel. Package for Bittersohn."

"Just leave it by the door," Sarah called out.

"You have to sign for it."

"Sign my name yourself. I'm in the bathtub."

If this was a bona fide UPS delivery, the driver would be in a mad rush to get back to his truck, which would be blocking however much of the narrow one-way street was still passable, and would do as she'd said rather than face Tulip Street again in this weather. If the messenger was bogus, Sarah preferred not to find out the hard way. Brooks could pick up the parcel when he came, if there was one.

She wished the door had one of those modern peepholes so she could see what the man looked like. It did have an old-fashioned keyhole, though, not used any more since a modern chain and deadbolt had been installed. Sarah knelt, flipped aside the tiny metal flap that covered the hole, and squinted through.

All she could see was a pair of hands in black leather gloves, carefully lowering a brown paper package to the floor. Since the package was about the size of the box of fudge she'd given the Purslanes, this seemed a remarkably delicate way to handle it. Maybe there was a "Fragile" label but even so—she

46

jumped as the messenger turned and leaped for the stairs, taking them three at a time from the sound of the thumps. She caught one fleeting glimpse of a black boot and something brown, but that was all.

Brooks had been gone a little over four minutes, she'd let the package sit there until he got back. Then Sarah remembered the absurdly cautious way those gloved hands had set the small thing down, and lame Mrs. Levits up above, and the pokey old elevator down below.

It was crazy, it was impossible. No matter, it was a risk she must not take. Sarah opened the door, bent her knees, and very, very tenderly picked up the package.

The box was neatly wrapped. Her name and address were clearly typed on what looked like a standard UPS label. The sender's name was obscured, the paper was not stuck down with tape, and the fancy red-and-green Christmas string holding it together was tied in a simple bow knot. In God's name, what did one do now?

Standing there with the box in her hands and her heart in her throat, Sarah glared frantically around the living room. Next to the gas fire sat a market basket she'd stuffed with greens and red alder berries as an apology for the tree they weren't going to have. As fast as she dared, she settled the box among the greens and carried it out to the fire escape.

On Tulip Street, the townhouses were set in a solid row with tiny backyards opening on a service alley. Across the alley stood the backs of the houses that faced on the next street over. Some previous tenant had rigged an endless clothesline on pulleys between Sarah's fire escape and the one opposite; surely not to hang out washing in this posh historic area, more probably to ferry small articles across to a friend.

With a piece of wide red ribbon she'd snatched in passing from among her gift wraps, Sarah tied the basket to the lower section of the filthy but still intact clothesline and pulled on the upper part to send it bobbing out into the empty space above the alley.

She could see the basket well enough in the glow from the street lamp beneath and the light streaming out from her own kitchen. It looked incongruously festive with its freight of greens and the perky red bow she must have tied, though she didn't remember doing so. An automatic reflex, everybody was tying bows this time of year. She stepped over to the telephone and rang the general again.

"This is Sarah," she told him. "Perhaps I'm overreacting, but somebody's just left a package at my door. The messenger said UPS, but the box is so insecurely wrapped they'd never have accepted it. No, of course I didn't open the door. I peeked through the keyhole. The messenger set the box down much too carefully and dashed off in a terrible hurry. No, I've hung it out on the clothesline. I just hope whoever lives across the way doesn't think—oh, I must have waked a pigeon, Shoo! Shoo!"

Boston pigeons do not shoo easily. This one settled on the edge of the basket, causing it to tilt a little, to Sarah's horror, and began picking off alder berries in a methodical and businesslike fashion. Sarah kept an eye out while the general asked questions she couldn't answer.

Now the pigeon had tired of alder berries and gone to work on the package. It had the red-and-green string in its beak, tugging with all the weight and expertise a tough, street-wise bird might reasonably be expected to possess. The pigeon braced against the handle and jerked harder. The knot gave way. The basket exploded with only a muffled pop, but the huge ball of flame lit up the whole area just for a moment, then charred fragments began drifting down, vanishing into the enveloping grayness.

She was supposed to be a fragment.

"Never mind the bomb squad, General," she said dully. "The pigeon set off the incendiary. I'm glad he got the alder berries."

She hung up on the general and was still standing there with her arms dangling limp when Brooks came back. Opening the door took all the nerve she had.

"Sorry I took longer than I meant to," he apologized. "Ms. Carboy was just coming in and waylaid me on the steps."

Sarah came alive again. "What was she wearing?"

"Eh? Oh. Black boots and gloves, brown coat, and a brown fur hat." Brooks was a birdwatcher, he noticed details. He wouldn't be wrong.

"I have to call the general again," she said. "This will mess up your sherry hour."

"Why? Sarah, what's happened? You're white as a sheet."

"Just a minute, Brooks. General Purslane, are those secret service men still with you? Wonderful! Have them come immediately to the Kelling house on Tulip Street and pick up a woman named—what's her first name, Brooks?"

"Virginia."

"Naturally, what else? Virginia Carboy. Tall, thin, long-faced, about forty-five. She's the one who put the negatives in the tea cozy, attached the note, and delivered the bomb. Now, please. She may try to bolt once she realizes she hasn't set this house afire."

Sarah reconfirmed the address, broke the connection, and dialed again. Charles answered, fortunately.

"Charles, this is Sarah. Don't so much as lift an eyebrow, but you and Mariposa make absolutely sure Ms. Carboy doesn't get out of the house. Somebody's on the way to pick her up, she has to be there when they arrive. Knock her out and tie her up if you have to, but do it quietly."

49

★ ★ ★ ★ ★

Evidently violence had not been necessary. Watching out the front window while Brooks reset the glass in the door, Sarah had seen the secret service men rush to the house, seen Charles let them in with precisely the right blend of unruffled dignity and patriotic cooperation. She'd seen Ms. Carboy being led from the house in handcuffs and stowed safely away in the unmarked vehicle that had managed during its brief stay to fill the lower half of Tulip Street with a Yuletide medley of honking horns and drivers' curses.

"I can't imagine it was Cousin Mabel's photograph that turned Ms. Carboy into a homicidal maniac," said Sarah. "It must have been Mr. Ronely who broke in and took the blue tea cozy, don't you think? Ms. Carboy wouldn't have had time to commit a robbery, then rush back for an incendiary bomb, even if she'd had one kicking around her bedroom where Mariposa would be apt as not to set it off when she cleaned."

"I quite agree," said Brooks. "They wouldn't have had time to liase, as General Purslane would no doubt describe the action. Anyway, the reason for that elaborate rigmarole with the tea cozy has to have been that they couldn't afford to be seen together. Otherwise, she could simply have walked up and handed him the negatives."

"So the bomb was a preplanned attempt to kill me," said Sarah. "Because Ronely, or whatever his real name happens to be, got the wrong tea cozy the first time around, I suppose. He may have thought I knew what he was up to and tricked him on purpose. Or else he was simply afraid I'd be able to identify him as the man who mugged me in front of the Ritz. Somehow or other he must have got word to Ms. Carboy that she was to deliver the fire bomb instead of just shooting or stabbing me because they didn't want it known I'd been deliberately murdered. If the arson squad had managed to detect signs of the bomb afterward, I suppose a story would have been gently leaked to the effect that Sarah Kelling Bittersohn was a known terrorist. Ugh!"

"Here," said Brooks, "you'd better have a nip of your own brandy. I don't know but what I might have one myself. What do you say we light the gas log?"

"You do it," Sarah replied. "I lit the last fire, I and the pigeon. It burned to death, poor thing."

"Better the pigeon."

That was a major concession from Brooks, who was normally on the side of his feathered friends. "Sit down and warm yourself, Sarah. I'd better start fixing that broken window."

While Sarah was finishing her brandy and Brooks was puttying the window, Charles snatched a moment from his service in the library to telephone that Ms. Carboy had been only too willing to rat on Mr. Ronely as soon as she realized the jig was up. Even now the secret service men must be closing in on him at a secluded rendezvous where he was trying to peddle Cousin Mabel and the alligator to a clandestine representative of an unfriendly foreign power. And Mrs. Brooks desired to ascertain whether Mr. Brooks would be back in time for dinner.

Brooks said Theonia had better not count on him because he still had Mrs. Sarah's curtain rods to hang. He then went on with his carpentry while Sarah roused herself from the gas log and began wrapping presents including Mother Bittersohn's tea cozy, which she now felt safe enough to take out of the freezer. Not to rock the boat, she used plain white paper and noncontroversial blue ribbon.

Max came home exhausted from tracking down clues and battling the storm, sorely in need of wifely consolation. She got him a drink and settled him down by the fireside with her and Brooks to discuss the case he'd been working on, which was a particularly intriguing one with many ramifications of interest to the analytic mind. Then Max got a telephone call that made him realize he'd inadvertently set up Sarah's uncle, of whom for some reason she was fond, to be the killer's next victim. Thereupon, all three of them charged off into the blizzard to ward off yet another disaster.

By the time they'd rescued the uncle, got the murderer safely jugged, and floundered their way back to Tulip Street, none of the three wanted to do anything except crawl into bed and stay there. Sarah had all but forgotten her own adventure until Max, warming his cold nose against the back of her neck, asked sleepily, "How did the shopping go?"

"All right," she replied. "I bought your mother a tea cozy."

"That's nice," he said, and fell asleep.

After a moment's reflection, Sarah did the same.

A Snatch in Time

I never did feel really comfortable with Carter-Harrison. I just wasn't in his class. I mean, I'm a Fellow in Gastroenterology and my mother thinks I'm the Mayo brothers, but actually I'm just one of the boys. Fellows, I mean. But Carter-Harrison is a Brain.

Everybody knew it from the day he entered the Research Center. Nobody could tell anybody what he was working on, but we were sure that when he finally published, it would be something big. So I suppose I was flattered when he started walking from the lab to the subway with me after work. Not that we had much in common, but we were the only two who didn't have cars, and I guess even a Brain needs some sort of human companionship.

He was a lot older than I. Almost forty, I'd say. When a man gets that old in Boston without forming a meaningful relationship with somebody or other, you can bet there's something askew somewhere. In his case, I think it was just preoccupation with his work. He didn't seem to have any social life whatever except what he got from our nightly strolls. When I realized this, I began trying to make them as interesting as I could. Had I but known, I'd have kept my mouth shut.

The hospital we work out of is in a pretty crummy section. "It's hard to believe," I remarked one night in early December as we passed a Southern Fried Pizzeria, "that this was once the classiest residential area in the city."

"Was it?" said Carter-Harrison with a polite imitation of interest.

"Yes, and not so long ago, either. This old guy I was running a GI series on once told me he used to be coachman to a rich family who lived here. The place was so exclusive they had big iron gates at the head of the street that used to be locked every night to keep the rabble out."

"They left them open once too often," snarled the Brain as a grubby kid on roller skates slammed into him and tried to pick his pocket. "That's interesting. Really interesting."

This was the first time he'd shown any genuine enthusiasm for a remark of mine. I embroidered the theme. "Don't you wish you could see the place as it was then, with the carriages hauling up to the doors and the girls swishing downstairs in their bustles?"

"It was an entirely different way of life, certainly. A gracious, ordered existence where a man could do his work without being under constant pressure to produce results."

He practically snorted those last words. I was surprised. Nobody had been pressuring him as far as I knew, but maybe I didn't know. Anyway, he got off on some train of thought and didn't speak again all the way to the station.

In fact, that was the last I saw of him for a week.

He hung a *Busy* sign on his door and just stayed inside. I wouldn't bust in on a Brain, of course, but I did wonder what he was up to. Then White Fang, my department head, started wondering what I was up to, so I buckled down to my ulcers and more or less forgot about him.

It was the following Tuesday night when he finally emerged. He stuck his head in at my door around half-past five, said, "Coming, Williams?" just as usual, and I came. He didn't say much else until we'd got to where the avenue makes a sort of circle with a fenced-in lot full of beer bottles and wastepaper in the middle. Then he stopped and looked at me in a funny sort of way.

"Do you recall what we talked about when we were last here?"

"Sure." I combed my gray matter frantically. "Oh, you mean about this being such a swanky place once."

"Yes, and you said you wished you could see it as it used to be."

"So?"

"Here." He pulled a little box out of his pocket. It had something like half a jump rope attached to each side. "Take a handle."

"What's this?"

"Did you ever read *The Time Machine*?"

"Oh brother," I said with my usual tact and savoir-faire.

"It's perfectly safe," he said earnestly. "I tested it on myself last night. It won't put us back more than seventy years or so, and the effect wears off in half an hour. Just keep hold of that handle and you'll be fine."

I wasn't scared, you understand. I merely assumed all that gray matter had jelled. Better humor him, I thought, so I grabbed the handle. "Okay, I'll swing, you jump."

He grasped the other handle. The box swung between us, suspended by its two wires, and began to buzz. I braced myself for a shock, but not for the one I got. As I stood there feeling like a nut, my eyes suddenly blurred. I blinked, and opened them in another world.

Another Boston, anyway. The chain-link fence around the traffic island had vanished. It really was a little park now, and the avenue was cobblestoned instead of blacktopped. The houses all looked spruce, the shops were gone. And sure

55

enough, a barouche with a pair of matched brown horses was pulling up in front of us. When the coachman jumped down to open the door, he almost knocked me over.

"Hey, watch it," I said, but he paid no attention.

"That man can't hear you," said Carter-Harrison, "or see you either. We haven't materialized."

"What?" I said stupidly. I could see the Brain all right, looking just as weedy as ever with a sticky handprint still on his coat where that kid had tried to pick his pocket. "What is this, hypnotism?"

"Oh no. We've actually been transported back in time, as it's popularly called. I'd have to get involved with what might be termed paranormal phenomenology to explain the situation. You could say we're sharing a dream if it makes you feel any better."

"Did you ever see a dream walking?" I did. She was getting out of the carriage. She was wearing a blue velvet coat and a hat freighted with a full cargo of white ostrich plumes. I wished I had my Chicken Inspector badge on.

Even the Brain was goggling. Looking back, I believe this must have been the first time he'd ever thought to take a good, close look at a woman. Nor was it pure scientific interest I saw gleaming in his eye.

"Come on!"

Dragging me by our strange umbilical cord, he loped up the stairs after her. A housemaid in a white cap and apron opened the door. We crowded in so close behind her we practically stepped on her skirt, but neither she nor the maid seemed to be aware of us. We found ourselves in a gaslit miasma of polished mahogany and aspidistras, with our fetching period piece peeling off her gloves and asking the maid was Uncle John home yet?

"Yes, Miss Arabella, and Mr. Martin with him. Will you

be wanting Mary to help you dress for dinner?"

Arabella said she supposed so, and headed upstairs. Carter-Harrison charged after her as Teddy Roosevelt probably hadn't yet charged at San Juan Hill. Not caring to strain the wire and blow a fuse among all these beaded lambrequins, I had to charge, too.

"What do you think you're doing?" I panted, as if I didn't know. "We can't go barging into her bedroom."

"Why not? She won't know."

"What if we materialize?"

"We can't. I haven't figured out how."

"Are you planning to?"

"I've got us this far, haven't I?"

At that moment, Arabella slammed the heavy paneled door in our faces.

"I dare you to open it," I said.

"I can't," he replied sadly. "We have no physical strength."

"Then how about if we just ooze through?"

"Don't be ridiculous."

Luckily—or not, depending on how you figure it—another white-capped maid came along and again we squeezed in after her. Don't ask me what Arabella's bedroom was like. I'm no good at describing anything but gastric juice. It's bright emerald green, if you want to know. Anyway, there was a lot of furniture and stuff, and Arabella was sitting in front of a dressing table with her head on a pincushion, having a good cry.

I'm no more comfortable around a weeping woman than the next man. My first thought was to get out of there fast. My second thought was, "How?" The door was shut again and Carter-Harrison wouldn't have budged anyway. He just stood there looking. Obviously this was one field in which he'd never done any research.

The maid started fluttering around with smelling salts. "Now Miss Arabella, don't go making your pretty eyes all red."

"I don't care. I wish I were hideous."

"Miss Arabella, you don't mean that."

"Yes I do. If I were an ugly old frump, that horrible Mr. Martin wouldn't be hanging around."

"Lots of girls would be glad of a rich beau like Mr. Martin."

"With that red face and fat stomach? I can't stand him. Honestly, if Uncle John makes me marry that man, I'll stab him on the wedding night. With my buttonhook, I think."

"Now Miss Arabella, it's wicked to talk like that." Mary unpinned the ostrich plumes and started taking down Arabella's hair. I heard Carter-Harrison catch his breath as it came tumbling down her back.

I remember my grandmother boasting that she could sit on her hair when she was a girl. Arabella could have sat on hers, I guess, but she didn't. She just sat there, sniffing and mopping her adorable face with a little lace handkerchief while the maid brushed out that cascade of light brown curls. Finally she sighed and stood up. The maid began unfastening her dress. It had about a million little hooks and eyes down the back. Every time another one let go, I felt a degree more fidgety.

I sneaked a look at the Brain to see what effect they were having on him. Believe it or not, he was blushing. He caught my eye and blushed even more deeply. "Damn it, Williams, I feel like a cad."

I have never before encountered anybody who felt like a cad. The only response I could think of was, "This was your idea."

About then, Mary reached the last hook. Carter-Harrison turned around and shut his eyes. Not wishing to be thought a cad, I did the same. Then I burst out laughing. I couldn't help it. There we were, conducting what must surely be the most amazing technical experiment of our age, standing in a woman's bedroom with our eyes shut. I was still laughing when the timer shut off and we found ourselves back on the sidewalk outside Madame LaFifi's Beauty Garden with traffic snarled all over the avenue and 1963 looking crummier than ever.

Carter-Harrison wound the two wires around the box, stuck it back in his pocket, and started walking toward the subway. I fell in beside him. His car came first. He said, "See you tomorrow," climbed aboard, and that was that.

Well, you can imagine the state I was in for the rest of the evening. I poured a drink, but it didn't have any kick in it. I tried a paperback thriller, but it failed to thrill. I even tried to study, but my head wouldn't work. At last I went out and bowled until I was tired enough to go home and sleep.

I had a particularly interesting batch of gastric juice the next day, which kept me from thinking much about Carter-Harrison and his time machine until he stopped by my lab just at closing time. When we got outside, I asked him, "Did you bring the jump rope?"

"Oh yes," he said perfectly deadpan. "It's in my pocket."

I didn't ask him anything else because he set such a pace I needed my breath to keep up. We made it to Madame LaFifi's in three minutes flat. Then darned if he didn't stop, pull out his box, and give me one of the handles.

"Here we go again," I remarked tritely, and sure enough we did. There was the park, there were the prosperous-looking brownstones with their lace curtains and Christmas wreaths, but no barouche this time. We stood there dithering on the cobblestones until I fancied a Keystone cop with a hard helmet and a walrus mustache was giving us the hard eye, but nobody went in or out of Arabella's house.

I'd have liked to stroll around and see more of the neighborhood, but the Brain wouldn't budge. First he'd look down the street, then he'd look up at the house, then he'd look over toward the iron gates, then he'd begin again. He got tangled up in the wires from turning around so much, but that was all the excitement for a while. Finally, Arabella peeked out from around the parlor curtains. She didn't see us, of course. That was a pity. It might have cheered her up to see Carter-Harrison with his beat-up hat pressed to his scraggy bosom and his mouth half open in silent worship.

"I wonder if Martin's coming to dinner again tonight," I speculated. "She sure looks down about something."

"Damn him!" The venom in the Brain's voice startled me so I broke the connection by dropping my handle.

"Oh hell, I'm sorry," I said.

"It would have run out in another minute or so anyway," he muttered. "I'll have to boost the—" something or other.

"So you can devote your full time to standing around on Arabella's sidewalk." I wanted to say it, but I didn't. After all, it was his time machine. And, for that matter, his time. "Could you project us into another period?" I asked instead.

"No I couldn't." He sounded quite peeved at the notion. "Not with this machine, anyway," he added grudgingly. "It's still very crude, you know."

"It's a fantastic achievement already," I said. "Are you going to publish?"

"Not yet. I want to spend some time working out the problems. You haven't told anyone?"

"I have not," I assured him. "They'd think I was either drunk or crazy."

The Brain snorted. "Very likely. A few fears ago, space travel was strictly science fiction stuff. Some day we'll move freely back and forth in both space and time. If I hadn't done this, somebody else would, sooner or later."

The thought was staggering, but the evidence was irrefutable. It could be done. I'd been there.

"When the time comes," he went on, "You'll get full credit for your share in the experiment. Until then, I must ask for your absolute silence."

"You'll have it," I said. "I haven't done anything but go along for the ride, anyway."

"You gave me the idea. That's all it takes, really. An idea."

He fell into another of his brown studies. I did some thinking then, myself. To conquer all-conquering time! I was rising to heights of poetry. "Try that on your balalaika, Nikita!" I exulted inwardly. James Carter-Harrison was the Yuri Gagarin of time, and I was both the Strelka and the Bjelka.

I never did get a chance to share these exalted thoughts with the Brain. He stopped inviting me on his journeys in time. I knew he was still going back to Arabella's because I saw him there twice. Both times he was just standing on the sidewalk. I didn't speak to him. He wouldn't have heard me.

It was two days before Christmas when he approached me again. In all my medical experience, including the time I took a first aid course at Boy Scout camp, I have never seen a person change so much in four days. He must have stopped sleeping altogether. His face was gray and there were wrinkles in his forehead that looked as if they'd been there forever.

"Williams," he said, "you've got to help me. I'm going to get her out."

I guess I stared at him. I know I couldn't speak.

"I need you." He was almost begging.

"Huh?" I managed to stammer. "Sure, anything I can do."

I was astonished. I was incredulous. But mostly I was sorry for the guy. To a man forty years old, falling in love for the first time is a desperate business anyway. But when he has to cross three-quarters of a century to call on his girl, he really has a problem. And now he was proposing to bring her together with him in a way that staggered the imagination. He couldn't do it, of course. But then nobody could build a time machine, either.

Another thought struck me. "You can't just transplant somebody into an entirely different time frame. You'd scare her to death, or drive her crazy."

"She's scared to death and half crazy now," he said bitterly. "Her uncle's forcing her to marry Martin. I've seen him, Williams. I've watched him try to make love to her. He knows she loathes him and he gloats over making her miserable. Damn sadistic devil! He'll kill her or she'll kill herself if I don't act now. I can't stand it."

He was telling the simple truth. I've never seen a man closer to cracking. I tried to reason with him, which was a waste of time, naturally.

"What year do you think it is? Was? You know what I mean."

"Eighteen ninety-nine. I saw a calendar in the house."

"Then why don't we look up the old newspaper records for 1900? We could find out if she did marry him, or—"

"No! Damn it, Williams, can't you understand? I'm not going to *let* it happen."

"But it's already happened. Whatever it was, it happened sixty-four years ago. You can't stop it now."

"Like hell I can't. Will you help me or shall I do it alone?"

"I said I'd help, didn't I?" And I hadn't had sense enough

to cross my fingers at the time, either. "What do you want me to do?"

"Come with me."

I followed him into his lab. We locked the door and went to work. Don't ask me what we did. I simply followed his orders and tried to keep from fouling up. He worked like a demon, first making alterations to the original box, then turning his attention to a different apparatus.

"What's this thing for?" I asked finally. By then it was after midnight and I was tired and hungry.

"This is the materializer," he explained. "She'll be invisible to us when we get her, just as we are to her now. We can't leave her in that state, naturally."

"It would be an awful waste of all that curly hair."

"She is lovely, isn't she?" He spoke so quietly, yet so feelingly, it was like a prayer. Then he grabbed a screwdriver and went back to work.

This was the first time I'd seen the Brain in his lab. He worked in a fury of concentration. Nothing appeared beyond him, from the most delicate mechanical adjustment to the most abstruse calculation. It made me nervous finally, like watching a high-wire performer doing a particularly dangerous balancing act. Surely he'd never make it. But he did, I guess. About three in the morning he straightened up, took off his lab coat, and said, "Thanks, Williams."

I yawned and rubbed my stubbly face. "When do we pull the snatch?"

"The . . . uh . . . oh. This coming afternoon at about half-past five, with any luck. She's going Christmas shopping and won't be returning till then, she told her maid. It will be dark by that time. If we can get her just as she's stepping out of the carriage, it should be quite simple."

That's what he said. We went and had ham and eggs at an

all-night diner, then I took a taxi home. I offered Carter-Harrison a lift, but he said he felt like walking.

I was late getting in, and I'm afraid my mind wasn't on the large intestine much of that day. As the hours ticked off, the thought of what we were trying to do took hold of me completely. Could we possibly pull off a kidnapping? If we did, what then?

That was where I stuck. Had the Brain applied his gigantic mental powers to the *What then?*

It was just after five on Christmas Eve when Carter-Harrison stuck his head in at the door and said, "Coming, Williams?" He had his machine in a green book bag slung over his shoulder. The parts we'd added last night made it too big to fit in a coat pocket. We started off in silence, but I knew I'd have to speak or pop.

"If we succeed—"

"We'll succeed."

"All right, we'll succeed. Then what?"

"We take her back to the lab in a taxi and use the materializer to materialize her."

"Yes, but I mean what happens after that? I'm sure you'll work the scientific part all right. I just want to know how you plan to cope with an hysterical woman in a bustle who's found herself among strangers in a new century."

That jolted him, I could tell. I honestly don't believe it had occurred to him that while he'd been falling in love with her, she still didn't even know he existed.

"Why, we'll simply explain to her who we are and what we've done." He was trying to sound confident. "She'll understand."

Which showed how much he knew about women. "Where's she going to live?"

"She can stay in my apartment." He caught me smirking

and added hastily, "I'll go to a hotel."

"And after that what?"

"Naturally I shall continue to consider her my responsibility until she makes a satisfactory decision as to her future."

You poor prune, I thought. You haven't a clue about what you're taking on.

But what's the use talking to a man in love? We were almost to Arabella's house now, and the butterflies in my stomach had put on their dancing shoes. The Brain seemed perfectly in control, though somewhat tense. As we reached the brownstone steps, he set down his book bag and opened the top.

"Here, Williams, take your handle and be ready to move fast when she comes."

He straightened up, holding his end of the wire, and a second later we were back in 1899. The avenue was empty. "I hope we haven't missed her," he fretted.

Two men came down around the park. They were both well-fed types with fur-collared overcoats buttoned across their corporations and curly-brimmed derbies setting off their handsomely curried mustaches. Seeing them, Carter-Harrison went white with fury.

"There are Uncle John and that rat Martin," he hissed.

Martin didn't look like a rat, he looked like a pig. He was talking loudly and flashing his dentures in a phony smile. "Maybe we ought to follow them inside," I said.

"We can't. We'd never get her out the door. Oh Lord, we should have come earlier. I don't know what to do."

Our problem solved itself just then, as the carriage appeared between the iron gates. We could see Arabella's white feathers bobbing up and down inside.

"There's the dear girl now," said Uncle John unctuously. He and Martin stood on the steps to wait for her. All together, we made quite a reception committee.

Poor Arabella looked positively nauseated when she caught sight of Martin. That ended my qualms.

Acting on Carter-Harrison's orders, I stepped forward as she descended from her carriage, fastened a heavy webbing belt around her waist and attached wires to her wrists while he worked feverishly at the time machine's controls.

"Come along, Arabella," urged her uncle. "We mustn't keep Mr. Martin waiting." You could hear the menace behind his jovial tones.

"I-I can't, Uncle." Arabella sounded puzzled, as well she might. "Something seems to have got hold of me."

"Nonsense!" He started down the steps. Carter-Harrison pressed the switch.

Just for an instant, I thought I could see Uncle John and Mr. Martin staring incredulously at an empty space on the sidewalk. Then they were gone and the Brain and I were back in 1963 with an oddly agitated webbing belt between us.

"We've got her!" Carter-Harrison waved wildly at a miraculously empty taxi. "Medical Building, Driver, and make it fast."

It was impossible to be gallant toward poor Arabella. We just shoved her, or what we assumed to be her, into the cab, out again, and up in the elevator to the Brain's laboratory. We had a vague feeling of a form between us, but it was almost weightless. Only the occasional jerk of the belt and the wires showed she was alive and kicking. With frantic haste, Carter-Harrison attached the wrist wires to the materializer.

"Now, Williams, pray," he said, and threw the switch to on.

There was no flash, no crash, no fizz, no fumes. There was just, after a moment, Arabella.

Everything had gone perfectly. Carter-Harrison had succeeded in transporting the woman of his dreams sixty-four years in time without mussing a flounce or a feather.

He had however, omitted one small calculation. If you take a pretty Boston lass of nineteen and move her ahead sixty-four years, you get—well, what we got was Mrs. Jared Fortescue Martin, who'd been a relentless perpetrator of good works ever since her bridegroom was mysteriously stabbed to death with a buttonhook on their wedding night. She was also the highly irascible sole trustee of the J. F. Martin Research Fellowship, presently awarded to James Carter-Harrison.

"I could not love thee, dear, so much, loved I not my fellowship more," the Brain murmured sadly as he reversed the materializer switch.

He got himself transferred to Stanford not long after that. As for me, I stick to the gastrointestinal tract and walk a block out of my way to avoid a kid with a jump rope.

Clean Slate

The only bright thing Henry Giles ever did in his life was to marry Sue Kilmer. Whether or not she took him solely to get Mrs. on her tombstone as some of her acquaintances alleged is beside the point. Granted, Sue was pushing forty by then and had never been a beauty. Nevertheless, it was a lucky day for Henry when he led her to the altar, or rather to the parlor of the Methodist parsonage. Sue wasn't one to waste good money on a fancy wedding.

She was a crisp little body, straight as a ramrod. The cotton print dresses and long white aprons she wore summer and winter were starched so stiff they rattled. After they'd been married awhile, Sue even managed to put a little starch in Henry's backbone.

Henry had bumbled along for almost fifty years before he got around to tying the knot. He'd skinned through grade school somehow, then gone to work full time in his father's general store. Twenty years later the old man was dead and the store was Henry's. He'd proved to be no great shakes about carrying on alone. Gradually Giles's Store had got seedier and seedier. The windows had filmed over with dust not thick enough to hide the litter of broken cartons and rusty cans inside. Folks had taken to driving over to The Corners for their groceries and dry goods.

The day after the wedding, though, things changed. At

eight o'clock sharp, Henry was out on the sidewalk washing the windows. Sue was inside, clearing away flyspecked posters announcing long-past bean suppers, scrubbing the long oak counter, sprucing up the shelves with fresh merchandise.

Little by little, Giles's Store perked up. Down came the dusty flypapers that had hung from the rafters since nobody could remember when. Out went the old sawdust box that had always stood beside the potbellied stove. In came a shiny new brass cuspidor. What was more, Henry kept it shined. He even black-ironed the stove regularly once a week.

Old Tige the store cat could no longer be found snoozing in the cracker barrel on a rainy afternoon. Sue kept him on the payroll because Tige earned his keep, but she made sure he took his catnaps in seemly dignity on a cushion behind the counter.

Ladies who'd shied away from dragging their flounces over Henry's splintery, tobacco-juicy floorboards could find no fault with Sue's well-varnished oilcloth runners. Dropping in at Giles's to look over the new calicos and muslins got to be a popular afternoon's entertainment. It was a real treat to be waited on by a scrubbed and smiling Henry all togged out in a gray alpaca shop coat and a new straw boater with a red ribbon around it.

So Sue and Henry throve and prospered. If they ever gave a thought to the children they might have had, nobody knew of it. The store was their baby. They lived over it, in two spotless rooms. They lived for it. They pampered it, gussied it up with every new fixing they could think of, kept it swept and dusted and straightened to a fare-thee-well. Gradually all the things his father had tried to teach him percolated back into Henry's consciousness. He became a competent storekeeper.

But Sue was the boss. She did the buying, handled the

cash, and kept her help up to the mark. She was no nagger; she didn't have to be. Henry had just about sense enough to realize his wife was the brains of the outfit, and good nature enough not to resent it. As a matter of fact, Henry's good nature was the only fly in their ointment. She had to bring him up short about letting people's bills run on more than once.

"You're a storekeeper," she'd snap, "not Santa Claus."

Still, Henry never could seem to put his foot down fast enough. One Saturday night, Sue ran out of patience. She took a slate out of stock and wrote on it, "Jos. Gibbs owes $19.73. S. Peters owes $8.59," and so on down the list of flagrant debtors.

"What you aimin' to do with that?" Henry asked her.

"I'm going to hang it right here over the till." And she did.

Henry fiddled uneasily with his apron string. "Folks ain't goin' to like havin' their names stuck up there like that."

"No," said his wife, "I don't expect they will."

They didn't, of course. One by one, red in the face and mumbling excuses, they paid up. By the end of the week, the slate was clean. Sue left it hanging as a gentle reminder, and it got to be a village joke. The first thing every customer who came in did was to sneak a peek in case somebody'd been posted. Credit problems at Giles's Store became scarce as hens' teeth.

Once in a while the slate got used again. Nobody could say the Gileses were mean about it. When Joe got laid off at the mill, they let his bill run on for months without a murmur. But then Joe went back to work and his wife appeared at church in a new Easter bonnet while there was still a sizable amount on the books. On Monday morning the slate read "Jos. Gibbs owes $57.16." Emma Gibbs kept her new hat out of sight after that until Joe had cleaned the slate.

In May the Gileses had the store painted fresh inside and out. On the first of June, they were robbed.

It was Henry who discovered the break. He'd come down early to sweep out and roll down the new striped awning he was so proud of. There was Tige, asleep in the cracker barrel as of yore.

"How'd you get in here? I put you out last night my—" Henry saw the open back window and stopped short. A cold sweat broke out all over him. "Somebody's been in here."

He raced up the stairs three at a time. "Sue! Sue!"

"Henry, what's the matter? Here, sit down before you fall down. Land's sakes, you're puffing like a engine."

"Sue! We been robbed!"

"Well, I never." His wife sank into the rocking chair. For once, all the starch was taken out of her. They stared at each other, stupefied by shock. Their store. *Their* store.

Sue came to her senses first. "What did they take?"

"I . . . I dunno. I just seen the back winder open an' came to get you."

"Just so."

Sue got up from the rocker, her apron crackling like a burst of grapeshot. "Come along, Henry."

She took his hand and led him downstairs as if he'd been her little boy. It was the first spontaneous gesture of affection that had passed between them since their wedding night.

At the sound of Sue's footsteps, Tige leaped from the cracker barrel and scooted out the open window. They both jumped.

"Consarn that cat!" Henry exploded. "See anything missin'?"

Sue pointed at the empty cash drawer left hanging open. "Somebody's been here, all right."

"They didn't get the money?"

"Of course not. The cash is where it belongs, upstairs under the mattress stuffed into one of your old socks. But they must have taken something." Her eye lit on the empty tobacco case. "That's it. There's what they stole."

Henry groaned. "Cleaned out. Cigars, cigarettes, pipe tobaccer, plug tobaccer, snuff an' all." He did some laborious mental arithmetic. "Forty-six dollars an' seventy-five cents' worth."

"Forty-nine dollars and fifty-seven cents," Sue amended. "See, there's one of those new Gladstone bags missing. They must have taken that to put the tobacco in."

Henry saw red. "I'm goin' for the constable."

"Henry Giles," snapped his wife, "you stay right where you are and keep your trap shut."

"But Sue!"

"Henry, you're not to breathe one word about this robbery to a soul. Not one living soul."

"But forty-nine dollars an' fifty-seven cents! All right, Sue. If you say so." The wretched storekeeper dragged his broom out to sweep the sidewalk.

June passed. Sue put up new flypapers and Henry changed them religiously once a week.

July passed. Customers straggled in, gasping from the heat. Sue's white aprons stayed crisp as ever.

August passed. Giles's Store did a lively business in corduroy knickers, plaid ginghams, and pencil boxes for the back-to-school trade.

September passed. Henry still fretted off and on about the forty-nine dollars and fifty-seven cents. Sue shut him up sharp every time he mentioned the robbery.

"You keep still about that, Henry. Just let me handle it."

October passed. Halloween night, all the kids in town

marched down the street shouting, "Shell ao-ut!" Henry tipped a barrel of cider apples on the porch. Sue passed out handfuls of stale cookies. Giles's Store didn't even get its windows soaped.

On November tenth, just about closing time, Dan Pottle dropped in.

Dan was the town sport. He grew sideburns halfway down his jawbone and slicked back his hair with Vaseline. He waxed his little mustache. Every girl in the village dreamed of having her reputation ruined by being seen in public with Dan Pottle. Dan stepped over to the cigar counter, bright-eyed and bushy-tailed in his new checkered coat.

"Evenin', Henry."

"Evenin', Dan. What'll it be?"

"A couple o' five-cent panatelas, if you don't mind me askin'. Can't go callin' on a pretty young lady smokin' them twofers o' yours. Smoke 'er right off the davenport." Dan guffawed at his own wit.

Henry took out the fancy box with the voluptuous brunette lithographed inside the cover, and held it over the counter. Dan carefully selected three cigars and stowed them in his waistcoat pocket.

"I'll give one to 'er old man. Good politics." He winked, plunked down a dime and a five-cent piece, and turned to go. Halfway to the door, he paused.

"Henry," he drawled, "did you ever find out who it was broke into your store that time?"

Henry's mouth drooped. He shook his head. "No, Dan, we never did."

Sue stepped to his side, her white apron snapping. "Not till just this minute. Thank you very much."

She took down the slate and picked up her slate pencil. In

clear block capitals she printed, "DAN POTTLE OWES $49.57."

Dan blustered, but he paid. One didn't try to weasel on a woman like Sue.

Felonious Courtship of Miles Peabody

"It's disgraceful," snorted my father. "She's got no right to keep taking them."

"Miles Peabody can certainly afford two pounds of melachrino creams a week," said my mother.

"But she's eating them under false pretenses."

"Now John, you know Aunt Julia's the last person in the world to do anything improper."

"If trifling with the affections of an honest man isn't improper, would you kindly tell me what is?"

Pop was getting mad. I could see the back of his neck turning red where it bulged out over his Sunday collar. In a minute, the ends of his mustache would start to twitch. They'd been twitching a lot since Miles Peabody got back to town.

It had all started one Sunday back in May. I'd skinned out of church ahead of Pop and Ma while they stopped to talk the way they always do. I was leaning against the big elm tree out front, wondering why it always has to rain on Saturday and be nice on Sunday when you can't do anything that's any fun, when I noticed a commotion over by the church steps.

A lot of people were buzzing around a dapper-looking old geezer I'd never seen before. I was just going over to see what the excitement was about when Mum and her Aunt Julia came out the church door. I have to admit they looked pretty

swell with their pinched-in waists and boned lace collars up
to their ears and new spring hats all over silk flowers and big
bunches of ribbon.

Aunt Julia's still vain about her looks even if she is almost a
million years old. Fifty, anyway. She was putting up her lavender parasol in case she might get a freckle or something
when she noticed the stranger.

"Miles Peabody!" She sailed down the steps with her long
skirts streaming out behind her and up to the geezer like he
was her long-lost brother.

"Julia! After all these years," I heard him say. "And more
beautiful than ever."

I decided any gink who could say something as sappy as
that to my great-aunt couldn't be much. Anyway, Jimmy
Hogan came along just then, so I went off with him. When I
got home, darned if I didn't find the guy sitting on our parlor
sofa with Aunt Julia.

"Miles," said my father, "this is my son Davy. Shake
hands with Mr. Peabody, son."

When I'm Pop's son Davy, that means he's in a good
mood. I stuck out my hand so as not to spoil it.

Mr. Peabody didn't make any smart cracks about fine
little chaps or favoring my Uncle Fred. He just shook hands
and said, "Glad to know you, Davy."

"I'm glad to know you, too," I said.

After a while, I really was. Mr. Peabody was just back from
out west. He'd panned for gold in the mountains and lived in
Indian camps and . . . well, he was just a snorter. He didn't
mind if a kid asked questions, even.

He had a stickpin in his necktie made out of a nugget from
his own gold mine and a genuine timber wolf's tooth on his
watch chain that he'd shot himself when it was sneaking up
on his cattle ranch. The wolf, I mean. He'd ridden horseback

through herds of buffalo and shot rapids in a canoe and been down the Mississippi on a steamboat. There wasn't much he hadn't done.

The trouble was, he kept stopping in the most interesting places to make some goofy remark about Aunt Julia. I wondered if maybe he'd got kicked on the head by a buffalo or something, but Ma and Pop didn't seem to notice anything strange so I had to make believe I didn't, either.

Mr. Peabody stayed to dinner and most of the afternoon and we got to be real good friends. Then we all walked him and Aunt Julia back to her house. Uncle Hiram left her this big place on Maple Street that she lives in all alone since she finally got Ma's two cousins married off. She asked Mr. Peabody in for a cup of tea, which is a sappy thing to offer a man who's shot a timber wolf if you ask me. He seemed real tickled, though.

"I don't see why she couldn't have asked us, too," I said after my parents and I started home by ourselves. "I wanted to ask Mr. Peabody some more about that train that he was snowed up in going through the Rocky Mountains."

"You'll have plenty of time for that, Davy," said Pop. "I expect we'll be seeing plenty of Mr. Peabody from now on. He's made his pile, now he's going to sit back and enjoy it, he tells me. Smart man."

"It's so romantic," said my mother. "In all those years he never forgot her."

"Her who?" I said.

"Aunt Julia, of course."

I don't know why Ma always gets sore when I ask the simplest question. "What in heck for?"

Pop snickered, but Ma give him a look. "They were childhood sweethearts, Davy. I remember my mother teasing Aunt Julia about her old flame Miles Peabody when I was a girl. I don't know why he didn't marry her, but he went out west instead and she married Uncle Hiram and that was the end of it."

"Looks to me as if it's only the beginning," said Pop.

He was right as usual. Mr. Peabody took a room at the Manor House and began sending Aunt Julia candy.

I got him going on that, I guess. We happened to bump into each other Monday after school and he invited me into the ice cream parlor. We had a real good time. Finally, while I was digging out the last of the strawberry syrup with my spoon, he asked me, "What does your Aunt Julia like best in all the world?"

"Melachrino creams," I said. "She's crazy about 'em."

So he went over to the candy counter and picked out the fanciest two-pound box they had. He told the clerk to wrap it up nice and send it to Aunt Julia.

"Do you want to put in a card?" the clerk asked him.

"Just write 'With Miles Peabody's compliments.' "

After that he kept sending her a box every week. He sent flowers, too, which seemed pretty dumb to me because she had a garden full already. He rented a buggy and took her driving. He took her to the Strawberry Festival and the County Fair. There wasn't hardly any place he didn't take her and all she ever did back was offer him a cup of tea once in a dog's age.

I finally asked Ma, "What's Mr. Peabody always hanging around Aunt Julia for?"

"Because he enjoys her company, naturally."

"Then why does he look so glum all the time?"

Ma was up to her elbows in bread dough and looking pretty hot and flustered or I don't suppose she'd have spilled the beans. "Because she won't marry him," she told me.

"Won't marry *Mr. Peabody?* She must be crazy," I said.

Ma got sore. "Davy, don't you dare breathe a word of that to anybody. It's nobody's business but Aunt Julia's. She's just not in a hurry to get married again, after Uncle Hiram. I mean, he left her comfortably provided for. Now go and play or something."

That night at supper I asked Pop, "Don't you think Aunt Julia's crazy not to marry Mr. Peabody?"

Pop choked on his soup, then he laughed. Not his big, jolly laugh but his short barking laugh he uses when he wants to cuss and can't in front of Ma. "Aunt Julia's got bats in her belfry, if you ask me."

"Now John," said my mother.

"Damn . . . I mean drat it, Alice, here's your aunt stuck with that big house and no man to take care of it for her. She calls me over there for some dratted thing or other about sixteen times a week and I'm pretty d-dratted sick and tired of it, I don't mind telling you. Now here's Miles Peabody, nicest fellow she'd ever want to meet, plenty of cash in his pockets, wanting to settle down and make her a darn sight better husband than she deserves, in my frank opinion. So what does she do but turn up her nose and go right on stuffing herself with his chocolates?"

"Now John," Ma said again, "don't go getting yourself all worked up."

But there's no use telling Pop not to work himself up when he's got a good mad started. He got so the ends of his mustache would start twitching every time he even heard Aunt Julia's name mentioned. The night she came over about the pump, I expected him to explode.

She came sailing up the walk in her lavender silk dress and her big hat with the purple bows on it. "John," she said, "I don't know what's the matter with that sink pump of mine. I can't raise a drop of water."

Ma and I held our breath. But Pop just grinned.

"Sure, Aunt Julia," he said. "I'll come right this minute. You probably just need a new washer. Run down to the cellar and get my tool kit, will you, son?"

I brought Pop his tools and tagged along to carry the box for him. I had a hunch he was up to something. Pop can think of the darnedest things when he gets going.

He started off quiet enough, tinkering away at the pump with his sleeves rolled up and one of Aunt Julia's aprons tied around his middle to keep his pants clean. Aunt Julia was standing beside him holding up a lamp so he could see what he was doing. I was handing him the wrench and stuff. All of a sudden he sort of grinned to himself and I knew it was coming.

"Seen the burglar yet, Aunt Julia?"

"What burglar?" I thought she was going to drop the lamp.

"Oh, haven't you heard?" Pop sounded so innocent I wanted to bust out laughing. "Broke into two houses out on the Millville Road, they tell me."

He held up the old leather washer, offhand-like. "See, there's your trouble right there. Won't take a minute to . . . hand me that jackknife like a good boy, Davy. Yep, they say he snoops around till he finds a woman living alone, then he forces his way in. I didn't mean to scare you, Aunt Julia."

"You're not scaring me, John," she said. But she didn't sound as if she meant it.

"Gosh, that's a relief. After all, a big house like this with so much nice stuff around, some women would be worried stiff about having no man for protection."

"I had twenty-six years of your Uncle Hiram. That's enough man to last me a lifetime, thank you."

"Not all men are alike," Pop argued.

"You don't know what they're like till you're stuck with

one, and then it's too late. If you think I'm going to make the same mistake twice, you've got another think coming."

"Well, it's your business, not mine," said Pop. "There, now she ought to do." He gave the pump a couple of tugs and it worked fine. "Got the tools packed, Davy? We'd better be getting along. I don't want to keep the kid out late," he whispered to Aunt Julia. "Just in case, you know. You sure you'll be all right here alone?"

"Quite sure," said Aunt Julia. "I'm much obliged to you, John."

"Think nothing of it. I expect Alice will drop over in the morning, just to make sure you're all right. Be sure to lock your doors and windows. Though they do say . . . but there, I don't want to get you worked up over nothing. You might want to take the dinner bell up to bed with you. You could ring it out the window for help, if you got the chance. Get a good night's sleep, Aunt Julia."

He waited till we were out of earshot, then he snickered. "If she does, I'll be a monkey's uncle."

"What are you going to do, Pop?" I asked him.

"None of your beeswax, kiddo." He ruffled my hair. "Just keep your flytrap shut, eh?"

I grinned. "Sure, Pop."

He came into the house whistling and scooted me off to bed. I didn't go to sleep, of course. I waited till it got good and dark, put my clothes back on, and shinnied down over the porch roof. I scrooched down in the lilac bush and kept my eyes peeled.

Sure enough, around midnight Pop came tiptoeing out and I tell you, if I hadn't known who he was, I'd have been plenty scared. He had on his old dark brown sweater that he wears around the yard, and a cap pulled down over his eyes, and a scarf or something tied around the bottom of his face.

He'd slung a sack over his back and you'd swear to goodness he was a real burglar.

For a big man, Pop can move mighty quiet. He snuck across the back yards like a cat after mice. I followed, keeping well behind so he wouldn't catch me and send me home. Of course Pop did all the things a real burglar wouldn't. He walked up bold as brass to the dining-room window that was right under Aunt Julia's bedroom, then he took a crowbar out of his sack and smashed the windowpane.

I don't think he realized how loud the crash would sound. But Aunt Julia sounded a heck of a lot louder. She leaned out the bedroom window in her nightgown ringing that dinner bell for all she was worth. "Help! Police!" she was screeching.

Pop was so startled, I guess, that he just stood looking up at her. She spied him, grabbed the pitcher off her washstand, and sloshed a whole gallon of water smack down on his head.

Then Jimmy Hogan's dog Spot came whooping over. Spot's got some bloodhound in him and I knew if he ever got hold of Pop's pant leg it would be all over. I made a flying leap and got him by the rump. Then I put my hands around his jaws and held his mouth shut so he couldn't do anything but whimper.

"Run, Pop," I whispered as loud as I dared.

He heard me and took off like a rabbit. By then, people were hollering out their windows. A couple of men were running down the street with clubs in their hands. I dragged Spot back to his doghouse and stayed there petting him to keep him quiet till they'd searched the neighborhood and gone back to bed. Then I streaked for home. When I shinnied up the porch pillar, Pop was waiting to haul me in the window.

"Davy, are you all right?"

"Sure, Pop. Are you?"

I sort of expected a bawling out for following him, but he

gave me a bear hug instead. "You saved my neck, old scout. What did you do with the dog?"

"Took him back to Hogan's and kept him quiet till the men went away."

"Good work, son. Do me another big favor, will you? Don't ever breathe a word about this to your mother."

"About what, John Turnbull?" There was Ma with her hair hanging down in braids over her pink kimono. "What are you two doing awake at this hour? John you're soaked to the skin!"

"Now Alice, don't go getting all haired up."

Pop might as well have saved his breath. Ma didn't let up on him till she'd wormed out the whole story. Then she gave us both a tongue-lashing that would take the skin off a brass monkey. Then she busted out laughing.

"Thank the Lord Davy has sense even if his father hasn't." Then she dragged Pop off by the ear as if he'd been a little kid to get out of his wet burglar suit.

It was all over town about the burglar next morning, which was Saturday. Jimmy was over to tell me before breakfast, even. He said the burglar must have doped Spot because Spot sure would have caught him if he hadn't. I said yeah, he sure must have. I was sort of glad when Ma called me in to breakfast.

After we ate, she put on her hat. "I'm going over to see how Aunt Julia survived the night," she said. "You're coming with me, Davy."

"Aw Ma," I said, "do I have to?"

"You certainly do. If you think I'm going to trust you out of my sight after what happened last night, you're just as loony as your father." Ma began to laugh again. "Honestly, you two!"

So we walked up Maple Street, but just before we got to

Aunt Julia's, we met the delivery boy from the ice cream parlor bringing the weekly box of melachrino creams. All of a sudden Ma got the same funny grin on her face Pop did when he started telling Aunt Julia about the burglar. She stopped the delivery boy.

"I expect those are for my aunt," she said. "We'll take them in for you."

The boy thanked her, handed her the package, and whizzed off on his two-wheeler. I was watching him go, wishing I had a bicycle, when Ma nudged me in the ribs.

"Davy, take this candy, quick, and get it out of sight."

I grabbed the box and stuffed it down my blouse. We boys all wear middy blouses with drawstrings that tie around our waists. They make handy sacks for swiping apples and stuff. I worked the melachrino creams around to the small of my back so they wouldn't stick out too much.

"What am I supposed to do with it, Ma?"

"Skin over to Miss Hatherton's and leave it on her doorstep, then ring the bell and run. Try not to let anybody see you."

"But Ma, they're for Aunt Julia."

"Don't argue, Davy. You were quick enough to help your father."

She giggled a little, then made her face all stiff and solemn and went on to the house. I slid over to Miss Hatherton's and left the box like Ma told me to, then I hurried back to Aunt Julia's. If there was going to be another rumpus, I wanted to be in on it, even if I didn't see anything funny about giving away two pounds of perfectly good chocolates to a sappy schoolteacher like Miss Hatherton.

I met Ma and Aunt Julia just coming out the door. "We're going to take a little walk," Ma told me. "Aunt Julia needs some fresh air and exercise to calm her nerves."

"My nerves are perfectly calm, Alice." Aunt Julia was fiddling with the catch of her parasol. "After living with your Uncle Hiram all those years, it would take more than a burglar to upset me. Anyway, I guess I taught him a thing or two. I only hope John remembers to bring over the glass and fix that broken windowpane."

Poor Pop! All he'd got for his trouble was another odd job. Ma and Aunt Julia started down the street. I tagged along behind. After they'd gone a little way, Ma said, "Do you mind if we stop in at Millie Hatherton's for a minute? I want to borrow one of her crochet patterns."

"I thought you hated to crochet," said Aunt Julia.

"Well, I'm trying to learn to enjoy it," Ma mumbled.

Anyway, they went up and rang Miss Hatherton's doorbell. The box wasn't on the doormat any more, I noticed. I hoped she'd have the decency to pass it around, at least.

I needn't have worried. We'd hardly got inside the door before Miss Hatherton was waving that fancy two-pound box of melachrino creams under our noses. She made sure Aunt Julia saw the card saying, "With Miles Peabody's compliments," too.

All of a sudden Aunt Julia was looking pretty sick. "No thank you, Millie," she said when Miss Hatherton offered her the box of candy.

"But Aunt Julia," I piped up, "I thought you were crazy over melachrino creams."

"I don't care for any, thank you," she said in a voice cold enough to freeze the whiskers off a polar bear. "Alice, I believe I'd better go home. My nerves are a trifle on edge this morning."

She was halfway home before she spoke another word. Then she let go. "That whey-faced Millie Hatherton!"

85

"Most people think Millie's rather an attractive young woman," said Ma.

"Young, indeed! She's thirty-five if she's a day. And how anybody could abide that sweet-sweet voice and those silly curls dangling over her forehead—" Aunt Julia flounced into the house and practically slammed the door in our faces.

"What's got into her?" I said. "She claimed she wasn't nervous before."

"Women's nerves are funny things." Ma was smiling again, don't ask me why. "Run on ahead and set the table, like a good boy. Your father will have to eat his lunch in a hurry if he's going to fix that window." She was laughing out loud by the time she finished talking.

"I don't see what's so funny," I said.

"You will, some day. Now if Miles Peabody only has sense enough to keep quiet."

"About what, Ma?"

"Honestly, men are so dense."

I didn't know whether she meant Mr. Peabody or Pop or all three of us, so I just went and set the table. Pop came home, gobbled down his grub, and tore off to set that pane of glass for Aunt Julia. He was pretty sore about it when he left, but he came back grinning like a catfish.

"Guess what, Alice? Miles Peabody stopped by to see how your aunt was doing after her scare, and she fell all over him. Asked him in for a bite, waited on him like a king, fed him two pieces of pie. Last I saw, she was sitting on the arm of his chair, tucking a pillow behind his head and lighting his cigar."

He grabbed Ma and gave her a big hug. "Guess your old man's not so dumb after all, eh?"

Ma stuck her head up over Pop's shoulder and winked at

me. "You're wonderful, John." The queer thing was, she sounded as if she meant it.

So that's how Mr. Peabody got to be Uncle Miles. Pop told him the real story about the burglar quite a long time after the wedding. Uncle Miles almost laughed himself sick. So then I told him about Miss Hatherton and the melachrino creams and that's when he gave me the genuine timber wolf's tooth. He said I'd earned it. I still don't quite see how.

Lady Patterly's Lover

"We'd be doing him a kindness, really," said Gerald. "You do see that, Eleanor?"

Lady Patterly ran one exquisite hand idly through the thick, fair hair of her husband's steward. "I'd be doing myself one. That's all that matters."

Born beautiful, spoiled rotten as a child, married at twenty-one to the best catch in England, wife at twenty-three to a helpless paralytic, bored to desperation at twenty-four; that, in a nutshell, was Eleanor, Lady Patterly. When old Ponsonby had retired and her husband's close friend Gerald had come to manage the Patterly estates, Eleanor had lost no time in starting an affair with him. Discreetly, of course. She cared nothing for the world, but she was vain enough to care greatly for the world's opinion of her.

Gerald had been only too willing. As handsome as Eleanor was lovely, he had the same total lack of scruple, the same cold intelligence, the same passionate devotion to his own interests. He took the greatest care of his old friend Roger Patterly's property because he soon realized that with Eleanor's help he could easily make it his own. It was Gerald who suggested the murder.

The killing part is the easiest. A pillow over his face, a switch of medicines, nothing to it. The big thing is not getting caught. We must make sure no one ever suspects it wasn't a

88

natural death. We'll take our time, prepare the groundwork, wait for exactly the right moment. And then, my love, it's all ours.

Lady Patterly gazed around the drawing room with its priceless furnishings, through the satin-draped windows to the impeccably tended formal gardens. "I shall be so glad to get out of this prison. We'll travel, Gerald. Paris, Greece, Hong Kong. I've always had a fancy to see Hong Kong."

They would do nothing of the kind. Gerald was too careful a steward not to stay and guard what would be his. He only smiled and replied, "Whatever you want, my sweet."

"It will be just too marvelous," sighed the invalid's wife. "How shall we go about it?"

"Not we, darling. You."

After all, it would be Eleanor, not he, who would inherit. Unless he married her afterwards, he hadn't the ghost of a claim. And suppose she changed her mind? But she wouldn't. With the hold of murder over her she could be handled nicely. If he were fool enough to do the job himself . . . Gerald was no fool.

"I shall continue to be the faithful steward. And you will be the dutiful wife. A great deal more dutiful than you've been up to now."

Lady Patterly inspected her perfect fingernails, frowning. "What do you want me to do?"

"I want you to start showing some attention to your husband. Don't overdo it. Build it up gradually. You might begin by strolling into Roger's room and asking him how he's feeling."

"But I do, every morning and evening."

"Then do it again, right now. And stay for more than two minutes this time."

"Oh, very well. But it's so depressing."

"It's not all jam for old Roger either, you know."

"How sententious of you, darling. Shall I hold his hand, or what?"

"Why don't you read to him?"

"He loathes being read to."

"Read to him anyway. It will look well in front of the nurse. That's our objective, Eleanor, to create the impression of devotion among the attendants. You must be able to act the bereft widow convincingly when we . . . lose him."

His mistress shrugged and turned toward the stairs.

"Oh, and Eleanor," Gerald lowered his voice yet another pitch. "We'd better postpone any further meetings until it's over. We mustn't take any risk whatever. And don't be surprised if I start a flirtation with one of the village belles."

She arched one delicately pencilled eyebrow. "Have you picked out anybody special?"

"One will do as well as another. Protective camouflage, you know. It's only for a few weeks, darling." He turned the full force of his dazzling smile on her, and went out.

Eleanor stood for a moment looking after him. It was hard on Roger, of course. Still, she had her own future to think of. Her husband had offered her a divorce as soon as the doctors had told him the sports car smashup had left him paralyzed for life. Naturally she had refused. It wouldn't have looked well, and besides, the settlement he'd offered was not her idea of adequate support.

No, she would have it all. She and Gerald. It was clever of Gerald to have found the way. She arranged her features in exactly the right expression of calm compassion and went to visit her husband.

Day by day she increased the length of time she spent in the sickroom. It was less tedious than she had anticipated.

For one thing, Roger was so glad to have her there. She took to bringing him little surprises: some flowers, a few sun-warmed strawberries from the garden. She had the gramophone brought into his room and played the records they had danced to before they were married. Nurse Wilkes beamed. Marble the valet scowled distrustfully.

Eleanor found herself looking forward to her visits, planning the next day's surprise, thinking of new ways to entertain the invalid. The weeks went by and Gerald began to fidget.

"I say, don't you think we ought to be getting on with it?"

"You said we mustn't rush things." And she went past him into Roger's room, carrying a charming arrangement of varicolored roses she'd got up early to pick with the dew on them.

As had become her habit, she took up the book she was reading aloud to him and opened it to her bookmark. Her eye, now attuned to Roger's every expression, caught a tightening of the muscles around his mouth. She put the book down.

"You hate being read to, don't you, Roger?"

"It's just that it makes me feel so utterly helpless."

"But you're not. There's nothing the matter with your eyes. From now on, you'll read to yourself."

"How can I? I can't hold the book, I can't turn the pages."

"Of course you can. We'll just sit you up, like this—" Eleanor slid one arm around her husband and pulled him up. "Nurse, let's have that backrest thing. There, how's that?"

She plumped a pillow more comfortably. "Now we'll prop the book up on the bed table, like this, and lift your arm, like this, and slip the page between your fingers so that you can hold it yourself." A pinching between the right thumb and forefinger was the only movement Lord Patterly could make. "And when you've finished with that page, we just turn it over. Like this. See, you've managed it beautifully."

"So I have." He looked down at his hand as though it were

91

something miraculous. "That's the first thing I've done for myself since . . . it happened."

For the next half-hour, Roger read to himself. Eleanor sat at his side, patiently moving his hand when he signalled that he was ready, helping to slide the next page into his grasp. She found the monotonous task strangely agreeable. For the first time in her life, she was being of use to somebody else. When Marble brought in the patient's lunch and Nurse Wilkes came forward to feed it to him, she waved the woman away.

"He'll feed himself today, thank you, Nurse."

And he did, with Eleanor setting a spoon between his thumb and forefinger and guiding his hand to his mouth. When he dropped a morsel, they laughed and tried again. At last Lady Patterly left Nurse Wilkes clucking happily over a perfectly clean plate and went to get her own lunch. Gerald was waiting for her.

"I've got it all figured out, darling," he whispered as soon as they were alone. "I've been reading up on digitalis. The doctor's been leaving it, I know, on account of that heart of his. All we have to do is slip him an extra dose and out he goes. Heart failure. Only to be expected in a helpless paralytic."

To her own surprise, Eleanor protested. "He is not helpless. He's handicapped."

"Rather a nice distinction in Roger's case, don't you think, sweet? Anyway, there we are. You've only to notice which is the digitalis bottle, watch your chance, and slip a table-spoonful into his hot milk or whatever they give the poor bloke."

"And what happens when Nurse Wilkes notices the level of the medicines gone down in the bottle? Not clever, Gerald."

"Dash it, you can put in some water, can't you?"

"I suppose so." Eleanor pushed back her chair. "I'll have to think about it."

"Think fast, my love. I miss you."

Gerald gave her his best smile, but for some reason her heart failed to turn over as usual. She got up. "I'm going for a walk."

She started off aimlessly, then found herself heading toward the village. It was pleasant swinging along the grassy lane, feeling her legs respond to the spring of the turf under her feet. Roger had loved to walk. For the first time since the accident, Eleanor felt an overwhelming surge of genuine pity for her husband.

She turned in at the bookshop. It was mostly paperbacks and greeting cards these days, but she might find something Roger would enjoy now that she'd found a way for him to manage a book.

That was rather clever of me, she thought with satisfaction. She liked recalling the look on Roger's face, the beaming approval of Nurse Wilkes, the unbelief in old Marble's eyes as he watched His Lordship feeding himself. "There must be any number of things I could help him do," she mused. "I wonder how one goes about them?"

She went up to the elderly woman in charge. "Have you any books on working with handicapped people? Exercises, that sort of thing."

"Physical therapy," Miss Jenkins nodded wisely. "I do believe there was something in that last lot of paperbacks. Ah yes, here we are."

Eleanor ruffled through the pages. "This seems to be the general idea. But don't you have any that go into greater detail?"

"I could always order one for you, Lady Patterly."

93

"Please do, then, as quickly as possible."

"Of course. But—excuse me, Lady Patterly—we all understood His Lordship was quite helpless."

"He is not!" Again Eleanor was startled by her own reaction. "He was sitting up in bed reading by himself this morning, and he ate his own lunch. You can't call that helpless, can you?"

"Why . . . why no, indeed. Good gracious, I can hardly believe it. Nurse Wilkes said—"

"Nurse Wilkes says entirely too much," snapped Eleanor. She would have a word with Nurse Wilkes.

She walked back slowly studying the book page by page. It seemed simple enough. Manipulating the patient's limbs, massage, no problem there. If only they had a heated swimming pool. But of course Roger wouldn't be ready for that for ages yet. And by then she and Gerald . . . Gerald was getting a bit puffy about the jawline, she'd noticed it at lunch. Those big, beefy men were apt to go to flesh early. He ought to start exercising, too. No earthly good suggesting it to him. Gerald made rather a point of being the dominant male. Roger was much more reasonable to deal with.

He was positively boyish about the exercises. When the doctor dropped around for his daily visit, he found them hard at it, Roger pinching on to Eleanor's finger while she swung his arm up and down.

"See, Doctor, he's holding on beautifully."

"She's going to have me up out of this in a matter of weeks."

The doctor looked from one to the other. There was color in Lord Patterly's face for the first time since the accident. He had never seen Her Ladyship so radiant. Why should he tell them it was hopeless? Life had been hard enough on that young pair. Anyway, who knew? There was always the off

chance the long bed rest had allowed some of the nerve end-
ings to mend themselves.

"By all means go on as you're doing," he said. "Just take it
a bit slowly at first. Remember that little heart condition."

Eleanor suddenly thought of Gerald and the digitalis. Her
face became a mask. "I'll remember," she said tonelessly.

Her husband laughed. "Oh, nonsense. Everybody's got
these idiotic heart murmurs. My father had and he lived to
seventy-nine. Gerald has, and look at him. Shoots, swims,
rides, all that."

"Gerald had better watch himself," said the doctor. He
picked up his bag. "Well, the patient appears to be in good
hands. You're doing splendidly, Lady Patterly, splendidly.
Don't be discouraged if progress is a little slow. These things
take time, you know."

"Time," said Lord Patterly, "is something of which we
have plenty. Haven't we, darling?"

His wife smoothed his pillow. "Yes, Roger. All the time in
the world."

"I'll leave you to it, then." The doctor moved toward the
door. "Watch his pulse, Nurse. Give the prescribed injection
of digitalis if it seems advisable after the exercises. You keep
the hypodermic ready, of course?"

"All in order, Doctor. Right here on the medicine tray if
need arises."

Gerald was right, Eleanor thought as she gently kneaded
the wasted muscles of her husband's arms. It would be easy.
Too easy. She drew the covers up over him. "There, that's
enough for now. I don't want to wear you out the first day.
Shall I put on some music?"

"Please."

She had taken to playing the classical records he liked. It
whiled away the time for her, too, sitting beside the bed, let-

ting the long waves of melody sweep over her, daydreaming of all the things she would do when she was free. Today, however, she found her mind dwelling on more homely pictures. Miss Jenkins's face when she'd dropped her little bombshell at the bookshop. The doctor's, when he'd found her giving her husband therapy. Her husband's now, as he lay with his eyes closed, the long afternoon shadows etching his features in sharp relief. He was as good-looking as ever, in spite of everything. That jaw would never be blurred by fat. What would it be like, living in this house without Roger? She tried to imagine it and could not.

After dinner the following evening, Gerald suggested a walk. "You're looking peaked, Eleanor. Needn't stay cooped up with your patient forever, you know."

His double meaning was plain. She rose and followed him out the French windows to the terrace.

"Rather an inspiration of yours, that therapy thing."

"What do you mean?"

"Easy enough to overdo a bit. Make the heart attack more plausible, eh?"

She did not answer. He went on, confident of his power over her.

"You were right about the digitalis, I decided. I've thought of something even better. Potassium chloride. I was a hospital laboratory technician once, you know. One of the jobs I batted around in after they turned me down for the army. Rum, when you come to think of it. I mean, if it hadn't been for my wheezing heart I shouldn't have drifted into this post, and if it weren't for Roger's I shouldn't be . . . getting promoted, shall we say? Anyway, getting back to the potassium chloride, it's reliable stuff. Absolutely undetectable. Do an autopsy and all you find is a damaged heart and an increased potassium rate. Exactly what you'd expect after a fatal coronary attack."

"Gerald, must you?"

"This is no time to turn squeamish, Eleanor. Especially since it's you who'll be giving it."

"Don't be a fool. How could I?"

"Oh, I don't mean directly. We'll let Nurse Wilkes do that. She keeps a hypodermic of digitalis on the table ready to give him a quick jab if he needs it."

"How did you know that?"

"I'm the old dear pal, remember? I've been a lot more faithful about visiting Roger than you ever were until your recent excess of wifely devotion. Nurse Wilkes and I are great chums."

"I can imagine." Men like Gerald were always irresistible to servant girls and barmaids and plain, middle-aged nurses. And rich women who thought they had nothing better to do.

"I took careful note of the type of hypodermic syringe she uses," Gerald went on. "Yesterday when I was in London, I bought one just like it at one of the big medical supply houses, along with some potassium chloride and a few other things so it wouldn't look too obvious. I'd dropped in beforehand to visit some of my old pals at the hospital cost and pinched a lab coat with some convincing acid holes in it. Wore it to the shop and they never dreamed of questioning me. I ditched it in a public lavatory and got rid of the rest of the stuff in various trash bins on my way back to the station."

"You think of everything, don't you, Gerald?" Eleanor's throat was dry.

"Have to, my love. So here we are. I give you the doings all ready for use. You watch your chance tomorrow morning and switch the syringes. Then you put old Roger through his paces till he works up a galloping pulse, back off and let Nurse take over, and get ready to play the shattered widow. The stuff works in a couple of minutes. And then this is all ours."

"It's all ours now," Eleanor told him. "Mine and Roger's."

"I say! You're not backing out on me, are you?"

"Yes I am. I won't do it, Gerald."

No woman had ever refused Gerald anything before. His face puckered like an angry baby's. "But why?"

"Because I'm not quite the idiot I thought I was. You're not worth Roger's little finger."

It was astonishing how ugly Gerald could look. "And suppose I go to Roger and let him know the loving-wife act was just a buildup for murder? Suppose you're caught with the evidence? You will be, Eleanor. I'll see to that."

"Don't be ridiculous. What would you get out of it?"

"You forget, my love. I'm the boyhood chum and devoted steward. I'll be the chap who saved his life. I'll be in charge here, far more than I am now. And with no wife to pass things on to, Roger just might be persuaded to make me his heir."

"How long would he survive the signing of the will?"

"That won't be your concern, my sweet. You'll be where you can't do a thing about it."

Eleanor stared at him, frozen-faced. He began to wheedle.

"Oh, come on, old girl. Think of the times we'll have on dear old Roger's money. You don't plan to spend the rest of your life in that bedroom, do you?"

"No," said Eleanor, "I don't."

Her mind was forming pictures, of Roger being carried down to a couch on the terrace to get the sun, of Roger being pushed around the garden in a wheelchair, of Roger taking his first steps on crutches. And some day, of Roger and herself walking together where she and Gerald were walking now. It would happen. She knew it would because this was what she wanted most in all the world, and she always got what she wanted.

"Very well, Gerald," she replied. "Give me the syringe."

"Come down into the shrubbery first so we can't be seen from the house."

She hesitated. "It's full of wasps down there."

He laughed and steered her toward the dense screen of bushes. Once hidden, he took the hypodermic out of his pocket. "Here you are. Be sure to handle it with your handkerchief as I'm doing, so you won't leave any fingerprints. Now have you got it all straight?"

"Yes, Gerald," she said. "I know exactly what to do."

"Good. Then you'd better go back to the house and tuck Roger in for the night. I'll stroll around the grounds awhile longer. We mustn't be seen going back together." He blew her a kiss and turned to leave.

"Wait, Gerald," said Eleanor sharply. "Don't move. There's a wasp on the back of your neck."

"Well, swat it, can't you?"

Lady Patterly's hand flashed up. "Oh, too late. Sorry, that was clumsy of me. Did it sting you badly?"

She left him rubbing his neck and walked easily across the terrace. The hypodermic barrel felt pleasantly smooth in her hand. She lingered a moment by the garden well, idly dropping pebbles and listening to them plop into the water far below. If one plop was slightly louder than the rest, there was nobody but herself around to hear it. She went in to her husband.

"How are you feeling tonight, Roger?"

"Like a man again. Eleanor, you don't know what you've done for me."

She slipped a hand over his. "No more than a wife should, my darling. Would you like to read for a while?"

"No, just stay with me. I want to look at you."

They were sitting together in the gathering twilight when the gamekeeper and his son brought Gerald's body back to the house.

"How strange," Eleanor observed to the doctor a short time later. "He mentioned his heart again this evening. It kept him out of the army, he told me. But I'm afraid I didn't take him all that seriously. He always looked so healthy."

"That's always the way," said the doctor. "It's these big, hearty chaps that go in a flash. Now, His Lordship will probably live to be ninety."

Lady Patterly smoothed back her husband's hair with a competent hand. "Yes," she replied. "I don't see any reason why he shouldn't."

Journey for Lady G.

"I'm afraid it will have to be Lady Gwendolyn this time," said Miss Henrietta.

Her brother Alexander looked up from his porridge, startled. "But Henrietta, I thought we had agreed to keep Lady Gwendolyn only for the direst emergencies."

"This is an emergency," replied his sister firmly. "The roof is past mending again, you simply must have a few weeks in the sun this winter for your bronchitis, and our bill at Brown's has run on so long I'm ashamed to face them. I hesitate to trouble you about it at breakfast, but we must have cash, a great deal of it, and soon."

"Couldn't the Admiral—"

"You know he wouldn't do. Nobody is going to give us anything for a Kneller these days. No, it will have to be the Romney."

"Very well, if you think it's absolutely necessary." The frail, elderly man touched an exquisitely darned napkin to his lips and rose from the table. "How I always hate seeing them go! You will make the usual arrangements, I suppose. We oughtn't to go through Bumbleby's this time."

"No, I quite agree with you. We must not impose on their good nature again, although they have been of greater service to us in the past than they can ever be aware. I made a discreet inquiry or two on my last visit to London and obtained the addresses of some other art dealers."

"But they must be reputable," Alexander fussed. "We dare not risk Lady Gwendolyn's getting into the hands of unscrupulous dealers."

"I think," reproved his sister gently, "that you may trust me to show as much care for our family treasures as you yourself would do."

"Of course you will." Her brother beamed at her fondly over his pince-nez. "Better, undoubtedly. Really, your efficiency never ceases to amaze me."

"Considering that we were neither of us brought up to lead useful lives, I think we do fairly well on the whole," said Miss Henrietta with a touch of complacency.

She was right. Their home might not have been maintained quite so impeccably as it had been in their mother's day, but still it remained both comfortable and attractive. Henrietta managed the housework with the occasional help of Mrs. Blount from the village. Alexander had developed all sorts of unexpected talents for mending taps and edging flowerbeds.

The elegant sufficiency with which their parents had fondly thought to leave them had all but vanished in the bewildering economy of a world they had not been reared to live in. Nevertheless, they stayed warm and well-fed. They wore their clothes an extra few years and darned their linen a little more industriously, but on the whole their standard of living had hardly changed at all.

This would not, of course, have been possible without the pictures. The family had always been fond of paintings and had always until now been able to indulge their tastes. One after another, the Johns and Marys had had their portraits done by the fashionable artists of the day. For generations these had gazed down benignly or, as in the case of the late

102

Admiral, ferociously upon their descendants. Now they were providing a reasonably comfortable income for the last of their line.

It was no wonder Alexander sighed with mingled affection and regret as he took the lovely Lady Gwendolyn from her place of honour over the drawing-room mantelpiece and wrapped her tenderly in a piece of old army blanket before boxing her up in a wooden packing case, to which he had thoughtfully screwed a carrying handle for his sister's greater convenience.

"I have often wished she were a full-length, but I must say just now I'm grateful she is only a head and shoulders," remarked Miss Henrietta as she juggled the awkward case into a seat on the 12:04 to London.

"You will be careful, won't you?" begged her brother. "And telephone as soon as you have anything to report."

"Don't worry. I shall be an astute bargainer." She waved a small, gloved hand at the slight figure on the platform as the train pulled out.

Alexander was beginning to show his age, she thought with a pang. He must have a new overcoat for his excursion to Antibes. How wonderful it was going to be to have some money again and how grateful she was to be able to help such a dear, good brother. She gave the wooden case containing Lady Gwendolyn a loving pat and settled back to enjoy the infrequent pleasure of a train ride.

The new art dealer, whose address she had written out and tucked into her glove, was not hard to find. The cab driver was most obliging about helping her inside with the packing case. As she had anticipated, the dealer pronounced the painting a genuine Romney and promptly made her a handsome offer for it.

"You are too kind," she fluttered. "I . . . it is such a tre-

103

mendous decision. Lady Gwendolyn has been in the family for so long, you see. I must be sure she is going to someone who will really care for her. One has a responsibility, you know."

Knowing how useless it is to argue with sweet little elderly ladies, the dealer pressed his card on her, renewed his offer with a shade more emphasis, replaced Lady Gwendolyn in her traveling case, and handed Miss Henrietta into a cab.

"By all means think it over," he urged, "but I don't think you will find a fairer offer in London."

"I am sure of it," she replied. "Believe me, it is not that. I simply feel I should like to sit down quietly with a cup of tea and think it over. You do understand?"

The dealer assured her that he did, and saw her off with a sigh.

Her driver was surprised at the address of the hotel she gave him. "You sure you've got the right place, ma'am?" His tone was paternal. "Mostly rich Yanks go there, and it costs the earth. Thought you mightn't know, ma'am."

"Yes, I know." Miss Henrietta smoothed down her shabby tweed coat and straightened her sensible felt hat. "It will be a refreshing change to spend a short time among people who have a great deal of money. One was brought up to believe it was vulgar to be preoccupied with such things, but we are all forced to be vulgarians these days, are we not?"

The driver agreed sadly that we were, helped his fare out with Lady Gwendolyn, and forgave the meagerness of her tip.

Miss Henrietta did not go to engage a room. Overcome by her exertions, she collapsed into a chair far more luxuriously padded than her father would have approved, and propped Lady Gwendolyn's case uncomfortably against her knee. A few minutes later, Lady Gwendolyn went tumbling into the path of a passing gentleman.

"Oh, I'm sorry. Clumsy of me." The well-dressed man stooped to retrieve the case.

"Do be careful. It's terribly precious," fluttered Miss Henrietta. "Thank you so much. Yes, perhaps it would be better against the chair, but I must confess I don't like letting it out of my sight, even for a moment. Only a short time ago I was offered a great deal of money for it."

"Really?" The indifference in the American's drawl was perhaps a shade overdone. "And what, may I ask, do you have in there?" he asked playfully. "The Crown Jewels?"

"Dear me, no." Miss Henrietta smiled shyly, showing an elderly woman's pleasure at being teased by a younger man. For an American he had rather a decent accent, she thought. She leaned forward with a pretty air of confiding. "As a matter of fact, it's a painting. I do not know if you have heard of an English portrait artist named Romney?"

Her new acquaintance's rather long nose seemed to quiver slightly. "Yes," he replied, "I have heard of Romney. I am, in fact, curator of an art museum."

"Fancy that!" Miss Henrietta smiled and nodded an amiable farewell. The American did not move away.

"About this Romney," he persisted. "You're quite sure it's authentic?"

"Oh yes," she replied. "It has been in my family ever since Mr. Romney painted it. And that gentleman today—let me see, what was his name? Ah, here it is, still in my glove. You see? There would be no point in his declaring it to be authentic if it were not," she added in rather a severe tone.

"Of course not," he half-apologized. "It's only that one doesn't often meet charming ladies in hotel lobbies carrying valuable paintings."

"Leaving them about for other people to trip over, you

mean. I do hope you are not bruised."

"I'll tell you what," he said with a gaiety that was somehow out of keeping with his personality, "I'll forgive and forget if you'll come and have a drink with me. Or would you prefer tea?"

"On the contrary, I should enjoy a glass of sherry very much," said Miss Henrietta. "I have had a most exhausting day." She took a firm grip on Lady Gwendolyn's handle and followed her new acquaintance into the bar.

Miss Henrietta had not one but two glasses of sherry. Halfway through the second, her cheeks had become flushed and she was chattering freely to her bosom friend of half an hour about the imponderable difficulties of keeping house on nothing a month.

"And so you see, Mr. Bargraves, I have decided to part with Lady Gwendolyn. What my dear mother would say, I do not know." She drained the last of her sherry with a defiant air. "But I'm going to do it nevertheless. Of course I shall see to it that she gets a good home."

Mr. Bargraves half-rose from his chair. "I wonder if you'll excuse me for just a moment, my dear lady. I have an urgent phone call to make. May I order you another glass of sherry while you're waiting?"

"Oh, I shouldn't," Miss Henrietta demurred.

"Nonsense," said the curator jovially. "One more can't hurt you."

"Very well, then. Just a little one."

Mr. Bargraves was back in a few minutes looking very pleased with himself. The art dealer's guarded replies to his cunningly worded questions had been more than satisfactory. He found Miss Henrietta in a state of fuzzy well-being. A few minutes later they were ascending in the lift to his suite, Lady

Gwendolyn's carrying handle clutched possessively in the curator's hand.

"And now let's see this wonderful Romney."

He drew the painting out of its case, studied it for a long time, ran experienced fingertips over the surface, finally took out a jeweler's loupe and studied every inch, both front and back.

"It's a Romney, all right."

His tone was matter-of-fact, but the hand that held the loupe shook slightly. Over Mr. Bargraves's horselike face crept a look his Yankee forefathers would have understood.

"Naow, Miz . . . that is, my dear lady, you've got a nice little property here. Mind you, I'm not saying it's one hundred percent authentic. That background was done by an apprentice, I'd say, with the finishing touches put in by the master, and of course being just a head and shoulders makes it less desirable than a full-length portrait. If she'd been a well-known historical figure, now—" He shrugged. "Nevertheless, it's a nice little painting."

"I have always been greatly attached to Lady Gwendolyn," said Miss Henrietta somewhat foggily.

"Just so. And I can appreciate your feelings about not wanting her to go into the wrong hands. It wouldn't do for your ancestress to wind up in the ill-gotten collection of some dissolute and lascivious millionaire playboy now, would it?"

"Oh no, that would be too dreadful."

"Well, that's the risk you take when you sell to those art dealers. They don't care who buys what, so long as they get the cash. I hate to say it, but they're a money-hungry lot."

"Alas, so am I just now," sighed Miss Henrietta. "I really do not know which way to turn. I simply must sell Lady Gwendolyn. But oh, if I could only make sure she gets into the right hands!"

A bright green light shone in Mr. Bargraves's eyes. "It so happens," he began cautiously, "that I might be in a position to help you."

"If you only could!" Miss Henrietta's hands in their mended gloves clenched imploringly. "I should be eternally grateful."

Mr. Bargraves cleared his throat. "I should perhaps explain that I am curator of a fine arts museum in that part of the United States which is known as New England." He dwelt on the last word lovingly. "An area, I may say, where we hold our ties with the old mother country very dear. I do wish you could see our museum, dear lady. A magnificent edifice, designed in the finest Graeco-Roman tradition by one of our great modern architects, filled with priceless art treasures from all over the world, visited by throngs of serious-minded art lovers daily from ten to five except Thursdays, and lavishly endowed by—" He checked himself hastily. "Of course it all goes into the building fund. We never have a nickel to spend on paintings. Nevertheless, I think I may take it upon myself to make you an offer for your Lady G."

He pulled out a bulging note case. "What would you say to five thousand pounds, cold cash?"

Miss Henrietta said nothing. She merely stared at the sheaf of notes in his hand.

"Think of it, dear lady. Your beloved ancestress would hang in a place of honour and dignity, viewed only by the worthy and deserving eyes of dedicated students of art and ladies and gentlemen from the best families. And—er—you needn't mention a simple cash transaction like this to the inland revenue man."

"But would you not have to show a bill of sale to Customs when you leave the country?"

"Nonsense! There are ways of getting around these things

if you know the ropes. We'll simply dispense with that little formality and nobody will be the wiser."

"Do you mean you simply give me the money and I give you Lady Gwendolyn and . . . and go away?"

"That's the ticket. No names, no pack drill, as you say over here. Come to think of it, you've never told me your name."

"Haven't I?" said Miss Henrietta absently. She was busy doing sums in her head. So much for the roof, so much for Alexander's vacation, so much for a nest egg to tide them over the winter. The figure was ridiculously low compared to what the art dealer had offered, but it was cash in hand and nothing in writing. It would do. She stretched out her small hand.

"Thank you, Mr. Bargraves. Lady Gwendolyn and I are deeply obliged to you."

Mr. Bargraves bowed her out. "It was my pleasure, dear lady." There could be no doubt he meant it.

He was still gloating over his bargain when a firm knock sounded at his door. Assuming it was the chambermaid, Mr. Bargraves opened the door, to find himself face to face with a frail, elderly man who brandished a rolled umbrella in a menacing attitude.

"I believe I am addressing Mr. Lucius Brutus Bargraves?"

"You have the advantage of me, sir."

"Yes," said Alexander, proffering his calling card, "I believe I have. That Romney on your dresser, sir, is mine."

"But I just bought it!"

"You cannot have done, sir, for I have not sold it."

Alexander pulled a sheaf of papers from his pocket. "Please study this inventory of my father's estate. As you see, everything is left to me as his only son, and the portrait of

Lady Gwendolyn by Romney is included herein. Here is a photograph of the portrait, and here is its provenance. You yourself certainly have no doubts of my painting's authenticity, or you would not have bothered to steal it."

"I did not steal it. I bought it fair and square."

"Perhaps you can show me a bill of sale, then? Ah no, I thought not. Let me tell you sir, the penalties for theft are severe in this country."

He glared at the dumbfounded curator over his umbrella. "Since Lady Gwendolyn was taken from my home, I have been in touch with London art dealers. When your confederate turned up with her this afternoon and you followed up the visit with a bogus telephone call designed, no doubt, to increase the price they might be willing to pay, the fact was reported to me. I came at once to you, sir, hoping to make you see the error of your ways and avoid criminal prosecution for what I sincerely hope was a rash impulse and not the act of a hardened felon—"

Mr. Bargraves wrung his hands. "But I had nothing to do with any theft. I never saw that old bat before in my life. I paid her five thousand pounds in good faith."

"If you paid her such a paltry fraction of the picture's true worth, you hardly did so in good faith," said Alexander severely. "As a self-styled expert in such matters, you must have realized at once that if she was willing to accept such a small figure, there must have been something fishy about the transaction. What was the woman's name?"

"I . . . I don't know."

"Really, Mr. Bargraves," a thin smile flitted across Alexander's lips, "I don't know what effect your taradiddle about an anonymous lady and a five-thousand-pound transaction without a bill of sale will have on a jury, but I must say it does not convince me. And quite frankly, I do not care whether

110

you are a thief or merely a receiver of stolen goods. My position is simply this: do I get my painting back *instanter* or do I call Scotland Yard at once?"

"Did you have any trouble with Mr. Bargraves?"

Miss Henrietta and her brother were enjoying a cup of cocoa in front of the drawing-room fire at the end of a trying but rewarding day.

"Not more than usual. He blustered of course but after all, I had the truth on my side. I must say however, Henrietta, that he referred to you in a language most unbecoming a man of his alleged position."

"One can hardly blame him." Miss Henrietta smiled. "The fox hardly expects to be bitten by the goose he is leading to the slaughter. It is curious how all of a pattern these people are, and how extraordinarily easy it is to find one in the right place at the right time."

"The shocking fact of the matter is that there are a great many scoundrels in the world," said Alexander. "Let me see, how many have we met so far? Forty-nine, I believe."

"Fifty," said Miss Henrietta. "Dear me, this is our golden anniversary."

She looked around the pleasant room at the unbroken row of ancestral portraits, safely retrieved one after the other from the hands of the predators. Then she raised her cup of cocoa to Lady Gwendolyn, smiling down again from her place of honour over the mantelpiece. "It seems appropriate to say, many happy returns. And may we all still be together to celebrate our Diamond Jubilee."

Force of Habit

I had been sleeping badly ever since my husband died. My first night in the new apartment was not likely to be a good one. I put off going to bed as long as I could, but at last it became pointless to sit up any longer.

It is a disagreeable business, taking off your warm clothes long after the heat has gone out of the pipes in a house that is not your own. Your nightgown is cold, the bathroom is cold, the sheets are coldest of all when there is no long-familiar though perhaps not greatly loved body sharing them with you. I had a hot water bottle, but it seemed a ridiculously small thing in the midst of so much emptiness. So I lay and shivered.

At least the place was quiet. Below me lived two deaf old sisters. Above was only the dressmaker's flat, empty now that the woman had died. I'd happened to notice the obituary notice in the paper because it was near my husband's. Suddenly while at work, it had said. There was still a dirty card reading SERAPHINE LABERES, DRESSMAKING AND ALTERATIONS stuck over the mailbox. If she'd gone a week earlier I could have had my choice of the two apartments. Perhaps the top floor would be lighter and airier. But the middle was always the warmest, my brother-in-law told me.

It certainly was quiet. "Next door to a convent," my

brother-in-law kept reminding me, as though this was an advantage. In fact neither one of us knew the first thing about convents, and very little about the Protestant church with which we fancied ourselves to be affiliated. My brother-in-law is one of those fat, red-faced men who like to point out the obvious in loud, hearty voices with a view to cheering one up. I was sick of him and his everlasting good intentions.

Gradually, as my body warmed the bed, I began to experience something like a sense of comfort. All was behind me now: Henry's illness, the hospital visits, the funeral, the awkward condolences and forced replies, the exhausting, and harrowing toil of breaking up my long-established household, the disagreeable business of the insurance. My brother-in-law really had been helpful over that. He enjoyed making the company disgorge money just somebody because had died, even though neither the loss nor the gain was his. "Nicely provided for," he'd kept repeating, pleased as though he'd been the farsighted one himself.

There was plenty for me to live on. Nevertheless, I should find something to do. I was not used to being idle. It might be pleasant to hold a job again, if one could be found in our gone-to-seed mill town. I could leave this quiet three-room flat every morning and not come back until suppertime. In between, there would be things to do and people to talk to. Not that I was much of a talker myself, but others would chat and I should hear the cheerful noise of voices. And on the weekends when my brother-in-law's wife telephoned to invite me to Sunday dinner, I could say, "Thank you, Martha, but I've been working all week and I have to stay home and clean my rooms."

Grateful to have a plan, I dropped off to sleep.

As I mentioned, I had not been sleeping well and it took

very little to wake me up. A flicker of lights on the ceiling did it this time. I lay for some while on my back, looking up at them, wondering what they could be. They were too small and feeble to be car lights; they moved in a confused, vaguely circular pattern. Finally I reached for my robe, stuck my feet into my slippers, and padded over to the window.

Two thoughts passed through my mind at the same time: "What on earth are they doing?" and "My brother-in-law was wrong."

Next door to a convent was not such a quiet place after all, it appeared. The nuns were conducting some sort of candle-light ceremony in the narrow, iron-railed garden below my window. I could barely make them out, ungainly shapes in their old-style long black robes, each with a lighted taper casting occasional yellowish gleams on her gray-white cowl. The flames looked so weak I wondered how they could possibly shine into my room, yet when I looked behind me, there were those tiny spots of light still reflected on the ceiling.

I tried to make out what they were doing, but there seemed no pattern or sense to their milling about. With some difficulty, I counted them. Fourteen. The number carried no significance that I knew of. After a while I got bored watching them and went back to bed. At once, as though I'd flipped a switch, the lights were gone. Out of curiosity I got up and went over to the window again. The garden was empty. I lay down once more, wondering if they did this every night and whether I'd get used to it.

The following day turned out far different and far busier than I had anticipated. To begin with, I still had a good deal of unpacking and settling to do. In the midst of this, the telephone man came. No sooner had he got the instrument installed than I impulsively picked it up and called the town library, where I'd worked before my marriage. Miss Harcourt was still there, quite old by now, of course, but she remembered me.

"Anna Harris. No, it's Anna Goodbody now, isn't it? . . . Indeed we'd rejoice to have you back. It's so hard to get anyone suitable nowadays, with all the halfway intelligent girls moving away where they can get higher pay." And so on, for quite a while. She asked if I could fill in at the North Branch that very evening, as it was the regular woman's daughter's birthday and she'd been hoping to get off.

Happy to be of use again, I said yes I thought I could manage all right and no I didn't mind a bit, though I couldn't make out whether I was not supposed to mind the short notice or the low wages. After a very complicated series of phone calls, it was arranged for me to be on duty at seven o'clock. This meant a quick pressing out of a suitable dress, a scratch supper, and a fast walk to the North Branch.

I got through the two hours easily, glad to be back in the musty-smelling old building I had been so glad to leave twenty-seven years before. Whoever was in charge of the North Branch these days had been sadly neglectful about reading the shelves. I managed to get quite a lot of the nonfiction straightened out as not many borrowers came in and only three or four teenagers giggled halfheartedly at the reference tables. I went home thoroughly tired and quite pleased with myself.

That night I had no trouble falling asleep, but I was awakened sometime after midnight by the nuns' little lights flickering on my ceiling. I tried to ignore them but I suppose I was too keyed up after my whirlwind day. Anyway, I got out of bed again and went to look. There they were, each with her candle, moving around in that same aimless, wavery circle.

115

Knowing nothing about Catholic orders, I was free to speculate. Maybe this was one of those cloistered convents where nobody spoke. They weren't speaking now, anyway, the sound would have carried up to me. Maybe they weren't allowed out in the daytime. To be sure, I saw nuns around town fairly often, but perhaps they were from a different convent, or perhaps some could go and others had to stay. It seemed odd, but the whole concept of the religious life is beyond me. I gave up wondering and idly counted them again. Fifteen. One more than the night before. Unless I'd counted wrong.

I had not. Every night after that, I witnessed the same performance. Every night there was one more nun in the yard. It got to be a sort of game. I dropped off about half-past ten, fully expecting to be wakened roughly two hours later. When the lights started to flicker on the ceiling, I got up, counted the number of candle flames—this was easier than trying to sort out the black shapes of the nuns themselves—and went back to bed. As soon as I was back under the covers, the lights would disappear from the ceiling. It was as though I controlled the amount of time those poor creatures were allowed to spend in the yard, and I must admit it gave me a queer feeling.

What with these nightly interruptions, my job, and keeping up the apartment, I found I was always tired, and I must have looked it. Miss Harcourt spoke to me.

"I hope the work here isn't too much for you, Anna."

"Oh, no," I said. As a matter of fact, it was nothing compared to when Henry was alive. "It's just I haven't been getting enough sleep on account of the nuns."

"The nuns?" She stared at me, quite startled. "Whatever do you mean?"

I explained about the nightly perambulations and the

lights on my ceiling. She shook her head.

"That is strange. I've lived here all my life, and I never heard of such a thing."

"I thought perhaps they couldn't go out during the day or something," I ventured.

"No, that can't be it. They are a working order. A number of them teach at the parochial school. You have seen them in here about the Catholic book lists. Some of the others run the thrift shop and that little place beside it that sells religious statues and whatnot. I believe they also go around visiting shut-ins and taking food to the needy. This is a poor parish, you know, since the mill closed down."

She didn't have to tell me that. One had only to walk down our main street and look at the dirt-streaked store windows, many of them empty except for torn paper signs with maybe a flyspecked cardboard display or a forgotten paper coffee cup, and see the women shuffling along in cheap, thin old coats with the hems dragging and sleazy kerchiefs tied over their curlers.

"I simply cannot understand what they'd be doing out there at that hour of the night," Miss Harcourt was still fussing. "Perhaps if you spoke to the Mother Superior, she could have them use the other side of the yard."

"How many are there?" I asked her.

"I really couldn't say for sure. Quite a large group, I believe, many of them fairly old. They were brought here not long after the war, when things were booming, and apparently just stayed on. Nowhere else to go, I suppose, like the rest of us." She sighed and went back to her dingy office, leaving me to cope with the week's circulation records.

Over the weekend it wasn't so bad, as I could sleep late both mornings. There was also the pleasure of refusing Martha's invitation to Sunday dinner. She and my brother-in-law took the news of my job as I had expected, pleased that they now had an excuse not to bother with me, annoyed because I'd taken the step without consulting them. I didn't care. Already my life was taking on a pattern in which they would have no part.

I did think of dropping a gentle remark to my brother-in-law that life next door to a convent was less rosy than he'd painted it, but I refrained. He might feel it his duty to take steps, and I did not want him interfering. After all, if the nuns chose to exercise in their own garden, whose business was it but their own?

By the following Wednesday afternoon, when I caught myself falling asleep over the books I was mending in the staff room, the mellow mood had worn off. My nightly count had reached twenty-two by then. The mailman had told me there were fifty—sisters, he called them—in residence at the convent. That probably meant I had twenty-three more nights of broken sleep to endure. Then, for all I knew, they'd be starting over again. Honestly, it was too much.

Glancing up from my work, I happened to see one of the daytime nuns passing toward the circulation desk I got up and went out to intercept her.

"Good afternoon," I said quite politely, all things considered. "I'm Mrs. Goodbody. I happen to be a neighbor of yours."

"A neighbor?" She was an elderly woman as Miss Harcourt had said she'd be, good-natured and not particularly bright looking, wearing gold-rimmed glasses that had been clumsily mended with adhesive tape. "Oh, you mean you live in the house next to the convent. Then you must have known our dear Seraphine." She beamed as though that made us friends.

"No, I'm afraid I never did," I told her. "I moved in just after she died."

I don't think the nun heard me. "We all miss her so," she went on, picking at the frayed edges of her sleeves. "She was so wonderfully kind to us."

She made the sign of the cross and wandered on to join another of her order who was talking with Miss Harcourt at the desk. I didn't like to go chasing after her again. Feeling defeated and cross, I went back to mending books. A few minutes later, Miss Harcourt came in.

"I asked Sister Marie Claire," she said abruptly, "and she says they don't."

"Don't what?"

"Sister says," Miss Harcourt explained carefully in her precise librarian's voice, "that the rules of the convent compel them all to be in their beds at half-past nine and not to leave their cells until six o'clock in the morning. She says none of them would dare disobey."

"I don't care what she says," I replied too sharply. "I've seen them out there every night since I moved."

She looked at me for a moment without speaking, then went back to the desk. I knew what she was thinking. "The shock of losing her husband, poor dear."

That evening I had the North Branch again. On my way into the house after I got off duty, I thumped at the door of my first-floor neighbors. Their television was blasting full force and I had a hard time making them hear. Finally one of the sisters, Miss Edith I believe it was, shuffled to the door.

"Come in, come in, Mrs. Goodbody. Helen, it's Mrs. Goodbody from upstairs," she screamed.

The other sister, who must have been even deafer, smiled and nodded but didn't turn away from the television set. She was watching a western and seemed to enjoy being able to hear the gunshots.

"I wanted to ask you," I shouted over the racket, "if you

ever see the nuns in the yard at night."

Miss Edith nodded briskly. "Fine. Not a bit of trouble since I started the new treatment. What I say is, you can't be too careful with all this—" I think the next word was *sickness*. Miss Edith had a trick of raising and lowering her voice between a bellow and a whisper without regard to the sense of what she was saying. Between that and the gunfire, I lost a great deal.

"—since she died. Though if you ask me, she plain wore herself to death sewing for those nuns."

"Yes, the nuns," I shrieked. "Do you ever—"

"Night and day. It was too much for a woman her age, but she was bound and determined. I never knew such a stubborn woman. Did we, Helen?"

Her sister smiled and nodded again, still not taking her eyes from the screen.

"We could hear that sewing machine of hers going at all hours. Some nights it kept us awake."

She must have been talking about the late Seraphine Laberes, I decided. It seemed incredible that any noise whatsoever could disturb this pair. Perhaps the empty apartment between had acted as a giant sounding board. I tried once more.

"They've been keeping me awake."

Surprisingly, she heard most of what I said, and gave me an odd look. "It can't be her. She's been dead for over a month."

"Not Seraphine! The nuns."

"That's what I said. It was doing for those nuns killed her, you mark my words. Working all day at the tailor shop and all night for them. And never getting a penny for it, I know for a fact. She even bought the material herself. She told me so. 'They're old,' she said. 'They won't give up their habits. But I can't stand to see them going around in rags.' I heard her," Miss Edith finished proudly.

The seamstress must have had stronger lungs than mine. I gave up and fell back, like Miss Helen, on smiles and nods.

"She made one a week, regular as clockwork. I'd meet her Sunday mornings going to the convent with a big black bundle over her arm. She didn't care. 'It's the Lord's work,' she'd say to me. She meant to make one for everybody, but she only got thirteen of them done. They found the thirteenth finished on her machine the night she died. That was an unlucky number for her all right, as I said to Helen. Didn't I, Helen?" Those last words were spoken in a whisper.

"You certainly did, Edith," replied Miss Helen.

I said good night and went upstairs.

That night I never shut an eye. I undressed and got into bed but all I could do was lie there waiting for those maddening pinpoints of light to appear.

I finally could stand the suspense no longer. I got up, pulled on the first clothes that came to hand, grabbed my black coat and a headscarf, and went downstairs. I found myself tiptoeing so as not to wake the house, then feeling silly for doing it with only Miss Edith and Miss Helen below and nothing above but the empty flat where Miss Edith claimed Seraphine Laberes had worked herself to death sewing for the nuns.

The garden was still empty when I got down there. I walked over and stood close to the iron railings, beginning to wonder why I had come. After a few minutes, though, I saw a glimmer of light over in the far corner, then another and another. I counted them one by one until the twenty-third appeared. To my annoyance, however, they stayed huddled over in the corner.

"I wish they'd get started with whatever it is they do," I thought crossly. I was getting chilly, standing there.

Immediately, as if I had turned on the power that moved them, the forms started moving around. Still they stayed away from me.

"Oh, come over here," I muttered.

They came, all twenty-three of them in a silent semicircle, looming toward me through the railings. No hands held the candles. No faces showed beneath the cowls. The robes were empty.

I believe I must have fainted. The next thing I remember, I was pulling myself up by the cold iron spikes, picking dirt and leaves off my good wool coat, staring in at the barren garden, empty now in the bleak dawn. I was not frightened. I only knew I should never sleep again until I had finished what must be done.

I went back into the house and took down the card over the top mailbox that said *Seraphine Laberes, Dressmaking and Alterations.* I carried it upstairs and burned it in an ashtray. Then I bathed, dressed, and put on a felt hat I seldom wore. It was still very early, so I puttered around making my bed, dusting a little, brushing my coat where I had fallen. Out of habit I made coffee, but I didn't drink any. As soon as the sky was decently light, I went next door and rang the bell.

The elderly nun who opened the door had on a neat, new habit.

"Seraphine made that," I said.

"She . . . yes she did," stammered the portress, quite startled by my brusque remark.

"She finished thirteen of them, I understand."

"She did, and may the blessing of Mary rest forever on her soul."

"But she still had how many to go?"

"Thirty-seven," the portress replied promptly, as though she had the number stamped on her tongue. "Me being on the door," she half apologized, "I got the first one."

"What is the name of your order?"

"The Little Sisters of the Poor."

Yes, it would be. I took out my checkbook.

Eyeing me with a mixture of hope and suspicion, she backed away from the door. "I'd better call Mother Superior. Will you step in, please?"

I don't know what I expected a convent to be like. The room into which the nun showed me reminded me of a dentist's waiting room. An elderly, not very successful dentist, like the ones in our town. One of those hideous pseudo-Renaissance tables stood in the middle with a couple of straight chairs drawn up to it. I pulled out one and sat down.

The Mother Superior didn't keep me waiting. She bustled in, her long rosary swinging from her waist. I thought it proper to stand up. What on earth did one call her? "Mother Superior" sounded rather a mouthful and plain "Mother" hardly suitable from a non-Catholic close to her own age. I bowed and said nothing. She waved me back into my seat and took the other chair herself. The portress left the room, but I could see her black skirts just beyond the door. I got right down to business.

"I must apologize for coming so early, but I have to do this as soon as possible for my own peace of mind."

The Mother Superior's lips formed the word, "Soul."

"My soul isn't involved," I said rather tartly.

"Oh, but the soul's always involved, Mrs.—"

"Goodbody, I live next door, in the apartment below where Seraphine Laberes used to live."

"God rest her soul," she sighed. "I wish we had more like her."

"I understand she was making you all new uniforms."

"Habits, yes."

"Can you tell me how much each one would cost to buy?"

"More than we can afford, I'm afraid." The Mother Superior was pretty shabby, herself. She named a figure that exactly corresponded to my weekly salary at the library.

"And you need thirty-seven more."

"Thirty-seven for the sisters. Thirty-eight counting me," she amended with childlike shrewdness.

I figured quickly on the back of my blank check. "Is that right?"

"It is, I've figured it often enough myself."

I filled in the amount, signed the check, and pushed it over to her, "Please buy them right away."

"But Mrs. . . . Mrs. Goodbody." She seemed hardly to know what to say. "This is an awful lot of money."

"The check's good," I answered shortly. "My husband left me"—a phrase of my brother-in-law's popped into my head—"well provided for."

"I don't know how to thank you."

"You must not thank me!" I think I frightened her with my vehemence. "You must take those thirty-seven nuns with you immediately into your chapel or whatever you call it, and give thanks that new habits have been provided through the efforts of Seraphine Laberes. I mean it! If you don't do this right away, I'll stop payment on the check."

"We'll certainly do it," she assured me nervously. "And we'll also say—"

"No. My name must never be mentioned. The gift is from Seraphine. Promise me, by all you hold sacred."

"I swear it on the Sacred Heart of Jesus." She made the

sign of the cross. Then she looked at me for what seemed a long time. Perhaps she saw something. "Seraphine Laberes was a very determined woman."

I nodded. Suddenly I felt drained of all my strength, as though I had sat up for many nights, sewing on black cloth that strained the eyes. "I must get to work."

She saw me to the door herself. That night I slept like a baby.

I often come across the nuns in their new habits now, but only in the daytime, thank goodness. Every so often, I slip into the Catholic church and light a candle. I don't quite know why I do it. Still, as Miss Edith says, you can't be too careful.

Better a Cat

"Puss, puss, puss."

"There she goes," said Miss Johnson. "That old cat of hers must have slipped his lead again. You might think she'd have more sense than to go looking for him at this time of night."

"Don't tell me," sighed Miss McGuffy. "I've begged and pleaded with her a hundred times. Mrs. Quinter, I tell her, no cat's worth getting yourself killed for. There've been five stranglings so far this year already. You stay off the roads after dark, I tell her, or you'll be the sixth. But will she listen?"

"You can't tell her a thing," said Miss Johnson. "I said the same thing to her myself only last Thursday. If you think so much of that precious cat of yours, I said, why don't you keep him indoors? But she only simpered in that featherheaded way of hers and said oh no, she couldn't do that. Tommy would be so unhappy if he didn't have his little run. Then let him run in the daytime, I said. But you might as well talk to a stone wall."

"She ought to be locked up, if you ask me," said Miss McGuffy. "Living on bread and tea herself and feeding that smelly old thing chicken and tinned salmon, if you please. It's a disgrace."

"Well, she'll get herself strangled one of these foggy nights while she's out there hunting for him," said Miss Johnson, tugging the tea cosy sharply down over the pot. "And then where will she be?"

Where was she now? Mrs. Quinter thought she knew, but she wasn't quite sure. She pulled her old black coat tighter around her bent body. There was a bone-chilling dampness coming up from the slimy cobblestones.

"Puss, puss, puss!"

She'd put a long way between herself and her basement flat by now. Still no lithe, shadowy form had bounded out of the blackness behind the dustbins. She slapped Tommy's thin nylon lead anxiously against the palm of her free hand. The empty collar dangled at one end. Miss Johnson had suggested that she buy the cat a smaller size, but Mrs. Quinter wouldn't hear of it.

"Oh, no, I couldn't do that. What if the collar got caught on something and Tommy wasn't able to squirm loose from it? A cat could strangle that way."

"Better a cat than a human," Miss Johnson had said. She'd meant well, of course.

"Puss, puss, puss!"

It would be warm at home. She'd set the teapot on the back of the stove and fixed Tommy's chicken on a blue willow plate. She'd been careful to remove all the bones. A cat might choke on a chicken bone. They knew how to make themselves cosy, she and Tommy.

She did wish they were both there right now, she in her comfortable chair by the fire and Tommy purring on her lap. It was no night for an old woman and a middle-aged cat to be prowling the streets.

"Puss, puss—oh!"

A figure loomed out of the mist, directly beside her. She had not heard footsteps.

"You'd best be getting home, Ma," boomed a not unfriendly male voice. "This is no place for a woman alone. Not with a mad strangler about."

"I know," she quavered, "but my cat slipped his collar and ran off. I daren't leave him out, in this neighborhood. There's no telling what might happen to him."

"A cat's got nine lives. You've only one. He'll find his way back all right, don't you fret. They always do. Get on with you, now. You're not safe here. Nobody is."

There was an edge of panic in the man's gruff voice as he tramped on past her over the cobblestones. He was much taller than she. Mrs. Quinter had to stand on tiptoe to fling the lead around his neck.

It was too bad he had to be the one this time. He had seemed a pleasant sort of man. But it cost so much to keep a cat properly fed these days. Her mended gloves fumbled awkwardly at his wallet. Twelve pounds. Excellent. That would take care of her and Tommy for weeks to come. She tucked the money inside her glove and replaced the wallet neatly in the dead man's pocket.

"Puss, puss, puss!"

She was almost home before the familiar, sinuous form pounced out of nowhere to wind its purring length around her weary legs.

"Tommy, you naughty cat," she cried. "I've been looking everywhere for you. Come home this instant and get your supper."

She snapped the collar under his jowls and took a turn of the lead around her glove. Miss Johnson, peering out from behind her curtain, saw the light go on in the entry across the way.

"Well, she's found him at last."

"And lucky she didn't find more than him," said Miss McGuffy. "A night like this, it isn't safe to be out."

128

More Like Martine

"You've got to feed the whole child," Martine spoke decisively, as always.

"It's about all I can do to feed the end that hollers." Betsy spoke wearily, as usual.

"I know, dear. If you'd only planned—"

"How can you plan to have twins?"

"But did you have to have them so soon after Peggy?"

"Jim and I wanted our kids to grow up in a bunch. It's more fun for them."

"But darling, fun isn't everything. You must develop their aesthetic awareness, too."

"I don't think mine have any."

"Oh, but all children do, dear. I saw the most charming exhibition of Guatemalan hand-weaving yesterday, done by six- to ten-year-olds. So fresh and spontaneous."

"Peg does hand-weaving. She made me this potholder at the playground."

"Sweet." Martine barely glanced at her niece's clumsy effort.

"Don't you think it's sort of fresh and spontaneous?" Betsy hung the red-and-green-and-yellow mess back on its hook. Martine was right, she supposed.

Martine was always right. Martine had been graduated from high school with all possible honors while Betsy was squeaking through third grade by the skin of her brace-laden teeth. Martine had been May Queen and Phi Beta Kappa at college and would soon be vice-president of her firm. Martine wore designer models and gave perfect little dinners to amusing people. Betsy handed out peanut-butter sandwiches.

"You mustn't vegetate in the suburbs," Martine was saying for the fifty-seventh time since Jim and Betsy had bought the house. "You have to keep broadening your horizons."

"Sorry." Betsy shoved another load into the washer. "I don't have the time right now."

"But you could do it in little ways, dear. Put some glamour into your meals, for instance. Dine by candlelight. Serve exotic foods."

"Jim likes steak and potatoes."

Her sister left, wearing that what-can-you-do-with-her expression Betsy had been seeing all her life. Somewhere, right now, some aunt or other must be wondering, "Why couldn't Betsy have turned out more like Martine?"

She slammed the empty coffee cups into the dishwasher. Betsy hated these unexpected flying visits. They always meant Martine had something to tell her for her own good. The awful part was, Martine always did. Maybe, deep down, Jim found his marriage boring. Maybe some day the kids would resent not having had a more well-rounded childhood.

The twins whooped in demanding lunch. "How about some nice cream of mushroom soup for a change?" she asked them timidly. The *yecch* was deafening.

Betsy tried again at dinner. She knew better that to tamper with the menu because if she served anything fancy, Jim would say in a sorrowful tone, "I thought we were having steak and potatoes." But she went all-out on gracious touches. She set the table with flowers and hand-embroidered place mats. She shut her eyes to the probable consequences and gave everybody, even the twins, crystal goblets instead of peanut-butter tumblers. She put on the green velvet hostess gown Martine had given her for Christmas a year ago, that she never wore because it was much too beautiful to fry an egg or scrub a twin in. She still hadn't got around to taking up the hem. Even with her highest heels, the skirt brushed the floor.

Her family reacted much as she'd expected. Jim grinned and rumpled the hairdo she'd fussed over. "Hi, Gorgeous. When do we eat?" Peggy demanded, "Is it a party, Mummy? Why, Mummy?" The twins yelled, "Who gets the presents?"

It was Mike who knocked over his goblet. Jim got most of the milk in his lap. "Why did you give it to him?" he roared, sopping frantically with his napkin.

"I'll get a sponge." Betsy jumped up, caught a spike heel in her too-long skirt, and went sprawling.

Jim was beside her, his big hands under her shoulders. "Can't you watch where you're going? Come on, kid."

"Jim, don't!" She hadn't meant to scream. "My leg."

"Let's see." He clawed away at the slippery velvet, cursing its endless folds. The angle of the bones sickened him. "Oh my God!"

He ran for the telephone. The children were all around her, trying to help by crying and patting her face with sticky fingers and offering to kiss it and make it better. Then Jim was back, shooing them off. "They say don't try to move. The ambulance is on its way. It's okay, kids, Mum's going to be fine. Oh Christ, who's going to stay with them?"

"Get Martine." She was talking from inside a tunnel. "Call Martine."

"That's it. Martine will know what to do."

From then on it was all bits and pieces: Jim's hand holding

hers too tight, voices saying things like dislocation and com-
pound fracture, then a needle in her arm, then nothing. When
she woke up, she was in traction.

"They'll have to get me out of this. I have to get home to
the kids."

She must have said it aloud. Somebody said, "Relax and
enjoy it, honey. You won't be going anywhere for a while."
Red hair and a red satin bathrobe with *I'm the Greatest* embroidered in white on it. Kind hands, raising her head,
holding a glass with a straw in it. Something cool and wet
going down her throat. Then more sleep, then a terrible business with a bedpan that started the hip and leg throbbing,
then it was night and Jim was with her. She held his hand
against her cheek and drifted into a pleasant nothingness
where the pain was something happening a long way off. She
could hear Jim talking. Sometimes it made sense.

"Martine was teaching the kids to finger paint. Peg did a
mural for the playroom."

"That's nice." She supposed it was her own voice an-
swering. "Did you eat?"

"Oh sure. Martine had a real gourmet meal waiting when I
got home." After a while, he kissed her and left.

The next day Betsy was less groggy, which meant she felt
the pain more. She was in a room with three other women.
She hadn't quite grasped that fact before. One was very old
and groaned a lot. One had a tube up her nose and lay
watching the little television set over her bed. The redhead in
the red satin bathrobe prowled around wearing a pair of white
gym socks for slippers. She had friends all up and down the
corridor. When they took their shuffling walks, they'd stick
their heads into the room looking for her. "Hi," they'd say to
Betsy when they saw her eyes open. "How's it going?"

It was a comfort having people around. Even the old lady

who groaned was nice, the redhead said. It was just the medication that made her like that. The redhead herself was feeling great and didn't see why they wouldn't let her out. Those goddamn doctors thought they knew everything. Betsy said she hoped they did. The redhead laughed.

"Hey, you're going to be fine. How about if I get you some juice?"

That night, Jim brought her ice cream. She ate a little, but the plastic spoon was too heavy to keep lifting. "Here, you finish it."

"Thanks, I couldn't. Martine put on a Spanish meal. We had gazpacho."

"What's that?"

"Cold soup with a lot of stuff floating around in it."

"Did the twins eat any?"

"Sure, they thought it was great."

"What else did you have?"

"Don't ask me. Some kind of chicken and rice thing. She served Spanish wine with it. Only half a bottle," he added rather embarrassedly. "She used those glasses Aunt Florrie gave us. She says it's a shame not to enjoy them."

"You yelled at me when I did that." Betsy just barely kept herself from saying it. Did Martine always have to make such a howling success of what she herself fell flat on her face trying to do? Jim misunderstood her silence, of course.

"Don't worry, she'll take good care of them. She's got the place shined up so you wouldn't know it." On the whole, his visit was less of a comfort than Betsy had expected it to be.

She'd just finished her lunch the following day when Martine blew in with a big box from the most expensive florist in town and a book on Guatemalan folk art. Martine stopped in the doorway and stared around the crowded four-bed ward, at the woman with the tube up her nose and her television blaring, at the old lady groaning in the corner, at the red-head's white gym socks and *I'm the Greatest* bathrobe. Before Betsy had a chance to ask her, "Who's staying with the kids?" she was gone. Maybe ten minutes later Martine was back leading a troop of doctors, nurses, attendants, technicians and an orderly wheeling a gurney.

"It's all fixed, Betsy," she caroled. "You're moving."

"To where?"

"A private room, of course. You can't stay in this rattrap. Now don't worry about the extra charges, darling. I know Jim's insurance won't cover them, but Big Sister's will. I carry a special rider just for you. Just lie perfectly still. You're going to be joggled around a bit, so they have to give you something for the pain first."

That was that. When Betsy woke again, she was in a tastefully decorated room with a handsome floral arrangement on the dresser, a book on Guatemalan folk art ready to hand on the bedside table, and no ministering angel in a red satin bathrobe and white gym socks to offer her a drink of juice. And who was staying with the kids?

She was still groggy from the shot, she supposed. She'd missed supper, but they brought her soup and some whitish stuff in a little plastic bowl. She picked at it, then turned her head away and shut her eyes. Jim didn't come. She wondered if he'd stopped by on his way home from the office and couldn't find her in the new room. She asked the nurse who came to fix her up for the night. The nurse said she wouldn't know; she wasn't on duty then. Maybe Jim had stayed home to take care of the kids. Betsy took her medication like a good girl. There was nothing to stay awake for, not in this lonesome place.

The next day lasted forever. When she couldn't endure lying there staring at her flower arrangement any longer, she got the attendant to turn on the television, and lay there watching soap operas, like the woman with the tube up her nose. They were all about people falling in love with people they weren't supposed to be in love with.

Jim came at last. He said he was sorry to be late. Martine had rearranged the living room furniture, taken the children to the art museum, and served coquilles St. Jacques with an amusing little sauterne. Betsy said how nice.

After that, one day was as bad as another. Betsy lay there watching men make love to other men's wives and women chase after other women's husbands. They started getting her up for physical therapy. It hurt, so they gave her something for the pain. She asked the nurse what would happen if she took two of the little red pills together instead of one at a time. The nurse put on her professional smile and said, "Oh, you wouldn't want to do that."

She got cards and flowers, but not visitors. The aunts were too far away. The neighbors were either working or taking care of their kids. Martine didn't come again, either. She must be too busy repapering the walls and feeding the whole child. The children couldn't have come even if anybody had tried to bring them. Nobody under eight was allowed in the rooms. Betsy asked for a telephone so she could at least hear their voices, but the floor nurse said she couldn't have one. Orders. The nurse didn't say whose.

Jim came every night but he never stayed long. He always told her what Martine had served for dinner, but he never told her what they talked about over the candlelight and wine after Peggy and the twins had been tucked in their beds with visions of Guatemalan hand-weaving dancing in their heads. He was beginning to look drawn and anguished, like all the Joshuas and Jeremies in the soap operas who dreaded having to hurt the Jessicas and Jennifers they'd married on a boyish whim and had to stick with on account of the children.

How could it have happened? Martine was years older than Jim. She'd always gone for suave, sophisticated middle-aged types who held important positions and got divorced a lot. But, the current fashion was for glamorous older women in important positions to form attachments with less glamorous younger men in relatively insignificant positions, some of whom had never been divorced at all. Betsy could see it happening every day, right there on the television screen.

Jim wouldn't walk out on Peg and the twins. He'd hang around looking anguished and noble, Jim who seldom looked anything but glad or mad or quietly content except when he did his barnyard imitations for the kids to laugh at. He wouldn't give up Martine, either. Martine wouldn't let him. Sooner or later, Martine would decide it was best for all of them that Betsy give Jim a nice, quiet, uncontested divorce.

Then what? Jim didn't earn enough to support two households. Even Martine wouldn't be able to make him live on her money. Betsy would have to get some scroungy, ill-paid job as a clerk or waitress and try to scrimp by. What sort of life would that be for Peg and the twins? And who'd look after them while she was at work? Inevitably, they'd wind up with Jim and Martine.

Martine would broaden their horizons. She'd break Peg of needing to run in out of the sandbox for a quick cuddle now and then, sand and all. She'd send her to boarding school, turn her into a slick young sophisticate. At least Peg wouldn't grow up listening to her great-aunts moaning, "What a shame she's not more like Martine."

Martines didn't mess up their lives. They took what they wanted and hung on to it while the Betsys floundered around breaking their bones and wrecking their marriages. When the nurse brought her the little red pill, Betsy asked for two. The nurse said sorry, she couldn't have two.

Her leg was progressing nicely. The therapist was proud of her. The doctor said she could go home Saturday. She told Jim that night and he said, "Great!" But he looked awfully anguished when he said it.

After that, when they brought her the little red pills, she pretended to swallow them and didn't. When she couldn't sleep, she lay there dredging up, one after another, all her memories of Martine acting for the best. Always Martine's kind of best, never Betsy's. Always having to knuckle under and be grateful. How she hated being grateful! Or was it Martine she hated?

How could she? Sisters didn't hate sisters. Except in soap operas. Would those millions of viewers stand for so much sororal venom if at least some of them didn't hate their sisters, too? By Saturday morning she had half a dozen red pills in her toothbrush holder. Six should be enough. Only she still hadn't made up her mind who was going to take them.

As far as herself was concerned, there was no problem. If she had to give up Jim and the kids she'd have nothing left to live for, so why bother trying? But why must she give them up? Martine didn't really love the kids, she'd barely glanced at Peggy's potholder. She'd do her duty by them the same way she'd always done it by Betsy, snatching them away from the dirty old sandbox, packing them tidily inside an impeccably tasteful cage.

Nor did she love Jim, not the way Betsy did, not the Jim who let his whiskers grow on the weekends and took the kids wading in the swamp to see the bullfrogs. Once the trend to not-so-handsome younger men had spent itself, she'd stack him away on the shelf with the rest of the back numbers and find somebody who'd do more to enhance her corporate image. It was appalling to think of murdering one's own flesh and blood, but if it was a matter of keeping Jim and the kids from being smothered in Guatemalan folk art, there was no choice Martine could make for her.

After Betsy was dressed and the nurse's aide had left her to pack her few things, she wrapped the six red pills in a tissue and stuck them in the pocket of her blouse. She'd know what to do when the time came.

And the time was at hand. When Jim came to get her, he was so wired up she wanted to scream at him, "Go on, say it. Get it over." But they were almost to the house before he pulled off the road.

"Betsy, before we get home, there's something I have to tell you."

When she spoke, the voice didn't sound like hers. "It's about Martine."

Jim took a deep, deep breath. "Betsy, I know how close you are to your sister. I fought it, Betsy. You've got to, believe me."

She could only wait.

"But goddamn it to hell, Betsy, I couldn't stand her! Japanese flower arrangements in my fishing creel. The kids whining for peanut butter and getting gazpacho. When I got home that third night and she threw it in my face how she'd gone to the hospital and got you switched to a private room because she could take proper care of her baby sister even if I couldn't support my wife, I went straight off the deep end. It was her own goddamn fault you got hurt in the first place, her and her goddamn crap about gracious living. I told her to butt out and let us run our own lives. I told her to take her god-damn gazpacho and . . . all right, get sore. But honest to God, Betsy, if I'd had her around for one more day, I actually think I'd have killed her."

His arms were trembling as he pulled her against him.

138

"The doctor said you needed absolute rest and no worries, so what could I do? I had to keep telling everybody you weren't allowed phone calls or visitors so they wouldn't spill the beans and get you all upset. But oh God, it's been tough! If you only knew the strain I've been under."

She got one hand free after a while and ran it over his face, making sure he was really there. "Jim, it's okay. Believe me it is. But who kept the kids?"

"I did, mostly. I called the office and told them I was on vacation as of then. We've been giving the hamburger stand a lot of business."

Incredibly, she could still laugh. "No candlelight dinners?"

He snorted. "I used to memorize a fancy menu out of your cookbooks every day so I'd have something to talk about. That wasn't what I wanted to say, kid."

His hands were exploring, confidently now that he knew she was still his. "What the hell? You're lumpy."

"Oh." Betsy shoved his hand away and grabbed at her breast pocket. "It's just some stupid pills from the hospital." She rolled down the car window and scattered them into the woods. "I won't need them now. Who's keeping the kids?"

Jim grinned all the way to his jawbones. "Our new maid. I stuck an ad in the paper for somebody to help out till you get your act back together. Damned if I didn't get an answer from that woman who'd been in the ward with you. She showed up in a T-shirt that had *I'm the Greatest* stamped on it. She was the one Martine really went up in flames over, so I figured she'd just about do for us. She's teaching the twins to box and Peg to referee. You know, broadening their horizons."

"Poor Martine. She really does mean well, Jim. At least she thinks she does."

"If you say so, baby. Just so she means it to somebody else. You know, I'd never realized how totally different you two are. Isn't it a shame Martine couldn't try to be more like you."

Assignment: Marriage

"That's the man," said the superintendent.

"Man?" The inspector's usually cool voice held a spark of anger. "Swine, don't you mean."

"He's a nasty one, all right. Four wives dead that we know about. Lord knows how many more we don't. And we can't lay a finger on him."

"It's abominable."

Detective Inspector Fanshawe's slender white fingers clenched so tightly around the photograph of the handsome young man with the wavy black hair that she came near to cracking the emulsion. This was almost the only sign of emotion her superior officer had ever seen her display.

"Men who prey on women," she went on in her level, beautifully articulated voice, "deserve to be exterminated like rats."

"Privately and personally, I couldn't agree with you more." Superintendent Pearsall sighed. "Our job would be a lot easier if we could do just that. Unfortunately, we have to keep muddling along, hoping to get some sort of lead on him while he's busy courting his next victim."

"It's absolutely certain he does kill them, I suppose."

"Four rich wives in five years and a handsome inheritance from each, not to mention the insurance settlements? Oh yes, I should say so. The problem is how does he manage it?"

"They all died in automobile accidents, you say."

"That's right. And in not one of the crashes have we been able to turn up the slightest clue that the vehicle or the woman driving it had been tampered with in any way. In each case, the husband was away from home with an ironclad alibi for every minute of his time."

"Which in itself is suspicious."

"Exactly, but they're all genuine. We haven't been able to put so much as a dent in any one of them. There couldn't have been any flummoxing of detour signs, or anything of that sort. On the books, Clayton Beardsley is innocent as a newborn babe. Possibly more so," he added with a lugubrious attempt at humor, "if one subscribes to the doctrine of original sin."

"But that's nonsense, of course," said Inspector Fanshawe crisply. "Wasn't there even some point of similarity in the four accidents?"

"Well, it was a real smashup in every case. Bits and pieces of the car scattered everywhere. In one instance, another motorist was technically at fault. That was a rear-end collision at high speed. The Mrs. Beardsley of the moment was impaled on the steering wheel column. Very messy. Both people in the other car were killed, so it was impossible to be sure what really happened. One witness claimed she'd stopped short for some reason in the fast lane, and the other driver was coming too fast to swerve."

"Surely nobody would be idiot enough to stop suddenly in a situation like that. Was there no possible clue as to why she did it?"

"None whatever. Most probably a sudden mechanical failure, though we couldn't tell what it might have been. Or she may have been given a delayed-action drug, but there again nothing showed up in the autopsy."

Inspector Fanshawe frowned. "Provoking. What happened to the others?"

"One simply went off the road at a bad curve and hit a tree. The other two both crashed over cliffs. The last wife had been drinking, as it appeared, but we couldn't lay that on Beardsley. She'd had a history of alcoholism long before the marriage. Beautiful woman, though."

He handed Inspector Fanshawe another photograph. She studied it in silence, then laid it back on the desk.

"Anything else?"

"Yes, the oddest part of all. In each case, the car had been in the garage for checkup and repairs just before it was wrecked. Two of the smashes happened when the victim was actually on her way home after having picked up the machine from the mechanic."

"Dear me," said Inspector Fanshawe. "That does pose an interesting problem."

"It does indeed. We questioned the mechanics, naturally, but it was the same story every time. Reputable people, known for sound work, had handled the car before and knew its quirks. Hadn't taken it down bit by bit, of course, but had checked it thoroughly and couldn't understand anything's going so drastically wrong in so short a space of time. A different garage each time. There might have been negligence in one case, but surely not in four. One mechanic might have been bribed to lie, but hardly all of them. Anyway, a bribe would have meant Beardsley's putting himself in another man's power, which would have been stupid. Whatever he is, he can't be that. No, he must have managed by himself. But—"

"Quite," said Inspector Fanshawe. "What do you want me to do?"

"I have no idea," said the superintendent. "I was hoping you might."

He had got into the habit of turning over the really impossible assignments to Inspector Fanshawe. Somehow, she always managed to pull them off. Not for the first time, he studied the slim, exquisite figure before him with bewilderment and a certain uneasiness. Fragile as she looked, she was as tough as any man on the force. She seemed to have no nerves and no feelings, only a cool intelligence and lightning reactions. She was invaluable and he wished to God she'd been transferred to another division. Frankly, she scared the hell out of him.

As always, she zoomed straight to the point. "Beardsley's between wives at the moment, right?"

"Yes. His latest bereavement was three months ago. It's about time for him to start looking for another victim."

"Then I assume what you really want is for me to make sure he finds her. Where would be the best place for me to get picked up?"

That was in truth exactly what he wanted, but hearing it stated so calmly appalled him. "Inspector Fanshawe, do you honestly mean you'd be willing to marry a man simply to get him pinched?"

She shrugged. "Women have married for sillier reasons. I shall need rather substantial expense money if I'm to be a good catch."

It was not that difficult for a single, lovely, and evidently affluent woman to become acquainted with Clayton Beardsley. From there it was just a step to the registry office.

The scoundrel had charm, there was no denying that fact. Had Inspector Fanshawe been the susceptible type, she could have been swept off her feet with no trouble whatsoever. But she wasn't.

Superintendent Pearsall thought her totally devoid of

emotions. In fact she had two. One was an ice-cold devotion to her duty as she saw it. The other was a burning-hot ambition to be Chief Inspector Fanshawe. Pulling off the single-handed capture and conviction of a four-time murderer would be another step up toward her goal. She couldn't understand why Pearsall had hemmed and hawed about letting her take on the assignment.

At the end of a month, though, all she had accomplished was to learn what it felt like to be a rich man's darling. Clayton Beardsley had done well out of his four previous wives and been lucky in Canadian oil. He had no pressing need for her hypothetical wealth and was being monotonously slow about making any move to get hold of it.

Another woman—almost any other woman—would have reveled in the attention she got. Her husband obviously delighted in showing off his new wife. He took her everywhere. He lavished furs and jewels on her, urged her to patronize the most fashionable dressmakers and never even winced when the bills came in. One would have thought he was as genuinely in love with her as he claimed to be.

Before taking up her perilous assignment, Inspector Fanshawe had done her homework. She'd pored over police reports of the four accidents, studied the gruesome photographs, learned all she could of Clayton Beardsley's four previous *ménages*. Her quick mind had picked up a couple of points.

Beardsley's love nests had all been either on high hills with steep, winding roads or near the sort of highway where every motorist who gets on it is impelled to drive much faster than he ought. And in every one of the four alleged accidents, at least one wheel had come off the car. How had Pearsall missed that? The only question was, how had Beardsley pulled them off? She puzzled over the problem all through the

145

honeymoon and the first six weeks, in her palatial new home.

Clayton, as she now found herself forced to call him, had always been far from the scene when the crashes occurred. The first time, he'd been driving a rented car, having left his own at the garage for his wife to pick up. After that, the Beardsleys had been two-car families. Sometimes it had been his wife's car that got wrecked, sometimes his own. Invariably, tires had recently been replaced or rotated, axles greased, brakes checked. Surely any tampering with the wheels would have been spotted by those skilled mechanics Beardsley always made a point of seeking out. Yet the wheels had come off.

The simplest way to make it happen would have been to loosen the cotter pin that held the wheel to the axle so it would fall out at an opportune moment. But could one depend on it to let go at a spot where the driver was most likely to crash? What if it fell out prematurely and went rattling around in the hubcap? Anyway, wouldn't at least one mechanic have noticed a loose pin?

It was the candles on the dinner table that tipped the fifth Mrs. Beardsley off to the way her husband planned to kill her. Candles were built up by dipping wicks into layer upon layer of melted paraffin. What if a too-small cotter pin were dipped the same way? The wax would harden and keep the pin snugly in place. A little extra axle grease smeared around the hub would serve for camouflage. Even the sharpest-eyed mechanic would be unlikely to notice such an insignificant detail on a routine inspection.

The pin would hold all right for a while, until the friction of high-speed driving or violent braking generated enough heat to melt the wax. Once it loosened, the working of the joint would quickly wear it through, especially if it had been flipped back and forth with pliers before the waxing, to weaken the metal even further.

"Really," said the newest Mrs. Beardsley to herself, "it's brilliant." She looked down the polished mahogany at her handsome husband with an admiration that, this once, was real.

From that evening on, she included the pins in her thorough safety check every time she took the car out. She had her own, of course, a sleek yellow Alfa Romeo. She had grown to enjoy it along with the other luxuries she was constantly having showered upon her. But the life of elegant indolence was boring her to distraction. She did wish Clayton would get on with the murder so she could make her pinch and move on to a more exciting case.

But her husband perversely refused to kill her. Far from tampering with her Alfa Romeo, he never even went near it. He was constantly cautioning her against driving too fast. His devotion showed no sign of slackening, but rather seemed to grow. He waited on her hand and foot. His lovemaking became even more sickeningly mawkish.

"You're so completely unlike anyone I've ever known, Pamela my darling," he'd gush. "So exquisitely detached, so serenely aloof, so infinitely above the messy emotional scenes with which other women always want to clutter up one's life. You're the most beautiful statue ever carved. I could look at you forever."

And as the weeks continued to roll by, it began to appear Clayton Beardsley intended to do just that. The fifth Mrs. Beardsley had to face the horrible truth: her husband was in love with her. She was furious.

"I came here to be murdered," she stormed to herself, "not idolized and fawned over and trapped into a lifetime of being dressed up and dragged around to expensive night clubs and restaurants. If he doesn't get on with it soon, I'll—"

She'd what? Divorce a devoted husband simply because he refused to kill her? Fat chance she'd have of getting any judge to swallow that one! Desert him and ruin her career on the force? Not bloody likely. Stay here and die of boredom?

"What a ghastly mess I've got myself into!" Her emotion was deep and heartfelt.

That evening, Clayton Beardsley found his lovely bride in an unusually pettish mood. He outdid himself trying to please her.

The following morning after he'd gone to his office, she spent more time than usual tinkering with her yellow Alfa Romeo. Then she drove it very carefully to the nearest garage.

"Something is making a queer noise down inside," she told the mechanic. "I wish you'd make it stop."

"Have it right in no time," he told her cheerfully.

Actually, it should take him a couple of hours to locate the screw she'd dropped strategically inside the engine. She enjoyed the walk back to the house. Naturally she cut across the fields. The highway was much too dangerous for pedestrians.

Clayton called from town later that afternoon. "I'm taking the 5:02 down, dearest. Is there anything I can bring you?"

"How good of you to ask, darling. Yes, would you mind terribly stopping at the garage on your way back and picking up my car? No, just a funny noise in its tummy. The mechanic said he'd have it ready by evening. Hurry home, sweet. I'll have a cocktail waiting."

"I suppose you'll be resigning from the force now that you're a rich widow." Superintendent Pearsall tried not to sound hopeful.

"On the contrary, I can't wait to get back to work." The former Mrs. Beardsley flicked a disdainful finger at the sable cuff of her black Balenciaga coat. "Soft living doesn't suit me at all. I do regret not having been able to pull off the arrest. I must confess I was rather hoping to get a promotion out of it."

"You have that anyway," he assured her, "for devotion over and beyond the call of duty." The affable smile cost him a considerable effort. "It was ironic, his getting caught in his own trap like that."

"Yes, wasn't it? When he told me to take my car into the garage, I naturally became suspicious, especially after I'd checked it over and found nothing wrong but a screw dropped where it had no business to be. I did as he said, but then pretended I wasn't feeling well and he'd have to pick it up himself. I took it for granted he'd either find an excuse not to or be extra careful driving home, then I'd have a chance to ferret out the evidence and confront him with it. But apparently he couldn't resist the temptation to speed on the highway. It's positively hypnotic, you know, watching everybody else whiz by. Clayton always drove much too fast anyway."

"The car was demolished, as usual." Superintendent Pearsall sighed. "I don't suppose we'll ever know precisely how he managed the murders."

"No," said Chief Inspector Fanshawe, "I don't suppose we ever shall. It's a pity. Now what did you have in mind for my next assignment?"

Father Knew Best

"Come along, Evangeline. You waste altogether too much time on that foolishness. A walk will do you good. Bring the *Mycologia*."

"Yes, Father."

Evangeline had been trained to obey. She laid down her brushes, fetched her gathering basket and the beautiful old manuscript book in which a long-dead ancestor had depicted the mushrooms of the British Isles. Each one was hand-drawn and coloured, with its name and pertinent facts lettered beneath in a minute and elegant hand. It was a work of art, a museum piece. To Mr. Chadwick-Byrne, it was something to identify mushrooms by.

When she came back, she saw he had torn a strip off the drawing she'd been toiling over for the past two days, and rolled it into a spill to light his pipe. She knew better than to protest. Even though her watercolours were as expertly done as any in the *Mycologia*, a woman could never be a serious artist. Women existed only to be dutiful wives, or to keep house for their fathers if the wife had failed so far in her duty as to die before her time.

There had been no question of Evangeline's marrying. Suitors had not been lacking twenty years ago. She'd been a sweetly pretty girl and the Chadwick-Byrnes were known to have money. But Mrs. Chadwick-Byrne was already ailing then, and the young men were not encouraged.

Now at sixty-eight, Mr. Chadwick-Byrne was a bluff, hearty man who showed every sign of living to ninety. He liked to be outdoors, hunting or taking nature walks of the sort that involved killing butterflies, taking birds' nests, uprooting plants, and picking things he could take home and devour. He was particularly fond of mushrooming.

Evangeline might have enjoyed these walks if she had been allowed to drift peacefully down the woodland paths, stopping where the fancy seized her to sketch or simply enjoy the loveliness of a flower, a bird, a pattern of branches against the sky without having to identify, uproot, or gather into her basket; but her father did not tolerate slacking. Naturally she was not allowed to use the field glasses except as an infrequent and grudging favour, or to do the serious work of identifying specimens. Her job was to carry the basket, the reference books, the cyanide jars, and to hover close behind her father's elbow, ready to hand them over as required.

Mushrooms were scarce that day. Mr. Chadwick-Byrne was annoyed. He did not exactly say the shortage was Evangeline's fault, but he snapped at her for dawdling even more frequently than usual. She was quite exhausted and immensely relieved when they finally came upon a clump of bright orange fungi.

"Ah, chanterelles," exclaimed the leader of the expedition.

"Do you really think so, Father?" Evangeline ventured. "I should have said—"

"When I want your opinion, I shall ask for it. Give me the *Mycologia*."

He flipped through the loose pages, regardless of their fragility. "Ah, there you are. *Cantharellus cibarius*. Beautiful specimens, perfect in every detail. Really, Evangeline, I had hoped, after all my patient efforts, to have taught you the rudiments of mycology. Here, see for yourself."

He thrust the *Mycologia* at her and knelt to gather his find into the basket. Cowed, she admitted the mushrooms matched the illustration and must therefore be chanterelles, one of the great delicacies among the edible mushrooms. Considering the smallness of the patch, however, it was doubtful whether anybody but her father would get to enjoy them.

After the chanterelles, they found scarcely anything except a few puffballs which had burst and were therefore inedible, and one deadly white *Amanita phalliodes* around which Evangeline made a wide, shuddering circle. Nevertheless, Mr. Chadwick-Byrne returned to the house in fine fettle.

"Well, don't stand there gibbering, Evangeline. Give the chanterelles to Mrs. Felt. We'll have them for lunch, with an omelette."

Mrs. Felt, who had cooked for them since Evangeline was a baby, peered doubtfully into the basket. "If you say so, sir." She, too, knew better than to argue.

Neither his daughter nor his cook was surprised when Mr. Chadwick-Byrne helped himself so lavishly to mushrooms at the table that none were left for them. Both were horrified a while later when he collapsed in agony on the drawing-room rug. He was retching so violently that he could not gasp out instructions to call the doctor, and neither of them dared take the initiative until it was too late.

After it was all over, Mrs. Felt explained to the police that she hadn't liked the look of those mushrooms.

"But the master was such a positive man, sir. It was no use trying to tell him anything once he'd made up his mind."

The sergeant nodded. Mr. Chadwick-Byrne had been well-known in the village.

"And what did you think, Miss Chadwick-Byrne? I understand you were with your father when he picked them."

"I . . . yes, I was. I did ask Father if he . . . I said I didn't think . . . but he showed me the picture in *Mycologia* and said they were—"

"What is this *Mycologia*? Could I see it, please?"

"Yes, of course." She fetched the precious portfolio and handed it over to him.

"Lovely thing this. Ought to be in a museum." The sergeant reached to turn a leaf of the yellowed parchment, hesitated. "Would you mind showing me which picture he identified the mushrooms from?"

She laid the book down on a small table and shuffled carefully through the drawings until she found the ones showing the trumpet-shaped cups of *Cantharellus cibarius*. "This is what Father said they were."

Her faint accent on the word *said* caught the sergeant's ear. "But you didn't agree?"

She flushed. "Father was so much more knowledgeable than I, I couldn't very well contradict him. But I did think they looked rather more like this picture here." She found another plate.

"*Clitocyde illudens.*" The sergeant made rather a hash of the Latin. "Jack o' Lantern. Poisonous. Same colour, more or less the same shape, specially if they'd begun to go by, say. Tricky things, mushrooms. Well, it appears to me that you were right and your father wrong, Miss Chadwick-Byrne. You mustn't take it too hard. Death by misadventure, I think we're safe in saying."

Death by pigheadedness would have been more like it. The things had probably tasted foul, but the old bastard would have died rather than admit he'd made a mistake. As in fact he had. And good riddance, as far as the sergeant was concerned.

After he had gone, Evangeline carried the *Mycologia* back up to her bedroom. From under her mattress she took the one page she'd slipped out of the portfolio before she carried it down. This was an exact replica of *Clitoclyde illudens,* with each venomous gill and spore rendered in meticulous detail. Beneath it, in that same exquisite, spidery lettering to be found on all the other pages, ran the description: *Cantharellus cibarius,* Edible. She'd have to burn it, of course, but she hated to. It was far and away the best thing she'd ever done.

Fifty Acres of Prime Seaweed

You know how it is around a medical research laboratory around half past five on a Friday afternoon. Or maybe you don't, but it certainly is. So when Carter-Harrison emerged from the fastness wherein he does whatever he does and suggested a spot of research involving a couple of boiled lobsters and a seidel or two, I cheerfully acquiesced.

We were nicely settled in a booth at Ye Olde Lobster Trappe, a Boston landmark since 1973, with bibs around our necks and our nutcrackers at the ready when Carter-Harrison remarked, "You ought to taste a real lobster."

"I'm about to," I replied as the waitress, whose name is neither Marge nor Myrtle but in fact Melpomene, set one in front of me.

My companion, being a man of science first and foremost, reached across the table and tore off one of its claws, which he proceeded to excavate and consume the meat thereof.

"Not bad, considering," he admitted, wiping melted butter off his chin. "But wait till you toss a bicuspid over a genuine Beagleport lobster, hauled from the briny blue Atlantic about fourteen minutes before you get your grubhooks on to it."

"You owe me a claw," I said. "Where's Beagleport?"

Carter-Harrison ate one of his own claws—or, to be scientifically accurate, one of his own lobster's claws—and wiped more melted butter off his chin. He has one of those long, bony New England jaws ideally adapted for getting dripped on. Then he punctiliously gave me his other claw. Then he uttered:

"Did I ever tell you about my family?"

"I never knew you had one," I replied. "I thought you sprang full-armored from the brow of Dr. Spock."

He thought that one over for a while. "Ah, I see. One of your jokes. No, Williams, I was born pretty much according to normal procedure, of not exactly poor and almost ridiculously honest parents, in the village of Beagleport, Maine."

"I'll bet you were a beautiful baby," I said with my mouth full of tail meat.

"My mother always thought so. That's why she insisted on splicing her maiden name of Carter to the paternal cognomen. My parents have now passed to the Great Beyond, namely Palm Springs, but the old family homestead is still occupied by my Aunt Agapantha and my cousins Ed and Fred. I was thinking we might take a run up there this weekend."

"Are you sure this is the right time of year to go?" I asked, gazing out the window at the lashing sleet that gives our city so much of its gentle springtime charm.

"The perfect time," he assured me. "We won't run into any tourists."

"I wouldn't mind running into some tourists," I said, but he wasn't listening. These excessively brainy types never do.

And that's why, some three hours later, we were groping our way up the Maine Turnpike in my old Chevy. I was groping, anyway, trying to sort out the road from the surrounding frozen wastes by the occasional glimpses I was able to get through my slush-caked windshield. Carter-Harrison was thinking deep thoughts. At least I assumed he was. He never said.

By ten o'clock, I'd had it. We found a motel open somewhere between Kittery and the Arctic Circle, and turned in. I woke expecting more of the same, but Saturday dawned crisp and clear. We got out of the motel early—there wasn't much there to hang around for—and fetched Beagleport around the middle of the morning.

Carter-Harrison started barking orders like "Left at the fire station" and "Right at the general store." At last he sat back with a sigh of satisfaction. "Now we're on the home road."

"This is a road?" I cried in startled disbelief.

He didn't answer. He was busy sniffing, his bony nose straight forward like a bird dog's at the point, his bony cheeks flushed the way they get when he's about to give birth to another bright idea. I felt an ominous twinge.

"What's eating you?"

"It's the air," he replied.

There sure was a lot of it. I tried a few sniffs myself, a rich blend of salt, pine trees, and ancient vehicle. We sniffed our way along until we came to two houses, one of them painted baby blue with scalloped pink shutters. The other was merely white. It was when we reached this latter that Carter-Harrison yelled, "Starboard your helm."

"Huh?" I said.

"Turn right. This is our driveway."

And so it proved to be. Ah, I thought, civilization at last. Then a powerful voice welled up from the bulkhead and ricocheted off my eardrums.

"What in time are you settin' there for like a pair o'ninnies?"

Carter-Harrison leaped from the car. "Hello, Aunt Aggie."

157

"Well, James. I might o' known. Couldn't you of wrote first?"

A woman of uncertain years wearing an awfully certain kind of expression emerged and confronted her nephew. She was almost as tall as he, though not so skinny. After a certain amount of glaring back and forth, he bent his head to kiss her on the cheek. She let him. Neither of them appeared to enjoy it much. I thought I might as well join the party, so I got out of the car and Aunt Aggie turned her glare on me.

"Who's the young'un?"

"My colleague, Dr. Bill Williams," Carter-Harrison told her. "I brought him up to see the place."

"Doctor, eh?" She hauled a pair of gold-rimmed spectacles out of her sweater pocket, gave them a wipe with her apron, put them on, and looked me over. "Huh, he don't even look dry behind the ears yet. Least he ain't all skin an' bones like you, James. Ain't enough meat on you to grease a griddle with. Well, come on in. Can't stand here lollygaggin' around the dooryard all day. Oh, drat an' tarnation! Go on, git! Scat! Shoo!"

At first I thought Aunt Aggie meant us, but it soon became clear she was addressing a large brown goat with white spots. As she pursued it across the yard, we could see the creature was chewing on a piece of rag. Aggie made pretty good time, but the goat was faster. At last she came back, her apron at half-mast, her expression one of mingled fury and despair.

"There went the last o' my good pillowcases. I'd like to wring that critter's neck."

"Then why don't you?" asked her nephew, ever the keen, inquiring mind.

" 'Cause he ain't my goat, that's why."

"Ergo, why do you let him into the yard?"

"I don't let him, you dern fool. He comes."

"Isn't there any way to keep him out?"

"Might try a deer rifle, but I misdoubt he'd just eat the bullet an' want another."

"Have you thought of building a fence?" I asked her.

She gave me a look. "Ed an' Fred spent fifty-two hard-earned dollars on barbed wire, an' three days' worktime stringin' it. He'd et his way through an' bit the tail off Fred's Sunday shirt before they'd got the posthole digger put away."

"You ought to sue his owner for damages."

"That's real bright o'you, Willie."

"Well," said Carter-Harrison, "why don't you?"

"Because," said Aunt Aggie, "that's why."

She nodded over toward the baby blue house with the pink shutters. A fluffy little blonde with a fluffy pink coat on was tripping winsomely down the steps. The goat ran to meet her and she flung her arms around its neck.

"Oh, you naughty Spotty," we heard her coo. "What have you got in your mouth?"

She came across the yard to us, snuggling the goat against her pink fluff. "Has Spotty been a bad boy again, Auntie Agapantha?"

I expected Auntie Agapantha to snap the blonde's head off and swallow it in one gulp. Instead, she only shrugged.

"Twasn't nothin', Lily Ann. Just an old dishrag."

"I've told him and told him." Lily Ann gave her curls a sad little shake. "I've said time and time again, Spotty, if you don't leave Auntie Agapantha's clothesline alone, I'll have to give you a spanking. But he never pays a mite of attention."

"Now don't you fret yourself," Aunt Aggie insisted. "Lily Ann, I don't believe you've met my nephew James that's a doctor down to Boston. An' this here's his friend William that helps around the hospital some. Lily Ann's the one that

159

married Claude, James. You remember I told you Claude got married?"

"Yep," said Carter-Harrison. "And killed. Did they ever find the murderer?"

Lily Ann burst into tears. Carter-Harrison began to look uncomfortable but didn't drop the subject.

"Stands to reason, doesn't it? Claude was supposed to have caught his necktie in the cream separator and been strangled to death. Whoever wore a necktie separating cream? Claude wouldn't have known how to tie one anyway even if he'd owned a necktie, which he didn't."

"He did s-so," sobbed Lily Ann. "He w-wore a tie at our wedding."

"Rented it with the suit," snorted Carter-Harrison.

"And I g-gave him another one for Christmas. He w-wore it because he l-loved me."

The young widow settled down to some serious bewailment. Aunt Aggie gave her eminent nephew what can best be described as a look.

Then she put her arm around Lily Ann's shoulders and led her away toward the baby blue house with the pink shutters. We two were standing there feeling like a nickel apiece when an old pickup truck clunked into what I had been assured was the driveway. Two men got out, one a clone of the other, though it would have been impossible to say which was the original and which the copy. They were both wearing ragged blue work shirts, ragged, gray work pants, and ragged navy blue pea jackets. Both looked a lot like Carter-Harrison.

"Hahyah, James," said one.

"Hahyah, James," said the other.

"Hahyah, Fred. Hahyah, Ed," said James, as I may as well call him now. "This is Bill Williams, a friend of mine from the lab. My cousins, Ed and Fred, Bill."

"Hahyah, Ed. Hahyah, Fred," I replied. "Mind my asking which is which?"

"We don't mind," said Ed, or Fred.

"But it wouldn't do no good," said Fred, or Ed.

"You'd mix us up anyway."

"Folks always do."

"So do we, sometimes."

"What ails Lily Ann?"

"She's cryin' again."

The first part of our conversation had been amiable enough, but these last two remarks were made in definitely accusatory tones. It was clear that both Ed and Fred had strong feelings about Lily Ann.

"It's because I just happened to ask who murdered Claude," James explained.

"Some Boy Scout, maybe," said one twin.

"Doin' his good deed for the day," said the other.

"Lily Ann done all right out of it."

"Got rid o' Claude."

"Got his folks' house."

"An' the farm. Fifty acres, prime land. Prime for Beagleport, anyways."

"Seaweed makes good top dressin'. Lot o' seaweed been spread over them acres down through the years."

"Raise anything you've a mind to."

"Lily Ann's not farming it herself, is she?" James broke in.

"Nope. Rents it to Abner Glutch."

"Abner Glutch? I thought he owned the hardware store."

"Owns the fillin' station, too."

"Gets men to run 'em for him."

"Got eight, nine workin' for him now."

"Makin' money hand over fist."

"Come to think of it," said James, "didn't I hear some-

161

thing about Abner's trying to buy Claude out when his parents died?"

"Ayup. Claude wouldn't sell."

"Claude would o' sold." It was the first sign of disharmony between Ed and Fred. "Mother wouldn't let 'im. Told 'im he'd blow the money in two, three years. Then where'd he be?"

" 'Bout where he is now, like as not. Damn shame the poor bugger never got the chance to spend it."

"Would o' left Lily Ann holdin' the short end o' the stick."

"Then she'd o' needed a new husband, wouldn't she?"

Aha, I thought. Now we were getting to the crux of the matter.

"She could hardly have picked a worse one than Claude," said James. "I can't imagine why she'd cry over a clown like that. Claude had an I.Q. of about fifty-six and looked just like that blasted goat. Beats me what she ever saw in him."

"Beats me," Ed affirmed.

"Beats me," Fred agreed.

At least they both said it beat them, though I'm not sure of the order. I was comparing one craggy face with another and it appeared to me that they all three looked about equally besotted.

You may argue that it was impossible for Dr. James Carter-Harrison to have become smitten by a fluffy blonde head and a weepy blue eye in so short a space of time, but that's because you don't know Dr. James Carter-Harrison. He'd already fallen in love three times during that same week, all three with semi-disastrous results. Maybe this was a family trait. Anyway, it made me nervous.

"Let's go take a look at that clothesline your aunt was complaining about," I suggested to divert his attention. "It's cold standing here."

None of the three cousins answered me, they just wheeled and stomped around behind the house, two of them wearing sea boots and the other walking as if he did. I was a little surprised they'd been so willing to let the subject be changed, then I wasn't. If in fact Claude Harrison had been willfully done to death by the unlikely instruments of a necktie and a cream separator, it was not beyond the bounds of possibility that one of Lily Ann's love-struck neighbors might have had a hand and possibly even a cravat in his sudden demise.

Since I was going to be their houseguest, I thought it would be rude to pursue the matter. Instead, I joined the cousins in grim contemplation of Aunt Aggie's clothes reel.

"Pitiful," was my diagnosis, and nobody disputed it. The upper halves of various items were hung on the lines that stretched among the various poles that poked out from the center like the ribs of an umbrella—only less so, if you get my drift. You've seen the things, you know what I mean. Anyway, the bottoms of said items were either hanging in shreds or missing altogether. Around the pole lay the remains of attempted fortifications: shattered picket fencing, tangles of chicken wire, oil drums, and suchlike futile measures.

"Have you tried land mines?" I suggested.

"Can't do that," said one twin.

"Lily Ann wouldn't like it," said the other.

"Can't say I'd go for 'em much, myself," snapped a now-familiar voice behind us.

"Oh hello, Aunt Aggie," said James. "Have you tried putting cayenne pepper in the rinse water?"

"He found it appetizin'. Speakin' of which, I s'pose you're hungry as usual."

"We had a snack at the motel."

"Huh!"

She tossed her head toward the kitchen. We followed.

163

This turned out to have been the correct move. She fed us home-cured ham, new-laid eggs, home-grown and home-hashed potatoes, homemade biscuits with homemade jam and a few other odds and ends. I attempted a little light conversation to be polite, but James sat lost in thought. At last he quit chewing and spoke.

"Aunt Aggie, is there any place around here we could buy one of those supersonic dog whistles?"

"Ed got me one. Spotty swallered it."

"Well, I'll think of something," he muttered, absentmindedly helping himself to a few more biscuits.

He continued to ponder. You could practically hear the brains churning, or maybe it was the biscuits. At last, as his aunt was making a pointed remark about did we think we was going to set here all day, he leaped from his chair like Archimedes from his bath.

"I've got it! Mind if I borrow your truck, boys?"

"We was goin' to pick up a mess o' lobsters," one of them demurred.

"Thought Bill here might like 'em," added the other.

"Might get a few extra."

"Ask Lily Ann over."

"We can go in my car," I said.

So we did, all but James, who drove off in the truck by himself whistling, "I'm a Yankee Doodle Dandy."

His aunt followed his departure with jaundiced eye. "Got another of his fool notions, I'll be bound. Been like that ever since he was knee-high to a sculpin. Beats me how James ever lived to grow up."

She was off on a stream of reminiscences. James had always been an ingenious little cuss, it appeared, right from the time he'd tried to hatch a clutch of duck eggs in his Sunday rompers.

"But he's one of the most respected men in his field," I protested. "We consider him a genius."

"Genius is as genius does," she sniffed, and went on picking out lobsters.

They steered me down the shore road so I could view the breaking waves dashing high on a stern and rockbound coast, then we went back to the house, arriving in a dead heat with James.

"Ah, good," he said. "I can use some help unloading."

"Go ahead, fellows," I said, quick-thinking as always. "I'll take care of the lobsters."

Aunt Aggie had taken advantage of my good nature to make a few extra stops, but I didn't care. There was a lot of nautical language coming from the back yard and I figured I'd got the best of the bargain. After I'd lugged in her manifold purchases, though, she remarked that if there was a worse nuisance than a man around a kitchen, she didn't know what it might be and I better go see what them three out there was up to. So I went.

One of the twins was up on a ladder screwing a pulley into the side of the house. The other was threading a vast amount of new manila rope through some more pulleys that had been attached to the center pole of the clothes reel. Carter-Harrison was horsing around with one of those heavy metal gas cylinders we see so many of back at the lab.

"Great idea," I exclaimed. "You're going to anaesthetize the goat."

"I don't think Lily Ann would go much for that," said the twin on the ladder.

"Me neither," said the one on the ground.

The goat wasn't saying anything, just sitting there waiting to see where his next meal was coming from.

"Then what's in the tank?" I asked. "Oxygen? Isn't there

165

enough of that floating around up here already?"

"It's helium," Carter-Harrison explained. "Would you mind stepping over to the truck and bringing us that brown baglike object we took the precaution of leaving locked in the cab? Got the keys, Ed?"

"Fred's got 'em," said the man on the ladder.

Ah, at last I knew which twin was which. Provided Ed stayed up on the ladder, anyway. I took the keys, said "Thanks, Fred," to flaunt my newly acquired knowledge, and went to get the brown baglike object, still unscathed by goatly tooth. I could swear Spotty snickered when he saw it.

When I got back to the scene of the activity, Carter-Harrison had both hands full of rope and an end between his teeth. "Gaha bawoo? Gooh!"

Being expensively educated, I was able to translate. "Balloon? What do you want that for?"

He spat out the rope end. "Elementary, my dear Williams. We hitch the balloon to the top of the clothes reel, Aunt Aggie hangs out her wash, we inflate the balloon with helium from the tank, then pay out enough line to raise the reel out of the goat's reach. The ropes will be fastened to those cleats up beside the window where she has her washing machine, so she needn't even go outdoors to raise or lower the reel, just haul it in as far as she wants."

By this time, his aunt's face had in fact appeared at the aforesaid window. Carter-Harrison hitched a short length of hose from the tank to the balloon, let the brown bag fill, then started paying out the guy ropes.

"See, Aunt Aggie, we've got 'er ballasted, and you can adjust the ropes to keep the pole upright. When you want to reel in, just give a tug on this hunk of fish line. That will pull the stopper out of the balloon and let the gas escape slowly.

You just keep hauling in your lines and she'll come up all standing."

He raised the reel about fifteen feet above the ground, then handed the guy ropes to Ed, who fastened them to the cleats beside the window, came down, and took away the ladder. Spotty made a few frantic leaps at the clothes flapping high above, then fell back, a shattered goat.

"I do declare, James," cried Aunt Aggie. "I b'lieve it's goin' to work. But what happens when that there gas tank gits empty?"

"Take it to Lem Maddox and he'll give you another."

"An' charge me a fortune for it, I'll be bound."

"Oh no. You're not paying for the tank, you know, just the gas."

"Huh. Forkin' out good money for a passel o' wind."

Spotty made another futile leap.

"But I guess it'll be wuth it. You know what? I'm goin' upstairs an' get that old dress suit Uncle Hector wore to Warren G. Harding's inauguration. It ain't had a good airin' since Lily Ann got that dratted goat. Could you just haul that reel down for a minute an' let it up again without emptyin' the balloon, James? No sense wastin' gas when you just filled it."

"I expect we can manage. Go get the suit, Aunt Aggie."

By the time she returned, we'd collected an audience. Lily Ann was back, pinker and fluffier than before, and she had a man with her. Quite a large man, who looked a lot like Teddy Roosevelt, in his later and portlier years. His name was Abner Glutch and he was wearing a necktie. In fact, as Aunt Aggie remarked, he was all togged out like a hog goin' to war.

"How come you're so fancy, Abner? It ain't Sunday till tomorrow, in case you lost count."

"Nope," he told her, "I ain't lost nothin'. I just gained me a helpmeet. Me an' Lily Ann snuck off quiet by ourselves an' tied the knot."

"We didn't want any fuss," Lily Ann explained, "out of respect for Claude." She strove manfully, or rather womanfully, to keep the quiver out of her voice.

"Well, I swan!" cried Aunt Aggie.

I swanned, too. So Abner Glutch had found a way to get his pudgy mitts on the late Claude's ancestral acres, Aunt Agapantha notwithstanding. I looked at his necktie and wondered where he'd been when Claude got snarled up in the cream separator.

Now, it appeared, all we could do was celebrate the event. As soon as she'd finished hanging up Uncle Hector's dress suit, to the admiration of all present except Spotty, Aunt Aggie invited everybody into the front parlor for tea and cake. The goat stayed outside, banging one of the oil drums around in hopeless frustration. Ed and Fred had been made to take off their sea boots before they joined the party, but I didn't think this was what made them so glum. They sat chomping down cake and looking as if they'd rather be out back with Spotty, banging oil drums around.

No doubt to disarm us into believing he loved Lily Ann for herself alone, Abner insisted on telling us what he was giving her for wedding presents. He'd already insured his life in her favor and deeded over both his store and his filling station.

"And I'm going to deed over the farm to Abner," said Lily Ann, sweet innocent that she was. "It's the least I can do."

"Not that I exactly what you'd call need it," said Abner, toying with his new wife's hand so everybody could get a good look at the sparkler she was wearing. "Business ain't been so bad."

He proceeded to tell us how good it was while Ed and Fred ate more cake and Aunt Aggie grew restive. As soon as she could get a word in, she started dropping a few hints about her own family.

"Well, us Harrisons ain't much on braggin' about what we got. Let's talk about somethin' more int'restin'. What was that you was tellin' me, Willie, about James flyin' clear out to California because all them bigwigs out there wanted to hear about the research he's doin'? Even paid 'is fare for 'im an' put a big piece in the paper, didn't they?"

"James, you never told us," cried Lily Ann.

"Oh, one honor more or less doesn't mean much to James," I said. "He's always winning some award or having some head of state or delegation of scholars drop in to offer him another research grant."

That was true enough, Carter-Harrison's activities being more inscrutable than anybody else's and scholarly veneration for those great brains who are doing that which nobody else can figure out the whereof or whyfor being ever immense.

"Can't be much money in it," Abner snorted, "or he wouldn't be drivin' that rattletrap out there."

"Oh, that's mine," I said. "My kid brother's, I mean." I felt I owed this to Aunt Aggie. "My Ferrari's in the shop. James never drives himself. It wouldn't be quite the thing, you know, for a man in his position."

That was true enough, anyway. Carter-Harrison was too subject to sudden fits of cerebration to be allowed behind a wheel, but I didn't explain that bit. I was enjoying the smug look on Aunt Aggie's face. Lily Ann was impressed. Abner was interested. Ed and Fred said they had to go and practice.

"Practice what?" snapped their mother.

"Pistol shootin'. Volunteer police. You shoot, James?"

James said no, but he wouldn't mind trying. Lily Ann said if there was any shooting she was going home and hide under the chesterfield because guns scared her silly.

"Let's not even talk about horrid old guns. Let's go look at the balloon again."

So we all trooped out to look at the balloon, Ed and Fred strapping on their holsters in a what-the-heck sort of way as we went. As we stood goggling at James's latest miracle of science, Abner Glutch expressed the opinion that it struck him as a mighty bothersome sort of way to hang out a few duds. Furthermore, he didn't see why all that foolishness about letting out the helium was necessary. Why couldn't they just pull it down?

"They did," Aunt Aggie told him. "Ed an' Fred got on one rope an' Willie an' James on the other—"

"Huh! Seems to me a man with a little beef to his bones could do it single-handed."

"I'll bet Abner could," cried Lily Ann.

"He's welcome to try," snarled Carter-Harrison.

"Yep," said Ed and Fred in unison.

So Abner took off his jacket, revealing a pair of lavender suspenders with baby-blue forget-me-nots on them, no doubt a gift from Lily Ann, and hauled. By George, he was a powerful cuss at that. In no time flat, he had Uncle Hector's pant legs dragging on the ground. Lily Ann applauded vociferously, then halted in mid-clap.

"Spotty, you bad boy! What are you—"

She got no farther. A shot rang out. Abner Glutch sprawled on the ground. Uncle Hector's dress suit, released from his lifeless grasp, soared again skyward.

As doctors, Carter-Harrison and I dropped at once to our knees beside the fallen man. Diagnosis was no problem. There's something all too obvious about a bullet through the back of the head.

"We'll have to call the police, Aunt Aggie," said Carter-Harrison.

"We're the police," said Ed, or Fred.

"Sort of, anyways," said Fred, or Ed.

"Yes, well." Carter-Harrison groped for words to explain tactfully that it wasn't the done thing for suspects to arrest each other. Before he'd succeeded, Lily Ann screamed and fell into a swoon beside her dead bridegroom.

Aunt Aggie took over. "Pick 'er up, Fred. Bring her in the house. Step lively, Ed, you call the state troopers. Some dern fool hunter takin' a pot shot at that balloon to be cute, I'll be bound."

If I were a mother who had two sons with revolvers strapped to their waists and a grudge against the man who'd married the object of their combined affections, I might have said the same thing. But why would the hunter have waited till the balloon was on the ground with a group of people clustered around it before he shot?

I was cursing myself for not having made Ed and Fred drop their guns before they took off when I noticed Spotty. Be cussed and be darned if that goat hadn't rolled his oil drum up against the house, directly under the cleat from which Abner hadn't bothered to cast off the guy ropes. He was up on top of it with his fore hooves braced against the clapboards and his neck stretched out like a camel's, yanking down lengths of that new manila line and gobbling them as if they'd been spaghetti.

"Hey," I yelled, but too late. The balloon was free, traveling low and fast over the treetops on an offshore breeze, carrying with it the clothes reel and Uncle Hector's dress suit. Carter-Harrison leaped to his feet.

"Williams, got your car keys?"

"Yes but—"

"No buts. Come on."

"The police will think we're running away," I protested as

he hustled me into the Chevy.

He didn't bother to answer, just licked his finger and held it out the car window to see how the wind was blowing. "South-southeast by a half east. She can't be making more than three knots. Full speed ahead to the harbor."

"But if it's blowing out to sea—"

"Step on it."

I could see why he wanted me out of the way. I'd seen gunshot wounds enough during my internship in the emergency room. Abner had been shot from only a short distance, obviously by either Ed or Fred. It didn't matter which. The twins would ditch both their guns before the state troopers arrived, get hold of two others—it wouldn't be hard in hunting country—and swear those were the ones they'd been carrying. Aunt Aggie would back them up. Lily Ann wouldn't know the difference. The bullet would never be traced. Aunt Aggie's yarn of somebody taking a wild pot shot at the balloon would hold. I was abetting a murder.

I knew it, and I kept going. I gunned that old can for all she was worth, praying the tires wouldn't pop or the engine fall out. We hurtled over rock and sand, through potholes and ditches, finally made it over the rise, and spied the balloon.

"Thar she blows!" cried Carter-Harrison. "Faster, Williams."

There was nothing ahead of us but a sharp slope and a lot of water. I whizzed downhill with my foot on the gas and my heart in my brakes, skidded out onto a wooden dock, and managed somehow to stop two feet from the end. Dead ahead of us, Uncle Hector's clawhammer coat was skimming the wave tops. Beside us, a lone lobsterman was standing in his boat with his mouth wide open and his eyes bulging. Again, Carter-Harrison grabbed my arm and hurled me aboard.

"Follow that clothes reel," he barked.

The lobsterman stared at Carter-Harrison, at the balloon, and at the twenty-dollar bill which I, with a flash of psychological insight, was waving under his nose. I added a second twenty. He nodded once, and cast off.

Out we pounded, into the chop. The clothes reel skipped along in front of us. Sometimes it was almost within our reach, then a ruffle of wind would send it skimming on ahead.

"Great-uncle Hector always was an exasperating old devil," muttered Carter-Harrison.

"I think I'm getting seasick," I said.

"Comin' on to blow," said the lobsterman.

With that, Carter-Harrison grabbed a boathook, poised it like a harpoon, and let fly. There came a giant pop, then a tangle of canvas and clothesline lay sprawled on the water.

"Oh, jolly good shot," I yelled.

"She's goin' down," grunted the lobsterman,

"Pole's too well ballasted," groaned Carter-Harrison. Waiting not to repine, he tore off his windbreaker, kicked off his boots, and dived. Seconds later, his hand popped up among the wreckage, waving Uncle Hector's clawhammer coat like a soggy banner.

"Catch, Williams," he shouted. "I'm going down for the pants."

I retrieved the coat, laid it over a lobster trap, and stood by to help him aboard. As he reappeared, dripping and triumphant, I held out my hands.

"Take these first," he spluttered.

I grabbed the pinstriped bundle, tossed it behind me on the floorboards, and hauled him over the gunwale. "Got a blanket or something?" I asked the lobsterman.

He didn't speak or move, just stood there gaping down at Uncle Hector's trousers.

"Great balls of fire, they're alive!" Carter-Harrison bent

and snatched up the writhing garment.

Out of the left leg slithered a six-pound haddock.

"Don't s'pose you'd care to set 'em again?" suggested the lobsterman.

"No," said Carter-Harrison through chattering teeth. "I think we've caught what we're after."

He shook the pants again. Out of the hip pocket dropped a gun, one like Ed's or Fred's. But it wasn't Ed's or Fred's. On the butt were carved in fancy letters the initials C.H.

"C.H.," I gasped. "Not-not Carter—"

"No, not Carter. Claude. Claude Harrison."

"You don't mean Lily Ann—"

"Oh yes." Carter-Harrison had got his windbreaker around him now, and taken a medicinal snort out of a flat bottle the lobsterman produced from behind the bait tub. "It was obvious from the start. Lily Ann, as you must have noticed, is a remarkably attractive woman. I asked myself what somebody like her could see in an oaf like Claude."

"You asked Ed and Fred, too," I reminded him.

"So I did. They didn't know, either. Therefore, there could be only one reasonable answer."

"Fifty acres of prime seaweed," I cried.

"Precisely. Claude then died under circumstances which would have been considered mysterious if Claude hadn't been such a clumsy lout and Lily Ann such a persuasive weeper. The widow was free to reopen negotiations with Abner Glutch, which she now believes herself, no doubt, to have concluded satisfactorily. She probably didn't intend quite such a brief honeymoon, but the chance came up and she took it. We needn't waste any blame on ourselves for providing the opportunity, Williams. If the fortuitous combination of the clothes rack, the balloon, and Great-uncle Hector's dress suit hadn't provided her with a way to get rid of the murder weapon, she'd have thought of something else."

"I don't doubt it," I agreed. "Lily Ann must be a pretty darn smart operator, to have hauled out that gun and shot Abner, then ditch it in the old man's suit and kick the oil drum over to where the goat could reach the ropes, all without anybody's noticing."

"I expect she already had the gun in her hand," said Carter-Harrison. "I noticed she had her hands tucked up inside the sleeves of that loose, fluffy coat she was wearing when we went outside. It's a natural thing for a woman to do on a chilly day, so why should anyone have thought anything of it? Then she yelled at the goat, and we all automatically turned our heads to look at him. That gave her a chance to shoot Abner. Of course he became the center of interest while she did her other little chores and pulled a faint so we wouldn't find her lacking in proper wifely concern. Well, we'd better get back to the house before she marries Ed or Fred."

I shook my head. "It won't be Ed or Fred. If you ask me, Lily Ann's looking forward to marrying a rich and famous doctor from Boston. Maybe I laid it on a bit too thick."

"Good God!" Carter-Harrison picked up the haddock, wrapped it thoughtfully in Uncle Hector's coat, laid it back with the pants, and took another swig from the lobsterman's bottle. "Well," he sighed, "some day perhaps I'll meet a woman who loves me for myself alone."

He was moody all the way home, sitting there with the haddock, the pistol, and Uncle Hector's suit in his lap. When we got there, Aunt Aggie was still doctoring Lily Ann for hysterics while the state troopers stood around looking helpless. When we showed them the revolver that had come out of Uncle Hector's hip pocket and explained the modus operandi by which we believed it to have got there, though, Lily Ann recovered fast and demanded to be allowed to call her lawyer. They said she could do it from the station. She began to cry again, but it didn't seem to be helping her much. State troopers are smarter than men like Claude and Abner Glutch.

As they departed, Aunt Aggie faced her nephew, tight-lipped. "Well, James, you've really done it this time."

"But Aunt Aggie," he protested, "what else could I do? That woman would have wiped out half of Beagleport and never batted an eyelash, if somebody hadn't stopped her."

"I ain't sayin' you was wrong. I'm just remindin' you of how Claude's father's will was wrote. When he died, the farm went to Claude. When Claude died, it went to Lily Ann. But a murderer ain't allowed to profit from 'er crime, which means Lily Ann never inherited at all. An' that means it comes back to us. An' that means the whole shebang, includin' that god-dern goat."

"Oh gosh, Aunt Aggie," cried Carter-Harrison, as well he might. "Well, never mind. I'll think of something."

"Do me a favor," said his aunt. "Quit thinkin'. Now git on upstairs an' take off them wet clothes."

So that was that and there we were: Ed and Fred out in the back yard building a goat house for Spotty, James crouched beside the stove wearing an old flannel nightshirt of his Cousin Raymond's and soaking his feet in a pail of hot water and mustard, Aunt Aggie boning the haddock for chowder. Nobody was saying anything. I felt uncomfortable.

Finally I broke the silence. "Say, James, you know those things they have at the laundromat, that you put a quarter in and—"

He was alive again, his eyes flashing, his flannel-clad arms flailing, his feet spraying mustard water all over the carpet. "That's it! Aunt Aggie, have you a mail order catalogue in the house?"

176

"I expect likely." She rubbed the fish smell off her hands with a hunk of cut lemon and went to get it. "Goin' to order yourself a new brain, James?"

"No, by thunder, I'm going to order you an automatic clothes dryer."

"A clothes dryer? Why, I never . . . well, now, that just might . . . you know, James, I always did suspicion there might be a speck o' common sense under all that intellect o'yours. Willie, go call in the twins an' tell 'em to get cleaned up for supper. I think it's about time we cooked you city folks a decent lobster."

The Mysterious Affair of the Beaird-Wynnington Dirigible Airship

"Well, Papa, so you have saved the Empire yet again." The Honourable Ermentine Ditherby-Stoat, irrepressible daughter of Britain's foremost cabinet minister, held up her face for the expected kiss of greeting. "How many rescues does this one make?"

"Jolly decent of you to take the trouble, sir, if I maybe permitted to say so," stammered Young Gerald Potherton, who was never far from Ermentine's side when propriety admitted his presence.

Lord Ditherby-Stoat allowed a hint of a smile to play about his patrician features as he handed his hat, stick, and dispatch case to Figgleton, his butler and trusted confidant. Then he stooped, for he was a tall man, and bestowed the awaited caress on his daughter's damask cheek.

"Have our guests arrived?"

"Her Ladyship is in the drawing room with Mrs. Swiveltree, Mme. Vigée-Lenoir, Mr. Hellespont, and Mr. Whipsnade, my lord," replied Figgleton. "Count Bratvuschenko has telegraphed that he will arrive on the seven o'clock train."

"But that will hardly give him time to dress for dinner," protested Ermentine. "Really, Papa, does England expect us to turn Haverings into a wild animal refuge every weekend?"

"England expects every man to do his duty," said Lord Ditherby-Stoat with quiet firmness, "and your parents expect no less of you, my dear."

With that, he passed through the massive oaken doors which Figgleton, having adroitly disposed of the hat, the cane, and the dispatch case, now held open for him. Ermentine and her adoring Gerald followed, she only somewhat subdued by her father's admonition and far more aware of her mother's stately presence.

Lady Ditherby-Stoat had been, and indeed still was, the fourth of the seven beautiful daughters of the Earl of Cantilever. Yet it was not the simply cut but sumptuous gown of deep green brocaded velvet or the modest parure of emeralds and diamonds that sparkled at ears, arms, fingers, and bosom, nor yet the matching tiara resting lightly upon her impeccably coiffed pale golden hair that betrayed her aristocratic origin. Rather it was the calm, unruffled patience with which she endured the conversation of Mr. Silas Whipsnade that provided the ultimate test of true breeding.

The Honourable Ermentine, infected with the reckless gaiety of the *siécle* now at its *fin,* was less circumspect. "Whatever do you suppose prompted Papa to invite that impossible Mr. Whipsnade?" she murmured to her doting escort once her father had moved away from them to greet his wife and the oddly assorted group he had caused to be assembled at one of England's stateliest mansions. "In my opinion, he's a bounder and quite possibly a cad."

"Ermy dear," drawled Mr. A. Lysander Hellespont with the familiarity of one who had known her since her pram-and-nanny days, "Whipsnade is merely an American. Let us not be intolerant."

"I at least shall not tolerate his insulting Ermentine by any unwelcome attention," stated young Potherton fiercely.

"Ah, our dauntless fire-eater. You are fortunate, Ermy, to have so stalwart a protector. Now I must go and make intelligent conversation with Mme. Vigée-Lenoir, though I fear that as, a confirmed bachelor, I am singularly ill-adapted to discussing the subject which has brought her to England."

"And what is that?" demanded Ermentine, favoring Hellespont with one of her *gamine* smiles.

"She is making a study of baby-care facilities for the working poor."

Unless Mme. Vigée-Lenoir was herself a nursing mother, the costume she had chosen seemed ill-adapted to reflect so serious a purpose. It was a diaphanous black tulle, cut remarkably low in the bosom and flashing with spangles along the edge of its many coquettish flounces. However, she and the dandified man-about-town appeared to be finding some common ground for conversation, judging from the merry twinkle in her dark eyes and the assiduity with which Hellespont twirled the ends of his dashing mustache as they chatted, he in flawlessly accented French and she in quaint broken English.

"I say, Mrs. Swiveltree looks smashing tonight," exclaimed Gerald Potherton, as well he might. The titian-haired beauty had chosen to array herself in a creation—for no such prosaic word as *gown* could suffice—of amethyst satin, cut extremely *décolleté* and slightly *en train,* its flowing breadths embroidered *á la japonaise* in a design of peacocks. Real peacock feathers nodded from her high-piled coiffure, their shimmering hues reflected in the heavy necklace of beryls and carbuncles that adorned her superb bust.

"Mrs. Swiveltree always looks smashing," said Ermentine dryly. "How else could she advertise the ever-growing wealth derived from her husband's vast shipping interests?"

"And where is the nabob himself? Off in one of his ships?"

"No, at home nursing his gout. Cadwallader Swiveltree is old enough to be her father, you know."

Older men did seem to take a fatherly interest in Mrs. Swiveltree, Gerald Potherton thought, though he had sufficient savoir-faire not to say so. Lord Ditherby-Stoat was at the moment giving the ship magnate's young wife his full and undivided attention. Could the rumors circulating about the club smoking rooms have some basis in fact? Despite his tender years, Potherton was not without some measure of sophistication. He knew men took mistresses, even cabinet ministers married to daughters of earls. But he thrust the notion from his mind. It would be the act of a cad to speculate on such a matter here at Haverings, with Ermentine at his side.

Little did he know that Ermentine was thinking along the same line! It was for this very reason that she was about to divert her father's attention when Figgleton forestalled her, entering the room with a large silver salver on which reposed a smallish oblong, wrapped in paper that bore the royal crest. Impassive as ever, the butler yet conveyed a feeling of pride as he approached Lord Ditherby-Stoat.

"From the Queen's Messenger, my lord."

"Thank you, Figgleton." Lord Ditherby-Stoat took the package into his hands and held it a long moment before, with a murmured apology to his guests, he divested the object of its gala wrappings.

"Why, it's a copy of *Leaves from a Journal of Our Life in the Highlands*," cried Ermentine, who had been shamelessly peeping over her father's shoulder. "Inscribed in Her own hand! Oh, Papa!"

Casting decorum to the winds, the company swarmed to view with their own eyes the magical signature, "Victoria R.," and the inscription, "With Our heartfelt thanks." Even Lady Ditherby-Stoat so far forgot herself as to exclaim, "Jolly well done, Edmund!"

"Then we may opine," said Mr. Whipsnade in a loud, ill-bred voice, "that you've pulled off the Beaird-Wynnington Dirigible Airship deal?"

"Since the newsboys are already braying out the tidings," Lord Ditherby-Stoat replied, "I believe I may not scruple to admit that such is the case."

"And Britain owes it all to you!" Mrs. Swiveltree's peacock feathers quivered with ill-suppressed emotion.

"I do not understand," said Mme. Vigée-Lenoir. "What ees thees airsheep?"

"Suffice it to say, Madame," A. Lysander Hellespont took it upon himself to explain, "that it is a lighter-than-air machine in which persons will be conveyed from one place to another."

"Ah oui, comme les fréres Montgolfier."

"That's it. Precisely like a Montgolfier hot air balloon, but with certain differences."

"Vive la difference! Ah, je vois, you weel weesh les couleurs britanniques. It weel be you who get to choose zem, Lord Dizzerby-Stoat?"

"That, my dear lady, is a closely guarded state secret, I fear," he replied whimsically, taking her dimpled arm in a manner that caused Mrs. Swiveltree's lips to tighten, a fact that did not escape the vigilant Ermentine.

Nor did it elude her notice that the despicable Mr. Whipsnade had edged himself yet closer to her father and his seductive companion, as if to catch any unguarded word that might fall from the statesman's lips under the influence of Mme. Vigée-Lenoir's too-visible allurements. Ermentine was about to thrust herself and her Galahad into the breach, assuming one could be found, when another diversion presented itself. Figgleton announced, "Count Bratvuschenko," and a dancing bear cavorted into the drawing room.

Such, at least, was the Honourable Ermentine's impression. The Russian diplomat, for diplomat he must be, else her father would hardly have offered him the hospitality of Haverings, appeared ill-fitted and certainly ill-barbered for his role. At least he was already arrayed in evening dress, far from impeccable but lavishly bedizened with a wide red sash across his corpulent shirt front, far too many gems on his fingers, and a galaxy of foreign orders pinned to his coat. He bowed so low over Lady Ditherby-Stoat's hand that the decorations clanked together like the clashing of arms on a distant battlefield, saluted the other ladies in like manner, shook hands among the gentleman with a vigor that left them wincing, then stood glaring about like a wild animal expecting to be fed.

As if divining the Muscovite's requirement, Figgleton reappeared, bearing a huge silver wine cooler filled with iced champagne. Following him were footmen bearing trays of crystal goblets and quantities of caviar heaped like tiny jewels in jasperware bowls from the kilns of Josiah Wedgwood, for Lord Ditherby-Stoat conceived it his patriotic duty to buy British whenever possible.

"A toast!" cried Hellespont when all were served. "To Lord Ditherby-Stoat and the Beaird-Wynnington Dirigible Airship."

His eyes were upon Mrs. Swiveltree as he spoke, since it was well-known that the elderly and irascible shipping magnate to whom she was so inappositely espoused was vehemently opposed to the mere concept of airborne vehicles in any form, and even forbade the feeding of pigeons in his park. Nevertheless, Mrs. Swiveltree drank with the rest, and held out her empty glass for more.

Not so the Russian. Having drained the bubbly to the dregs, he hurled the empty goblet straight at the fireplace.

183

Fortunately, the omniscient Figgleton had prudently stationed there one of the footmen, a shining light of the local cricket crease in his off-duty hours. John dexterously fielded the fragile bit of crystal without cracking either the glass or Lady Ditherby-Stoat's composure.

"Right smart operator, that butler," Mr. Whipsnade remarked audibly to Mrs. Swiveltree. "Poor relation, I opine? Favors His Lordship a lot, don't he?"

Even the uncouth Whipsnade could hardly have uttered a more ill-chosen remark. The resemblance between the great statesman and his major domo was indeed obvious, and the reason not far to seek. Among the buxom lasses of the countryside, the gallantries of His Lordship's late grandfather—and indeed of a certain more recent member of his family—had been notorious. The bond between master and servant was indubitably strengthened by ties of blood.

And was that cause for opprobrium on either side? As butler in so stately a home as Haverings, Figgleton had risen to the same eminence in his sphere of life as had Lord Ditherby-Stoat in the loftier halls of Parliament. Why should any find it remarkable that a well-deserved mutual regard might exist between two men of such stature? Still, it was an embarrassing moment. A hasty babble ensued as everybody strove at once to change the subject. Under its cover, Lady Ditherby-Stoat made her way to her husband's side.

"Edmund," she murmured, "you have brought the plans for the Beaird-Wynnington Dirigible Airship to Haverings, have you not?"

He inclined his leonine head gravely. "How you divined the ruse, my dear, I do not know, but the fact remains that I have."

"Are you totally mad?" she all but hissed. "Could you not have left them under lock and key at the War Office?"

"Quite frankly," he replied, "I durst not. Even before negotiations had been fairly completed, bombs had been planted by the Anarchists, the Nihilists, the Separatists, the Prohibitionists, and the Folklore Society. I had an uneasy premonition that mischief might be afoot. Fear not, my dear. The plans are perfectly safe. Only we and Figgleton know where they now repose."

At that moment, the unspeakable Whipsnade, who had sneaked close during their private conversation, was so unfortunate as to sneeze, thus calling attention to his unprincipled tactics. It was at once apparent to all that Lord and Lady Ditherby-Stoat had been discussing the whereabouts of the invaluable documents for which Lord Ditherby-Stoat had labored so adroitly and successfully. Lady Ditherby-Stoat immediately recovered her customary composure, but it was too late. Everyone present had caught the slight crisping of her gloved fingers, the slight tightening of her lips.

She masked it well. "Figgleton," she said imperiously to the butler, who was assiduously engaged in refilling Count Bratvuschenko's glass for the fourteenth time or thereabout, "the Dowager Lady Ditherby-Stoat is not yet down. Go and ascertain whether she requires assistance."

As Figgleton passed out of the room, Lord Ditherby took occasion to intercept him and add in a tone too low for even Whipsnade's ears, "And make certain our confidential matter is securely disposed of."

Too discreet to reply by word or sign, the butler went about his mission. It could not but be observed that Lord and Lady Ditherby-Stoat hovered thenceforth close to the massive oaken doors, ostensibly to greet the dowager when she made her entrance, but in fact to make sure the butler was not trailed by the regrettable Whipsnade. Or so, at least, it

185

was surmised by the Honourable Ermentine and her young knight-at-arms!

Needless to say, all were agog for Figgleton's reappearance. It was, therefore, an anticlimax when the drawing room was next entered not by that august figure but by a mousy wisp of a middle-aged woman in a limp garment of some unappealing gray fabric. She approached Lady Ditherby-Stoat with humble steps and half-whispered, "My lady, I am sent to inform you that Her Dowager Ladyship will not be coming down."

"Nonsense, Twiddle," said the mistress of the great house crisply. "Return at once and remind her that we go in to dinner in precisely three minutes' time."

"I fear the summons will be of no avail, my lady. Saturn has gone retrograde."

"How bothersome of Saturn," drawled Mrs. Swiveltree. "Couldn't it have waited until after dinner? Now your table won't balance, Honoria."

"Her Dowager Ladyship will not emerge from her rooms again until Mars enters the house of Leo," Miss Twiddle explained with that meek stubbornness which the rich and powerful find so exasperating in the genteel poor.

"Then you must take her place, Twiddle," said Lady Ditherby-Stoat. "I cannot allow Saturn to upset my seating arrangements. Mr. Whipsnade, you will take in Miss Twiddle."

"And serve him right," whispered the incorrigible Ermentine.

Whatever retort Gerald Potherton might have made was lost in the stir that greeted the butler's return. Abandoning all pretense at detachment, Lord Ditherby-Stoat hastened to meet him at the drawing-room door. Almost at once, it became apparent to the entire company that the majestic, the impassive Figgleton was in a state of near-collapse. "My lord," he gasped to the eminent statesman now so anxiously confronting him, "the plans for the Beaird-Wynnington Dirigible Airship are—"

Even as the word *gone* formed on his lips, the faithful retainer collapsed and expired at his master's feet.

" 'E 'as—'ow you say — faint!" cried Mme. Vigée-Lenoir.

"I fear not," responded A. Lysander Hellespont, whose dilettante manner masked keen powers of observation. "That trickle of gore on his shirtfront and the knifelike object protruding from the region of the heart would rather indicate that Figgleton has been stabbed."

"You are right," confirmed Lord Ditherby-Stoat. "With a chastely ornamented gold-handled dagger such as might with propriety be carried by any lady or gentleman in full evening dress. My dear, I confess myself at a loss as to the handling of this untoward occurrence."

"There is only one thing to do," said Lady Ditherby-Stoat. Touching the bell, she summoned a footman. "James, remove Figgleton's corpse to the butler's pantry and tell Frederick to pour the hock. Mr. Hellespont, will you give me your arm?"

Picking up her cue, Lord Ditherby-Stoat offered Vigée-Lenoir, leaving Mrs. Swiveltree, much to her dismay, to be escorted by the bear-like Russian count. Ermentine and Gerald, needless to say, were not to be parted. Nervous but ever-dutiful, the mouselike Miss Twiddle brought up the rear with Mr. Whipsnade.

One could hardly have expected gaiety to prevail among a company that had just witnessed the dreadful consequences of a murder, for murder it must have been. Even Lady Ditherby-Stoat appeared a trifle *distraite* as she discussed the novels of Lord Beaconsfield with Mr. Hellespont. It was

Mme. Vigée-Lenoir who managed to choke off Mr. Whipsnade's dismal rehashing of the horrendous event and save the occasion from degenerating into a mourning party. With flashing smile and vivacious wit, she managed to lift all spirits save those of Miss Twiddle, to whom gaiety would have been inappropriate, and Count Bratvuschenko, who continued to deplore the barbarous English custom of not allowing glassware to be smashed while he gourmandized freely among the many dainties proffered by the assiduous footmen who were valiantly upholding the hospitable tradition of Haverings even as their mentor Mr. Figgleton lay stiffening behind the baize doors with his pantry book laid upon his dagger-pierced bosom as a final token of respect.

Nor did Whipsnade enter into the spirit of stiff upper-lip and play-the-game. His countenance grew steadily more dour as he responded in curt monosyllables to Miss Twiddle's feeble attempts to make proper dinner-table conversation.

"He's worried about which fork to use," Ermentine murmured wickedly to Gerald.

But Whipsnade's perturbation pierced far deeper than any fish slice. At last, to the astonishment and dismay of the company, he rose to his feet, overturning a glass of claret in his agitation. Heedless of the spreading crimson stain, he croaked in a tone more raucous than the cawing of the rooks on the battlements, "Enough of this heedless frivolity. A dastardly crime has been committed here tonight and I, Silas Whipsnade, can no longer stifle the stern voice of conscience that cries aloud for redress. The name of the evildoer is—"

He got not farther. With a wild cry of "Arrgh!" Silas Whipsnade clutched at his throat and fell forward into a serving of *riz à l'emperatrice*.

Count Bratvuschenko glanced up from his own plate.

"One of zoze untraceable Asiatic poizonz. It happen all ze time at zese diplomatic dinnerz." He went on eating his dinner. Lady Ditherby-Stoat rang for another footman. Ermentine addressed her father.

"Papa, we shall have to call the police, shall we not?"

"My dear, how can that be?" her father answered. "Have you no apprehension of the dread consequences that would ensue should it become generally known that the plans of the Beaird-Wynnington Dirigible Airship have been stolen? But lest you deem me to have been culpably negligent, I must reveal to you that the late Silas Whipsnade was in fact the noted detective Augustus Fox, whom I myself engaged to guard the plans. The gallant fellow appears to have been on the verge of unmasking the malefactor when he was foully done to death by some as yet undiscovered agency. Let us only remember that, however uncouth his methods of procedure, the alleged Silas Whipsnade gave his life in the service of his country. Take him away, Frederick, and fetch the port."

Lady Ditherby-Stoat gathered the eyes of the female members of the party and led them away from the dining room, leaving the men to find what solace might within the depths of the cut-glass decanters. Circumstances being as they were, it was not surprising that they did not sit long over their port. Hardly an hour later, Lord Ditherby-Stoat, A. Lysander Hellespont, and young Gerald Potherton entered the drawing room.

"But where eez ze Count Bratvuschenko?" demanded Mme. Vigée-Lenoir.

"M'yes," said Lord Ditherby-Stoat thoughtfully. "That is a penetrating observation of yours, Mme. Vigée-Lenoir. It seems to me Count Bratvuschenko has been absent from our gathering for sometime. Hellespont, have you noticed him lately?"

"Not I," disclaimed of the suave man-about-town. "Potherton?"

The junior member of the group answered only by a shake of the head and a barely suppressed hiccough.

"But zees ees terreeble," exclaimed the Frenchwoman. "All ze men deesappear."

"It is a pity," Mrs. Swiveltree agreed with an ironic glance at Mme. Vigée-Lenoir's exuberant decolletage. "Why should it not have been one of the women?"

Ditherby-Stoat touched the bell for a footman. "James, go and see whether Count Bratvuschenko has retired. He may have become indisposed, being unused to British cooking."

"Considering how much of it he ate," Ermentine observed sotto voce, "I shouldn't be surprised."

Gerald responded by another hiccough and a shake of the head. "He was in fine fettle over the port. Dearest, I fear there may have been yet more foul play. Might you not drop a hint to your father about calling in another private detective?"

"Better still," cried Ermentine, "let us turn detectives ourselves. Come, a-sleuthing we shall go!"

Potherton held out a restraining hand. "Wait a moment, the footman is returning. Perhaps he has news of the count."

Much the same thought must have crossed Lord Ditherby-Stoat's mind, for he inquired, "Well, James, do you bring news of the count?"

"Yes and no, my lord, in a manner of speaking," the servant replied in a tone of utter befuddlement. "What I mean to say, my lord, is that some of him's there and the rest of him isn't."

"How very unusual. My dear, if you will excuse me, I believe I ought to go and view this astonishing development myself."

"Oh, let's all go," cried Mrs. Swiveltree, sensing that

Mme. Vigée-Lenoir was about to say the same thing.

Nobody, however, said what was in everybody's mind; namely that since all the servants were faithful old retainers except the drab and mousy Miss Twiddle, whom none could dream capable of a stabbing, a poisoning, or indeed of any action calling for boldness and cunning, then the vicious murderer who was so adroitly decimating their numbers must, ipso facto, be a member of the house party.

Was it Hellespont, that enigma of the clubs and fashionable salons, whose source of income was cause for conjecture and whose predilection for such diversions as slow horses and fast women was well-known? Was it Mme. Vigée-Lenoir, whose reason for crossing the Channel might in truth have been something far, far removed from baby care? Mrs. Swiveltree had already intimated pretty strongly that she herself considered the voluptuous *gauloise* "little more than a foreign adventuress."

And what of Mrs. Swiveltree herself? Was old Cadwallader's absence from this gathering prompted by gout or by guile? Could his known antipathy to the Beaird-Wynnington Dirigible Airship have driven him to send his wife here tonight ostensibly in defiance of his wishes but in fact to obtain and destroy the plans that could threaten his shipping interests? Mrs. Swiveltree might have her reservations about old Cadwallader as a *preux chevalier,* but of his generosity in the matter of jewels, frocks, millinery, country houses, carriages, and the other small amenities of his life she had no cause for complaint and no desire to disoblige her source of supply.

Gerald Potherton was a younger son, with his way to make in the world. His attachment to the Honourable Ermentine might exclude him from suspicion, but how could he know His Lordship's daughter might not suddenly transfer her affections elsewhere, and who was to say that madcap miss hadn't put him up to it?

As for Count Bratvuschenko—well, they would just have to see.

And see they did! The door to the room that was to have been occupied by the foreign nobleman had been left open by the footman in his agitation. Through the orifice, all could see a heterogeneous group of objects dropped carelessly on the bed. There was a furry something that proved on closer inspection to be Bratvuschenko's bushy brown beard, as well as his luxuriant head of hair. There was his eyeglass. There were his medals, his sash, his tail coat, and even his embonpoint.

"A padded waistcoat, by George!" exclaimed Hellespont. "The blighter was heavily disguised."

"But why would any man weesh to make heemself fat and ugly?" demanded Mme. Vigée-Lenoir.

"That, madame, is a question we must all ask ourselves," replied Hellespont, "though I deem it more pertinent to consider where the former inhabitant of these trappings may be at this moment."

Well might he consider. Little did Hellespont know that even as he spoke, a figure far removed from the guzzling buffoon he had last seen at the dinner table was searching assiduously through Hellespont's own personal effects. Nor were the discoveries thus made of a particularly edifying nature. What was an intimate of Lord Ditherby-Stoat doing with a pack of marked cards in his possession, not to mention a threatening letter from his bookmaker and several photographs of the sort of young women who are only facetiously referred to as ladies? And why should a cabinet-size portrait of the Honourable Ermentine be found in such less than dubious company? Lastly, what was contained within this box of a mysterious powder, that had a picture of a horse crudely limned on the cover?

Already, the rooms of the other guests had been searched. Mrs. Swiveltree's had yielded a large bill from her milliner, a still larger one from her dressmaker, a picture of her husband looking stern and relentless, another of a foreign-looking gentleman with a pencil-thin mustache and a languorous eye, this latter inscribed with words in a foreign tongue that had caused the searcher's eyebrows to rise in sardonic amusement. There was also a box of a mysterious powder in a pale pink color, delicately scented and enigmatically labeled "Coty."

Mme. Vigée-Lenoir's room had contained, aside from the expected feminine fripperies, certain articles of interest to the inscrutable searcher. Notable among these were dunning letters in French from her *modiste,* her *coiffeuse,* and her *boulanger;* a cachet of some mysterious powder labeled "For Teething Infants," and one glorious pendant earring of blazing rubics and sparkling brilliants, along with a note which, translated from the French, read simply but meaningfully, "You know what you must do to get its mate."

The late Silas Whipsnade's luggage, as might have been expected from His Lordship's recent revelation, contained an identification card from the Eye-Spye Detective Agency; made out, however, in the name of Silas Whipsnade rather than Augustus Fox. It would appear that the detective was determined to preserve his alias at any cost. There was a letter from Lord Ditherby-Stoat engaging the detective to come to Haverings on the weekend of the house party, and enclosing a personal cheque for a sum that sent the eyebrows soaring again. The soidisant Whipsnade had used the letter for certain private jottings, scribbling Hellespont's name with a large question mark after it, and Mme. Vigée-Lenoir's under a caricature that can best be described as rude. He had even added a whimsical bar sinister to the family crest engraved on the letterhead. Other than those vagaries and a box of a mysterious gray powder labeled "For Fingerprints," the luggage carried nothing of interest.

Gleanings from the mean apartment of Miss Twiddle were more surprising. Drab and mousy though her outer garments might be, it transpired that the companion possessed unmentionables of flaming scarlet. Cunningly disguised in plain brown paper jackets were a whole row of sensational novels. The searcher had not been able to suppress a low whistle as he scanned the torrid pages of Ouida and the passionate outpourings of Mrs. Aphra Behn. He had also taken a cautious sniff at a small bundle of mysterious packets of a white powder labeled "To Be Taken with Meals."

A hasty trip from that secret haven of romantic rodomontade to Figgleton's basement room was a study in contrasts. Aside from his pantry book and the daily newspaper, the late butler's reading matter appeared to have been confined to the "Peerage"; and his correctly butlerian wardrobe to have contained but one incongruous item—namely, a baby's diaper embroidered with the crest of the family he had so loyally served; a Stoat Rampant on a Field Vert. His well-polished shoes had recently been fitted with patent arch supports, and his collar box contained not only the expected neckware but also a small box of a mysterious powder bearing the inscription "Pep-U-Uppo (Patent Applied For)."

Gerald Potherton's room had contained little of interest save several fruitless attempts to pen an ode to his "lost love," a somewhat surprising theme considering Ermentine's obvious though possibly temporary attachment, a dunning letter from his tailor couched in terms far from poetic, a lurid spy novel, and a tin of a mysterious powder represented as "Mustache Strengthener."

Lord Ditherby-Stoat's sumptuous quarters were hardly more fruitful. Aside from the empty dispatch-box and the copy of *Leaves from a Journal of Our Life in the Highlands*, there were only such accoutrements as might have been expected: a signed portrait of Her Gracious Majesty in a heavy silver frame, another of Lady Ditherby-Stoat in her presentation gown, a photograph of Lord Ditherby-Stoat himself in full dress with orders standing beside a bust of his great ancestor, a baby's diaper embroidered with the Ditherby-Stoat coat of arms, and a phial of a mysterious substance labeled "Rhinoceros Horn," no doubt the gift of some foreign emissary.

Lady Ditherby-Stoat had not been spared in this relentless search, and some surprises had eventuated. Little would her acquaintances have divined the vein of sentiment that ran behind that "icily regular, splendidly null" façade. Hidden beneath the scented padding in her hosiery drawer were an unsigned lace valentine, a faded rose, and a much-creased note bearing the poignant words, "Although you can never be mine, I shall cherish you in my heart forever," and signed with the single initial P, these precious tokens all folded inside the sheet music of Tosti's touching ballad, "Goodbye." Beside them lay a packet of a mysterious powder marked "For the Nerves."

The Honourable Ermentine's boudoir had revealed all the froufrous and whimsies to be expected of a pleasure-loving young lady. There was a box of bonbons, half its sugary contents devoured. There was a veritable snowstorm of dance cards, on which the names of General Potherton and A. Lysander Hellespont appeared frequently. More surprisingly, on the topmost card, Count Bratvuschenko had written himself down for a *galop*. And shuffled in among the heap, as if to conceal it from the eyes of her maid or possibly her mother, was an unsigned note on lilac-coloured paper bearing the perhaps teasing, perhaps ominous, words, "I know your secret."

Also attracting the searcher's notice was an ornate crystal jar full of some mysterious scented substance labeled enigmatically "Bath Salts." He was turning this bit of evidence over in his strong, well-shaped hands when, as chance would have it, the Honourable Ermentine flew into the room on the urgent mission of tucking up a stray ringlet. Catching sight of the intruder, she stopped short, her eyes blazing fearlessly.

"What," she demanded imperiously, "are you doing with my bath salts?"

"I am doing this."

The tall man snatched up a delicate porcelain pin tray, ruthlessly dumped its contents on the dressing table, sending hatpins and glove stretchers in every direction, and spilled out the bath salts into the tray. Picking up an ivory-handled buttonhook, he then stirred the crystalline mass, wafting a fragrance as of violets throughout the chamber. In horrified fascination, Ermentine watched. Then she gasped.

"What is that?"

Her quivering finger pointed to a small glass ampoule that now glistened atop the heap of bath salts.

"Well you may ask," said the unknown in portentous tone. "Unless I am mistaken, which I must say has never happened thus far, this little ampoule contains at least one more lethal dose of the unknown Asiatic poison by means of which the late Silas Whipsnade was so recently and efficaciously done to death under our very eyes."

"Then don't tell me who did it. If you dropped dead in the midst, like Mr. Whipsnade, I should never be able to explain to Mama how a strange man's corpse got into my bedroom."

She was to have trouble enough explaining the presence of a live one; judging from the expression on her mother's face as Lady Ditherby-Stoat entered the room, followed by the rest of the party.

"Ermentine, who is this person?"

"I have not yet got round to asking him his name, Mama," replied the minx. "I found him fishing an unknown poison out of my bath salts."

"Confound you, villain!" cried Gerald Potherton, springing to the fore with his fists at the ready for a knockdown blow. "How dare you attempt to defame the name of a lady?"

"Nothing was farther from my mind, I assure you," replied the stranger. "I am but attempting to defend my own."

With a low bow, he proffered an engraved calling card, which Potherton could not but read.

"Augustus Fox, forsooth! Ruffian, you are making sport of me. Augustus Fox lies a stiffening corpse in the . . . Ermy dearest, would you happen to recall what the footman did with Mr. Whipsnade?"

"Mr. Whipsnade is in the butler's pantry with the late Percival Figgleton," Fox informed Potherton. "Though this was not the first time he has taken my name in vain, Whipsnade was in fact none other than himself, an insignificant employee of a third-rate detective agency. His only genuine ability lay in his adroitness at aiding unscrupulous persons in their fell designs and blackmailing them when their perfidies had been accomplished."

"What perfidies?" demanded Lady Ermentine.

"Any perfidies," Fox replied with a tolerant smile. "Let us suppose, for instance, that an unlucky gambler determined upon doping the Derby favorite but needed help in obtaining the requisite potion. Or a cocaine smuggler wished to expand her already thriving market. Or the young wife of an elderly tycoon had fallen in love with a handsome adventurer and required a means of rendering the old man unconscious so that she could join her paramour in the happy task of turning her gems to paste so that he and she would have a tidy nest egg with which to elope."

He shrugged. "But this is mere speculation. And so, I fear, is the question of what prompted Whipsnade's impromptu funeral oration. Did such scruples as he might still possess prompt his attempted denouncement of a crime too heinous even for him to stomach? Was it rather part of a subtle ruse devised between himself and his final employer? Or was he endeavoring to make a public example of his latest victim in order to stimulate the payment of Danegeld from the others? We shall never know. May I suggest that we descend to the drawing room before we attack the problem of who concealed the poison capsule in Miss Ermentine's bath salts? I quite agree with Mr. Potherton as to the unsuitability of polluting these chaste walls with further sordid revelations."

With one accord they made for the staircase, Fox stooping to retrieve the delicately perfumed lace handkerchief which Mme. Vigée-Lenoir dropped at his feet, and restoring it to her with a gentlemanly gesture that yet made plain he was not the man to be trapped by so transparent a ruse.

When all were reassembled in the majestic salon, Fox indicated that he was ready to resume his narrative, though not before the Honourable Ermentine had observed, "I never knew Figgleton's given name was Percival."

"Ah," said Fox, whom the aside had naturally not escaped. "But therein lies the gist, or nub, of my tale. Miss Twiddle, you are, are you not, the sister of the late Percival Figgleton?"

As though by necromantic means, the drabness and mousiness disappeared. An inch of scarlet petticoat showed beneath the drooping gray hem as Miss Twiddle drew herself up proudly. "I am."

"Then you must know what weighty secret it was that your brother carried for lo, these many years."

"Figgleton carried lots of secrets," Lord Ditherby-Stoat interrupted peevishly. "I trusted him, damme."

"And worthily did he uphold that trust," said Lady Ditherby-Stoat most unexpectedly.

"Percival could do no other," cried Miss Twiddle. "Ne'er drew he an ignoble breath."

"What does she mean, ne'er drew he?" Gerald muttered to Ermentine.

"I don't know. I think it's poetry." For once, that ebullient young woman was sober, gazing at Miss Twiddle's scarlet petticoat as if gripped by some force she could not understand.

"Trustworthy is an adjective that cannot be applied to at least one other person in this room." Fox's keen, penetrating eyes traveled among the assemblage, resting first on Mme. Vigée-Lenoir, then on Hellespont, and lastly on Mrs. Swiveltree. "To get at the root of this matter, we must ask ourselves, who benefits most from the theft of the plans for the Beaird-Wynnington Dirigible Airship? Or, as we used to say at Harrow, *cui bono?*"

"Mrs. Swiveltree," said Ermentine promptly. "Mr. Swiveltree will be so pleased they're gone that he'll pay her dressmaker's bills without a murmur."

"I should be rather inclined to vote for Mme. Vigée-Lenoir," drawled A. Lysander Hellespont. "I fancy a certain cabinet minister in a certain country not more than a Channel's swim from here will do rather more than pay her dressmaker's bills."

"And I, on ze ozzer hand, wondaire how zese plans may affect ze plans of Monsieur Hellespont's bookmakaire," retorted the Frenchwoman viciously.

"These are all points to consider," said Fox blandly. "And now let us ask ourselves who benefits the least."

"Cui malo," interjected Gerald Potherton, much to Ermentine's admiration.

"The *malo* is mine, naturally," said Lord Ditherby-Stoat. "Unless the plans are recovered, I am a ruined man."

"However, my brother is in any case a dead man," rejoined Miss Twiddle sharply.

"My dear," Lord Ditherby-Stoat turned to his wife, "might you not drop a hint to Twiddle that she oversteps herself?"

"She does not," replied Lady Ditherby-Stoat. "Her logic is irrefutable."

"There is also the matter of the defunct Silas Whipsnade," Fox went on, "although strictly speaking it was not the loss of the plans that hastened his demise."

"Then what was it?" demanded Ermentine.

"It was his rapacious greed," the famous detective responded. "You see, Whipsnade had ferreted out that weighty secret which the late Percival Figgleton and the discreet Miss Twiddle had guarded so jealously for so many years. He planned not to guard it, but to exploit it to the hilt."

"You mean more blackmail?" cried Hellespont.

"I do."

"How dastardly!"

"And how dangerous. Whipsnade reckoned not with the primitive ferocity that lies beneath his intended victim's suavely correct facade."

All eyes turned toward Hellespont.

"Don't look at me," he drawled, essaying a light laugh. "I'm not all that correct."

"Then it was Count Bratvuschenko," exclaimed Mrs. Swiveltree, who appeared not yet to have grasped the import of those grotesque habiliments so recently discovered in the vanished guest's bedroom. "One sensed the primitive ferocity merely from the way he attacked his soup. But where is he now?"

"If you will wait one moment, I shall bring him to you."

Fox wheeled and ran lightly up the majestic staircase. In little more than the promised moment, the bearlike Bratvuschenko was back among them, glowering around in search of the brandy decanter.

"And now," cried a merry voice, "I shall make him disappear again."

With an airy gesture, the brown wig was lifted, the bushy beard detached. Behold, Augustus Fox stood before them!

"When I learned through dark and devious sources," he explained, "that Silas Whipsnade was up to his old tricks at Haverings, I determined to safeguard my own unblemished reputation and foil his evil scheme by being on hand myself to ferret out whatever *miching mallecho* had brought him here. The true Count Bratvuschenko, who I may say owed me a little service for reasons I am not free to divulge, was only too happy to have me take his place while he remained in his secluded country seat poring over his chessboard and making notes for the novel he plans some day to write. I foxed you, did I not?"

"He is a veritable master of disguise," ejaculated Gerald Potherton, in whom clear signs of dawning hero worship were now discernible.

"If the ladies will forgive me," said Fox, "I shall also divest myself of this somewhat uncomfortable padded waistcoat. It spoils the drape of one's coat. As does a bulky sheaf of papers, such as the plans for the Beaird-Wynnington Dirigible Airship. May I relieve you of them, Lord Ditherby-Stoat?"

Before anyone could make a move, the plans were in the hands of Augustus Fox. Amid the startled cries he calmly tucked them inside his own impeccably tailored garment.

"I have a hansom cab waiting. Within the hour, I shall have hied myself straight to Buck House and placed these documents in Her Majesty's own hands. As for you, Lord Ditherby-Stoat, I fear the *cui malo* you thought to avoid by your stratagem has caught up with you. When you staged a cunning robbery as a pretext to drive your gold-mounted dagger into the most loyal heart that ever beat even as Figgleton was in the act of informing you that the plans were gone, you sealed your own fate."

"How so?" cried Hellespont.

"For one thing," replied Fox, "the hilt of the dagger bore His Lordship's own monogram. No such slip would have occurred, of course, had you been able to rely on your accustomed guide and mentor, Lord Ditherby-Stoat. Few persons realized that the brain behind the Beaird-Wynnington coup, and indeed behind all your brilliant acts of statesmanship, was that of your elder cousin, the alleged Percival Figgleton, who was in fact the true Lord Ditherby-Stoat."

"Good heavens, Honoria," drawled Mrs. Swiveltree. "You married the wrong cousin."

"Oh no," replied Lady Ditherby-Stoat with her usual calm aplomb. "I married the right one. No doubt Mr. Fox will be able to explain."

"I believe so," said the great detective. "The original contretemps arose from the fact that the late Cedric Ditherby-Stoat, eldest son of the third Lord Ditherby-Stoat, was killed in the hunting field at the age of thirty-one, supposedly unmarried although not without issue. In fact, Cedric had been united in lawful wedlock seven years previously with the daughter of a publican in a neighboring village, by whom he had a son and a daughter, both of them quite legitimate but not recognized as such by Cedric's parents because of their mother's lowly origin. Upon Cedric's death, therefore, the succession passed not to his son Percival, the rightful heir but to Cedric's younger brother, the present Lord Ditherby-Stoat. I may say in exculpation that I believe the present Lord Ditherby-Stoat to have been kept in ignorance of his nephew's legitimacy until he was apprised of the truth by the late Silas Whipsnade not long since."

"Bloody beggar wanted five hundred thousand pounds to hush it up," whined Lord Ditherby-Stoat, from whom the mien of rank and dignity seemed already to be falling.

"To continue my painful narrative," Fox went on, "the true Lord Ditherby-Stoat, though fully aware of his rights, was astute enough to realize he had no real hope of succeeding to the position that should have been his. However, the blood of the Ditherby-Stoats ran high in his veins. Rather than bring scandal upon the family by forcing himself, the grandson of a publican, into the public eye as the rightful claimant, he took the nobler course of dedicating himself to its service. Using a false name, he engaged himself to the household as boot boy and worked his way steadily up through the ranks until his obviously superior qualifications earned him, young as he was, the exalted position of butler and confidant to His False Lordship. Inspired by her brother's example and aided by his increasing influence with the family, Percival's younger sister also anonymously obtained a post here, as companion to that elderly dowager whose malign influence over her sons had been a primary factor in preventing Cedric from securing the rights of his own legitimate offspring. Entitled though she is to the dignity of a family member, she has meekly and dutifully endured the scorn and ignominy of a lowly paid companion. Miss Twiddle, I salute you."

"How did you fathom my secret?" gasped the erstwhile drab and mousy underling.

"Elementary, my dear Miss Ditherby-Stoat, for thus I must henceforth style you. I noted the tearstains on your well-worn copy of *Oroonoko, or the Royal Slave*. Immediately, all was clear to me."

It was clear to A. Lysander Hellespont, too. A new light dawning in his eyes, he bent low over Miss Ditherby-Stoat's formerly careworn hand.

"But there is more," said Fox. "Shall I go on, Lady Ditherby-Stoat?"

"You must, must you not?"

"Yes, I must. I believe the next chapter in our saga must have taken place when Lady Honoria, fourth daughter of the Earl of Cantilever, already betrothed to Lord Ditherby-Stoat, visited Haverings with her parents and the soi-disant Figgleton announced their arrival."

"We exchanged but one glance," said Lady Ditherby-Stoat in a gentle, wistful tone nobody had ever heard her use before, "and we knew. Later, under pretense of visiting the ladies' cloakroom, I tiptoed down to the butler's pantry. There I learned that Figgleton was the true Lord Ditherby-Stoat. There we plighted our troth. There we planned what was clearly the only thing to be done. The following day, under pretext of visiting my old nanny, I slipped away to a tiny church in an unfashionable street and married my darling Percival."

"And after that you had the gall to marry me?" cried Lord Ditherby-Stoat.

"Ours has been no true marriage. You went through the ceremony under a false title and false pretensions. And I kept my fingers crossed as I said my vows."

"And you had a terrible headache on the wedding night," Ditherby-Stoat added bitterly. "And you've had one ever since. I've always wondered how we managed to come up with Ermentine."

"You had nothing to do with Ermentine's birth. She is the legitimate daughter of my beloved late husband, Percival Ditherby-Stoat. As such, she is now also the true heiress to Haverings."

"Then where does that leave me? Honoria, what shall I do?"

"Obviously, Edmund, there is only one thing for you to do." She opened her evening bag and handed him a small, pearl-handled revolver such as might properly be carried by the fourth daughter of any nobleman. "I suggest the library, and you might take a footman with you this time. One does get so weary of ringing bells."

The Dastardly Dilemma of
the Vicious Vaudevillian

The audience stirred restlessly before the closed curtain on which were painted in large, ornate letters shading from softest pink to vibrant cerise the poignant words, MOTHER SHIPTON'S SOOTHING SYRUP—GOOD FOR WHAT AILS YOU. To the left of the slogan was the spirited depiction of a wan, elderly, bald-headed man writhing in obvious agony and visited by a multitude of maladies. Beneath it was the single ominous word, BEFORE. To the right was a portrait of the same man, but ah, what a difference! Young, vital, bursting with robust health and boasting a full head of wavy chestnut hair, it was labeled succinctly, AFTER.

One might have thought this artistry, with its inspirational message of hope and rejuvenation, would suffice for the entertainment of those assembled before it, but not so. Impatient utterances and restless stirrings might be heard, especially from those in the front rows who could catch certain mutterings from behind the curtain. These sounded suspiciously like, "Your deal," "I'll take two cards," "Raise you," and similar ejaculations pertaining to some uncouth game of chance.

Suddenly the curtain parted. BEFORE was banished to the left, AFTER to the right. But instead of the awaited spectacle, the audience saw only two unkempt stagehands, both startled, one irate. This latter was yelling, "Hey, fathead, lay

206

off them ropes. The show don't start for another two minutes."

Finding the opportunity to play to a filled auditorium irresistible, however, he fanned his cards to display a king-high straight and laid it before his partner. "Okay, Gus. Let's see you beat that."

"You cheated," cried the man thus addressed. "That ain't the hand I dealt you."

His further expostulations were drowned in loud outcries from offstage, uttered in a female voice with a strong French accent.

"Qui, moi? Jamais! Nevaire! Pas du tout! Not on your teentype! I am no spy, no sneak, no pigeon de stool. In vain you lure me wiz meenks, wiz gold, wiz diamonds and pearls all fake like you. I am a trouper, not a snooper."

Then came a crash, as of a scent bottle or a pomade jar smashing against a wall dangerously close to some would-be tempter's ear. Their own altercation forgotten, the two stagehands rose. He of the inside straight dashed for the wings. The other paused only to show the audience a hand of five aces, toss the cards carelessly down among the other appurtenances of what could only be a magician's act, and hasten after his partner.

Little did the audience realize they had just been in the presence of one who was in fact no mere stagehand but in reality the famous detective Augustus Fox. His appearance in this rude guise was at the behest of Victor Virtue, far-famed manager of Virtue's Victorious Vaudevillians, in a desperate attempt to stem the plague of misfortunes that threatened to bring about the company's ruin.

A motive for these perfidious acts was not far to seek. It must have been obvious to everyone from the call-boy to the newest member of the chorus that some member of the company had been bribed to perpetrate the calamities by Virtue's hated rival, one Samuel Slime. Slime's motive, of course, was to usurp Virtue's place in the forefront of vaudeville, replacing his wholesome entertainments with the sort of filth that, under Virtue's aegis, would ne'er sully the eyeballs of honest men, respectable women, and innocent children. Left to Slime, the stage would become one seething fleshpot of undraped limbs and swelling bosoms, interspersed with vulgar comedians posturing in the rudest manner while they turned the air blue with their ribald anecdotes.

Already serious onslaughts had been made: itching powder in the tightrope walker's tights, garlic in the lead soubrettes nosegay, peach fuzz glued to the metal plates on the tap dancers' shoes. Chopped onions had been thrown down from the balcony to make the audience cry instead of laugh during Tom Tripp's impeccably pure but generally hilariously received comedy act, aggravating the comedian's habitual melancholia and causing him to drown his sorrows in a too-liberal dose of Mother Shipton's Soothing Syrup.

But the show must go on, and on it went. The curtain parted in earnest, revealing The Great Mysterioso, in frock coat, top hat, and sweeping black cape, together with his piquant aide, Miss Mopsy Muffet, in winsome peasant costume, her green bodice laced snugly around a tiny waist and pink skirts frothing out beguilingly (and, it must be confessed, somewhat, abbreviatedly) over bright pink stockings and dainty slippers.

All went well at first. Mysterioso produced coloured handkerchiefs by the dozens from the end of his magic wand. He caused an egg to vanish from his own hand and turn up in Miss Mopsy's pompadour. He did incredible things with the deck of cards so recently cast down by the two recreant stagehands. He produced a somewhat sullen white rabbit from the depths of his top hat. Miss Mopsy brought a tiny flowerpot, held it out so the audience could see that it was completely empty, then waited with eager, shining eyes while the magician draped a pink silk handkerchief over the pot and made mysterious passes.

Hey, presto! Change-o! The kerchief began to bulge, to rise. Of a sudden, it was wafted aside. There in that empty pot grew a magnificent paper flower fully eight inches in diameter, on a tall stem. With a gallant bow, Mysterioso plucked the posy and presented it to Miss Mopsy. She in turn raised it to her dainty nostrils, took an appreciative sniff and fell into a fit of uncontrollable sneezing.

"Pepper!" she gasped.

"Ah me," sighed the magician whimsically in an attempt to carry off the mishap as part of the act, "those wicked imps of air and fire have been at it again."

He handed her an assortment of coloured handkerchiefs and busied himself with some sleight-of-hand tricks while Miss Mopsy retired to the wings to recover her composure and repair the ravages to her greasepaint, but it was clear he had lost his audience's attention.

Sensing this as any good showman should, he hurried along to his last and most spectacular illusion. A long, coffinlike box had been sitting at the back of the stage throughout the performance. This was now pulled forward. A member of the audience was invited up to inspect the box inside and out, making sure it was free of any hidden compartment. This person was allowed to assist Miss Mopsy into the box, then politely thanked and dismissed. Miss Mopsy put her head through an aperture in one end of the box, her green-slippered feet through the opposite end. The lid was closed, securing her within a wooden prison. Amid gasps of horror from certain ladies in the audience, Mysterioso picked up a large saw and declared his intention of sawing Miss Mopsy in half!

The saw was without doubt a sharp one. It cut through the wood cleanly and quickly. The audience held its breath. Surely the magician would slay his charming assistant! Yet Miss Mopsy Muffet continued to smile quite self-assured, as the saw came nearer and nearer.

But now her eyes widened, a grimace of fear contorted her face. Her lips parted in an earsplitting shriek.

"Stop! Stop! You're killing me."

Mysterioso's arm froze in mid-thrust. Victor Virtue himself rushed onstage. The two halves of the great curtain swung together. BEFORE scowled, AFTER beamed, as the audience babbled together in frightened anticipation of dreadful news. But in a matter of moments, Victor Virtue stepped through the folds and held up his hand for silence.

"Ladies and gentlemen, I am happy to announce that Miss Mopsy Muffet sustained only superficial injury during the recent unfortunate episode, which was caused not by any lack of skill in the part of The Great Mysterioso, but through careless mishandling of the equipment by a negligent stagehand who has already been dismissed. Gallant trouper that she is, Miss Muffet declares herself quite able to perform her starring role as the heroine in our smashing grand finale, that stirring melodrama, NUGGET NELL, OR THE GOLD MINER'S DAUGHTER. And now I have the honour to present the act that took all Paris by storm, directly from the Moulin Rouge, the darling of the boulevards, Mlle. Fifi LaPuce and her Trained Fleas!"

He bowed and withdrew, amid somewhat tentative applause. The curtains parted again. Gone was the magician's equipment, including the ill-omened wooden box. In its place hung a backdrop of the Champs Elysées, in front of which came tripping a saucy, black-eyed mademoiselle wearing a jaunty red bow in her jetty locks, a flirtatious costume of vivid scarlet, and black pumps with heels fully two inches high. She was wheeling what looked like a glassed-over tea cart, and smiling as only a Parisian *gamine* can smile. If it was Mlle. La Puce (and who else would it have been?) who had made that tempestuous scene before the show began, there was no sign of perturbation in her manner now.

"Bon soir mesdames, messieurs. Tonight you weel see some feats ze most amazing. But first you must meet my so talented entertainers."

She proceeded to introduce her fleas, holding them up one by one. There were sweet little Clothilde the tightrope walker, brawny Pierre and agile Armand, the daring young fleas on the flying trapeze. There were Babette the coquette and handsome Eugene who apparently chose to invent their own impromptu routine, for she broke off her exposition to exclaim, "Ah, naughtee! Naughtee! Pas devant ze audience," and put them hastily back into the tea cart.

Mlle. LaPuce was clearly fond of her fleas and it might have been presumed that her fleas in turn were fond of her. Certainly she won all hearts as she described, though not in over-tedious detail, what wonders her troupe were to perform.

"But you must wondaire, mesdames et messieurs, 'ow you weel be able to see mes chers petits performing zair pretty treecks. So now I show you. Be'old ze giant magnifying glass."

She glanced expectantly toward the wings. Instead of the stagehand with the magnifier, out galloped a huge dog of unnameable breed. As Mlle. LaPuce vainly endeavored to restrain him, the vicious mongrel contrived to overset the cart and then ran offstage, carrying the entire flea circus within his

211

shaggy pelt. Screaming hysterically, "Ma pauvre Clothilde!" Mlle. LaPuce rushed after him as from the opposite wing Victor Virtue rushed onstage to announce the next act.

Troupers to the core, the Bathos Brothers danced onstage, twirling their canes and waving their straw boaters to the tune of "Waltz Me Around Again, Willie." But alas, their waltz became a mad fandango as it was made evident that their feet were utterly and completely out of control. While Augustus Fox was backstage removing pins from the actors' greasepaint, some archfiend had been buttering the Bathos Brothers' boots.

Stalwart souls that they were, the brothers tried to pretend their wild antics were part of the act, but the audience was not deceived. For the first time in their hitherto distinguished theatrical career, the song-and-dance team was booed off the stage. Victor Virtue was forced onstage again to quell the tumult.

"And now, ladies and gentlemen, the event you've all been waiting for. Virtue's Victorious Vaudevillians present that soul-stirring saga of love and hate in the badlands of gold and greed, *Nugget Nell*."

It was the old, old tale of the harried heroine, the handsome hero, and the venomous villain. True, the gold miner himself was to have figured in the drama. Sad to say, however, he had been so plied with strong drink immediately before the performance, no doubt by the same dastardly hand that loosed the dog and buttered the boots, that he spent the entire act slumped on a rustic bench that formed part of the stage setting, emitting only lugubrious hiccoughs and an occasional snatch of "Whoa, Emma."

As the drama unfolded, it became apparent to all that the true hero of the performance was in fact the alleged villain. Finding the actor who was to have essayed the role stretched prone in his dressing room helpless from a sudden attack of poison ivy, his face towel having been clandestinely rubbed with that noxious weed by the unknown evildoer, Augustus Fox himself had donned the frock coat, the opera cape, the high silk hat, and the black crepe hair mustache with its over-dandified curling ends. Flawlessly he executed the demanding role, declaiming his fell intent to foreclose on her father's gold mine or else work his evil will with Nugget Nell as the case might be. Convincingly did he recoil in sinister ire as the stainless, unflinching heroine told him to go his wicked way, and might fortune grant him grace to find repentance ere doom o-ertook him.

Instead of repenting, however, Fox whipped out a dagger which he proposed to plunge into the hero's back as that young man enfolded Nugget Nell in a fervent though chaste embrace.

Because of the series of near-disasters that had already cast their blight on the entertainment, Fox thought it best to explain in an aside to the audience that the deadly-looking knife was but a trick dagger with a collapsible blade, and that he would only *pretend* to stab the hero. Notwithstanding this disclosure, he performed the action with a most convincing display of histrionic talent. The hero fell gasping to the floor. Shrieking in anguish, Nugget Nell threw herself on her adored one's supposedly lifeless corpse.

In a moment, however, it became known that her screams were no mere feigning. She rose up, considerably ensanguined about the bodice, holding aloft the gore-encrusted dagger. "You meathead," she cried, "you got the wrong prop!"

Yes, it was a real knife. The hero was dead, and Augustus Fox was his murderer. Here was drama with a vengeance! Once more Victor Virtue rushed onstage, this time accompanied by two helmeted policemen, both brandishing their nightsticks in a threatening manner and shouting, "You're under arrest!"

Without losing a jot of his aplomb, Fox raised his hands in surrender. But Mopsy Muffet, still in her blood-smeared costume as Nugget Nell, hurled herself between him and the policemen.

"Officers, I beg of you, do not arrest his man. Little can you know what succour he has granted me, a frail and fragile female forced to yield day after day to the uncouth embraces of this alleged hero, who was in real life a cad and a rotter to whom I wouldn't have given the time of day if I didn't have a dear widowed mother to support. Pray let him go free, with the blessings of a wronged woman and her sweet old mother upon his noble head."

"But he killed him," one of the policemen pointed out.

"I know, but he didn't mean to," argued Miss Muffet. "Somebody messed around with the props, that's all. It happens."

"Not in my company," Victor Virtue retorted. "Not unless somebody makes it happen. I'm not blaming you, Fox, but I must say you've let me down sadly. You were supposed to apprehend the miscreant, not fall victim to his wiles."

"I did not fall victim to anyone's wiles, and I have apprehended the miscreant." Quick as lightning, he seized the wrist of Miss Mopsy Muffet. "This is she."

"But . . . but the pepper in the flower."

"A ruse to divert suspicion from herself."

"But she almost got sawed in two!"

"Humbug! She was wearing a steel corset, proof against the keenest sawtooth. As in fact she still is, not having dared to risk leaving it about her dressing room. I felt it just now when I was required in my role as villain to force my doubly

214

unwelcome attentions upon her. And as for stabbing your hero, do you think Augustus Fox would have been fool enough not to make sure the collapsible dagger was in perfect working order before he employed it upon the person of another? You will find that dagger—or a police matron will find it—cunningly concealed somewhere about her costume, probably in that same hiding place whence she extracted the real dagger when she fell upon her pretended lover and actual victim, who of course was still living until she stabbed him during her feigned paroxysm of grief."

"But why would she kill him?" demanded Victor Virtue in bewilderment. "I know Reginald Rapture was no plaster saint, but he wasn't the skunk she'd made him out to be. And he was crazy about her."

"Ah, therein lies the crux of the matter. Reginald Rapture was indeed crazy about Miss Mopsy Muffet—crazy enough to fall in with her reprehensible schemes to undermine your troupe. It was because Rapture had been her accomplice that she was compelled to destroy him. You see, she planned to jilt him for another, richer man."

With purposeful stride, Fox approached the sodden miner, still huddled on his bench, snoring in a manner that had seemed convincing enough until Fox, with one deft motion, reached out and stripped away the great bush of false beard that had totally masked the man's countenance.

"Samuel Slime!" cried Victor Virtue.

"None other," said Fox. "It was Slime's callous intention to preside in person over your final discomfiture and gloat over the ruin of your theatrical fortunes from which he thought to obtain his ill-gotten gains. And in which Miss Mopsy Muffet obviously expected to share. Arrest them, officers."

Nonchalantly, Augustus Fox resumed his top hat and

opera cloak and turned to the stunned audience. "So you see, ladies and gentlemen, that in real life as in melodrama, true virtue does in fact triumph and true villainy receive its just punishment. Go your ways, remember the lesson you have learned today, and come back next week for another thrilling performance by Virtue's Victorious Vaudevillians. I thank you, one and all."

And thus did the curtain close on the one and only, never-to-be-forgotten on-stage appearance of that dauntless detective, Augustus Fox.

Rest You Merry

"I do think, Professor Shandy, you might show some consideration," sputtered the bursar's wife.

"It's only once a year," pleaded the Dean of Women. "I'd be only too glad—"

"I thank you," said Professor Shandy. "I shall keep Christmas in my own way, as usual."

"But you don't keep it," wailed the bursar's wife, sounding like Scrooge's nephew only less cheerful.

The professor did not reply, "Bah, humbug." He merely backed his visitors out the door. His adroitness was the result of long practice.

This was the seventy-third such interview. Professor Shandy had kept count. He had a passion for counting. He would have counted the spots on an attacking leopard. If the hairs on his head were indeed numbered, he would have known the exact number. As it happened however, he was bald.

Every Christmas season during the eighteen he had spent teaching natural science at Bemis College, he had been tackled by virtually every faculty wife and civic leader in Bemisville. Over the years faces had altered, come and gone, but the plaint was ever the same.

"We have a tradition to maintain."

The tradition dated back, as Professor Shandy's research

had revealed, no farther than 1907, when the wife of the then president of the college had found herself stuck with a box of Japanese lanterns left over from the alumni ball. Being of a temperament which combined artistic leanings with Yankee thrift, she conceived the notion of staging a Grand Illumination of the Common on Christmas Eve, producing a dramatic effect at practically no expense. As the years wore on, the professor had come to feel a deep sense of personal injury because it had not rained that night.

In fact, the event had attracted so much attention that it had been repeated with ever-accumulating embellishments ever since. As time went on, the village green had become a positive welter of blue lights, red sleighs, and whimsical figurines of carolers in quaint costume.

The householders around the common, and eventually throughout the village, had thrown themselves wholeheartedly into the jollification. Of late years, Bemisville had become one multicolored blaze of Yuletide spirit. People drove miles to look at the lights. Pictures appeared in national magazines.

However, the photographers always had to avoid one dark spot in the gala scene. This was the home of Professor Shandy. He alone, like a bald, pudgy King Canute, stood firm against the all-engulfing Christmas tide.

In the daytime, as even the bursar's wife admitted, it was not so bad. In fact, the small house of rosy old bricks looked quite festive in its frame of snow-covered evergreens. This was what really galled the ladies of the village.

"You could do so much *with* it," they moaned.

Their fingers itched to hang Styrofoam candy canes on the professor's gleaming brass knocker. They yearned to bedeck his magnificent blue spruces with little lights that winked on and off. One after another, they had volunteered as decora-

218

tors. They had showered the professor with garlands of gilded pine cones, with stockings cut out of red oilcloth, with wreaths of sour balls that had tiny pairs of scissors dangling whimsically on red satin ribbons to snip off goodies as required.

He thanked them all courteously and passed on their offerings to his cleaning woman. By now, Mrs. Lomax had the most bedizened place in town, but the brick house on the common remained stubbornly unadorned.

Left to himself, the professor would have been perfectly willing to make some small concession to Christmas: a spray of holly on the door, perhaps, and a wax candle flickering pleasantly after dark in parlor window. No matter what the bursar's wife said, he rather enjoyed the holidays. Every year he sent off a few carefully austere cards to a few old friends. He then avoided as many as he decently could of the Christmas festivals, Christmas dances, and Christmas cocktail parties, and went to visit relatives.

These were a cousin and his wife: quiet, elderly people who lived a comfortable three hours' journey from him. They would thank him for the cigars and box of assorted jellies, then sit him down to an early dinner of roast beef and Yorkshire puddings. Afterward, the cousin would show his stamp collection. The professor did not care for stamps as such, but they were splendid things to count. As soon as he had finished his tabulation, the cousin's wife would serve tea and her special lemon cheese tarts and remark that he had a long ride ahead of him. Professor Shandy considered his cousin to have married exceptionally well.

About nine o'clock, agreeably stuffed, he would sneak home and settle down with a glass of good sherry and *Bracebridge Hall*. At bedtime, he would step outside the back door for a last whiff of fresh air. If it was a fine night, he would feel an urge to stay out and count stars for a while. However, if he indulged the whim, some neighbor was sure to spot him and insist on inviting poor, lonely Professor Shandy over for a drink.

Altogether too many of his Christmases had been spoiled in just such ways by the overwhelming holiday spirit of Bemisville. When the wife of the head of the chemistry department showed up on the morning of December twenty-first with a pot of poinsettias fashioned from bits of old detergent bottles, something snapped. He thrust the loathsome object at Mrs. Lomax, grabbed his coat, and ran for the Boston train.

The following morning, two men drove up to the brick house in a large truck. Professor Shandy met them at the door.

"Did you bring it all, gentlemen?"

"The whole works. Boy, you folks sure take Christmas seriously out here, don't you?"

"We have a tradition to maintain," said the professor briskly. "You may as well start on the spruce trees."

All morning long the men toiled. Expressions of delighted amazement appeared on the faces of passers-by. As the day wore on and the men still toiled, the amazement remained but the delight faded. Neighbors began to peer nervously from around the edges of their curtains.

It was after dark when the men got through. Professor Shandy saw them to the door. He was wearing his coat and hat, and carrying a suitcase.

"Everything in order, gentlemen? Lights timed to flash on and off at precisely fifty-three-second intervals? Amplifiers turned up to full volume? Switch boxes provided with sturdy locks? Very well, then, let's throw the switches and be off. I'm going to impose on you for a lift back to Boston. I have an urgent appointment at the waterfront."

"Sure, glad to have you," they chorused, feeling the pleasant crinkle of bills in their hands. It had been an interesting day.

On the evening of December' twenty-fifth, Professor Shandy stepped out on deck for a breath of air. Around him rolled the mighty Atlantic. Above him shone only the lights from the bridge and a skyful of stars. The captain's dinner had been most enjoyable. Presently he would go below for a chat with the chief engineer, a knowledgeable man whose hobby was counting the revolutions of the ship's engines.

Back in Bemisville, the floodlights would be illuminating the eight life-size plastic reindeer on the roof of the brick house. The twenty-three plastic Santa Claus faces would be glowing, one to each window, above the twenty-three sets of artificial candles, each containing three pink and two purple bulbs.

He glanced at his watch. At that precise moment, the seven hundred and forty-two red, green, blue, and yellow oversize bulbs on the spruce trees would have flashed on and off for the four thousand, five hundred and eighty-seventh time; a total of three million, three hundred eighty-eight thousand, seven hundred and fourteen flashes.

The amplifiers would by now have blared three hundred and thirty-five renditions each of "I'm Dreaming of a White Christmas," "I Saw Mommy Kissing Santa Claus," and "All I Want for Christmas Is My Two Front Teeth." They would at this moment be on the seventh bar of the three hundred and thirty-sixth performance of "I Don't Care Who You Are, Fatty, Get Those Reindeer Off My Roof."

Professor Shandy smiled gently into the darkness. "Bah, humbug," he murmured, and began to count the stars.

Homecoming

Heads turned as the tall man in the impeccably tailored London gray suit with the almost imperceptible plaid overlay of a deeper slate color strode off the plane from Budapest, his only impediment a well-worn mackintosh nonchalantly slung over left arm and the insouciant half-smile that curved his sensitively molded lips. Little did the heads know that those keen gray eyes with their haunting tinge of deep sea blue (or were they blue with a hint of gray?) felt like boiled eggs after nights of sleepless watching, or that the orifice behind those finely chiseled lips seemed to be lined with some sort of reddish fuzz from all that paprika.

No matter. He was home now, his mission completed, the priceless Inglefeather emerald safely restored to its rightful owner. Her Noble Highness had been most gracious. Having dealt with gracious nobilities before, Max Bittersohn—for this was none other than the renowned tracker-down of priceless objects—had courteously declined the Order of the Gauntleted Gnu and requested a certified cheque.

He did not follow the throng to the baggage carousel. His luggage would be sent on to him by trusted emissaries once the recovered Canaletto had been safely extricated from the secret compartment and the Cellini salt cellar from among his dirty shirts. Their rightful owners would not be gracious about their return, but the insurance company they were trying to collect from would.

Bittersohn headed toward the taxi station, still at a brisk pace despite the silver bullet lodged in his left hip. Silver bullets were always a hazard of doing business in Transylvania. Momentarily distracted by a twinge of agony, he did not at once perceive that the taxi he was about to enter already held an occupant. As he murmured his apology, a waft of Inchoate #19 assailed his nostrils and a low, thrilling laugh reached his ears.

"Au contraire, Monsieur Bittersohn. I beseech you to enter."

He recognized the voice and the perfume, but not the elegant robe of costliest sables in which the sultry Lady Ychs had swathed her voluptuous form. A new sable coat. Her soi-disant Ladyship ought to have known better. Here in Boston, women of the social class with which she aspired to connect herself did not wear sables, unless the sables had been their grandmothers'. "Sorry, Lady Ychs," he replied curtly. "I'm on my way home."

"But no, you must listen! Monsieur Bittersohn, I am in deadly peril."

He sighed and entered the vehicle, not trying to avoid the sumptuous swirl of fur that covered the shabby seat. It would be soft against his bullet. "So what else is new?"

"Ah, you can joke. But moi—" She leaned closer, letting the rich pelts fall away from her luscious throat and bosom. "Regardez."

"Very pretty," said Bittersohn. "Mind if I open a window?"

"Merde, you are cruel. Do you not observe that I am without the Du Barry diamonds?"

"Then hadn't you better button up your sables? You might catch cold with your neck all bare like that."

Now that he thought of it, which in fact he seldom did, Bittersohn found that he could call to mind every tiniest detail of the dazzling five-strand collière, each of its three hundred and sixty-eight unflawed diamonds at least a carat in weight. He could not, however, recall having seen it off Lady Ychs, not that the necklace had excited any particular remark. Boston women did wear their family diamonds, to get the good out of them, although others would have found the Du Barry jewel a trifle flashy for everyday wear.

"Monsieur Bittersohn, you do not understand," Lady Ychs was protesting. "I am without my diamonds because they have been stolen from me. And the theft was committed for the sole purpose of luring me into the snare of the infamous Dr. Yang."

"And you don't want to go? Think it over, Lady Ychs. Dr. Yang is the last of the wicked mandarins, a vanishing breed. This is your chance to get in at the end of an era."

"Mon ami, I do not weesh to get in at the end of an era. I weesh to have back my beautiful necklace. Enfin, mon cher Monsieur Bittersohn, I weesh to hire you to recover the Du Barry diamonds for me."

"But you still haven't paid me for recovering the Montespan bracelet."

"Bah! Are we petit bourgeois clerks to concern ourselves with such pettifogging details? I need you, mon amour."

Suddenly her arms were about him, her lips were against his—and a pad reeking not of Inchoate #19 but of chloroform was pressed against his nostrils. As Bittersohn slid into oblivion, he cursed himself for a fool. He might have known Dr. Yang would have one of his villainous henchmen concealed among the sables.

When he regained consciousness, his tongue was still furred, but not with paprika. He had been thrown, as he had

barely had time to anticipate before the noxious fumes over-
came him, into a dank cellar. Even as the thought, "Now
they're going to flood it," flashed through his mind, a valve
could be heard opening in the far corner of the improvised
dungeon, and a gush of foul-smelling water spewed forth.

Springing to his feet and leaping nimbly to the top of a
nearby tea chest, Bittersohn shouted, "Hey, you nincom-
poops, that's not the water main. It's the sewer drain."

From somewhere in the impenetrable blackness, a startled
outcry could be heard. "Oh Jesus, Lum Fong, we opened the
wrong valve."

"Our heads will roll for this," was the gloomy reply.

Sure enough, not a moment later, two severed pates
dropped to the cellar floor with two sickening thuds. Again
out of the stygian gloom came a voice known and loathed,
speaking in flawless English with the sinister sibilance that
had aye been the infallible mark of the wicked mandarin.

"Ah so, Dr. Bittersohn. We meet again. Please do accept
my abject apologies for the despicable error committed by
those two worthless bunglers. Faugh! The odor of this miserable dungeon must be inexpressibly repugnant to the nostrils
of one so fastidious and highly cultured as your estimable
self. Would you prefer to remain and endure the unspeakable
stench, or would you honour me by ascending to my humble
quarters? There is a spiral iron staircase immediately behind
the tea chest on which you have been forced to take refuge
from the vile filth which by now threatens to engulf your
standing-place, not to mention your honourable person. If
you would care to step across and save yourself? I should
perhaps warn you that the edge of each step has been honed
to razor sharpness. Any slight misstep in this Cimmerian
fulginosity could mean instant and I fear most painful ampu-
tation."

225

Bittersohn's lips curled in silent contempt. Did Yang actually believe him stupid enough to fall for that ancient ruse whose object, of course, was to make the intended victim grab for the iron handrail? This latter, needless to say, was electrified and would fry the unwary grabber faster than a noodle in a wok.

From above, he could hear the impatient clicking of gold filigree fingernail guards as the archfiend rubbed his bloodthirsty hands together in eager anticipation of the fireworks to come. He would get them. With one deft movement, Bittersohn whipped out the Swiss army knife he always carried in deference to his former scoutmaster's sage injunction, "Be prepared." Among its multiple blades was one designed for removing stones from horses' hooves, never yet found occasion to use. At last it would serve a purpose. Horse-hoof hook at the ready, he struck a match from the booklet he had pocketed at the Budapest Arms. Its glimmer was feeble, but sufficient to show him the point of vulnerability. In a trice, he had dropped the hook on the live rail. As soon as the sparks from the short circuit had quit fizzling and the smoke died down, he nimbly ascended the now perfectly harmless though not very well-maintained staircase, retrieving his helpful pocketknife on the way.

By the time he got to the top Dr. Yang had, as anticipated, discarded his gold filigree nail guards, exposing dreadsome talons with their sides filed to sharpness and their tips to deadly points.

"En garde, Dr. Bittersohn," he hissed. With a burst of fiendish laughter, the mandarin slashed like a panther at the detective's jugular.

Bittersohn was ready for him. Having hastily switched blades from the horse-hoof hook to the fingernail cutter, he began a nerveless game of parry and riposte, snipping with cool precision at the ruthless nails until these once-lethal weapons were reduced to mere blunted stubs. Now the declawed mandarin's Oriental impassivity was totally shattered. Bittersohn knew why. By losing his nails, Yang had also lost face.

"Seize him!" Yang was screaming. "Seize him!"

"Who's supposed to do the seizing?" A smallish, thinnish elderly rogue had emerged from an inner room, absentmindedly pocketing the beaded curtain as he passed. "You're out of henchmen, Boss. I kept telling you, you can't go around decapitating faithful servitors right and left at whim without creating yourself a manpower shortage. It's not like in the old days. I'm sorry to say it, Boss, but you're a has-been. Oh hi, Max. What brings you here?"

"I'm supposed to be looking for Lady Ychs's diamond necklace," Bittersohn replied casually, dusting off his trusty Swiss army knife on his impeccable linen handkerchief and stowing it back in his pocket. "How's business, Lightfingers?"

"Slow. It's these damned unisex clothes they're wearing now. Shove your hand in a hip pocket and you never know whether you're going to come up with a fat wallet or a rap for attempted rape."

"Things are tough all over," Bittersohn rejoined sympathetically. "I've had a silver bullet in my own hip since Tuesday."

"Genuine silver?" The pickpocket's interest was clearly whetted. "Wait a second. Was this in Transylvania by any chance?"

"Where else?"

"Took you for a vampire, eh?" Lightfingers nodded in understanding as he glided around behind the famous detective and shuffled away down the richly carpeted corridor. "See you around, Maxie."

"Sure, Lightfingers."

Bittersohn smiled inwardly. The bullet was gone and he hadn't felt a thing. Too bad a talent like this had been reduced to working for scum like Yang. The mandarin was now sneaking furtively toward him, carrying a flute and a tall woven basket from which protruded a hideous hooded head.

"All right, Yang," he said wearily. "Quit waving that idiotic snake around. Don't you think I know a defanged cobra when I see one? Now do you hand over the Du Barry necklace or do I step over to Beach Street and begin spreading it around every chop suey joint in town that Dr. Yang has lost face to a roundeye?"

A long, indrawn hiss in which the disgruntled cobra joined was the mandarin's only answer. Reaching into the sleeve of his heavy silken robe, somewhat awkwardly because of the unaccustomed shortness of his fingernails, he drew forth the fabulous diamonds and held them out to his conqueror.

Bittersohn nimbly avoided the trap door under the silken carpet, kept a tight hold on the necklace until he had made sure he was well clear of Lightfingers, then walked briskly—more briskly than before now that he was free of that annoying bullet—to a nearby pawnshop. There he greeted the pawnbroker.

"Hi, Sol."

"Hi, Max. What are you after today?"

"Money." Bittersohn tossed the magnificent handful of fabulous gems on the worn oaken counter. "What am I offered?"

"How hot is it?"

"Not very. Anyway, you won't be keeping it long."

"Maxie, is this one of your ingenious subterfuges?"

"Trust me, Sol. Here's the exact sum I want." Bittersohn named a figure. The pawnbroker, after a bit of a struggle for they were unusually luxuriant, managed to raise both eyebrows simultaneously.

"Precisely that?"

"Precisely that."

"If you say so."

The pawnbroker paid over the money and made out the ticket. Bittersohn, still striding briskly albeit beginning to experience a sense of fatigue, pocketed his gain, left the shop, and hailed a passing hackney, being careful to inspect the interior for exotic foreign ladies and any henchman who might still have escaped Dr. Yang's impetuosity. He gave a fashionable address, then sat back and braced himself against the impact of Boston's historic potholes. It did make a difference, having that bullet out.

Lady Ychs was at home. Her maid Ylyse said so. There was little Ylyse did not know about Lady Ychs. "You weesh to see her, M'sicu?"

"Not particularly," said Bittersohn, stifling a yawn. "Just give her this with my regards."

"A . . . —ow you say? . . . a pawn teeckeet? Mais, M'sieu!"

The maid vanished, clearly nonplussed. A moment later, Lady Ychs herself appeared, trailing yards of black chiffon and marabou.

"Monsieur Bittersohn," she cried imperiously, "for why you offer me zeese . . . zeese insult?"

"For why you want your diamond necklace back, that's for why. All you have to do is apply at the address on the ticket and pay my friend Sol the stated amount."

"But why so strange an amount? I do not comprehend."

"It's elementary, my dear Lady Ychs. You simply add my standard fee for recovering Du Barry necklaces to my outstanding invoice for retrieval of your Montespan bracelet, plus one percent brokerage fee for the gentleman behind the counter, and voila! Next time you feel an urge to use your diamonds as bait to lure some unsuspecting victim into the nefarious toils of your confederate, Dr. Yang, perhaps you'll pause and reflect. Oh, and the sable coat. I'd let it age for a decade or two before you start wearing it around Boston. Adieu, Lady Ychs. Please note that I didn't say au revoir."

It was with a sense of deep personal satisfaction that Bittersohn strode over the bricks and cobblestones of Beacon Hill, to the brownstone house where one surpassingly lovelier than any languorous adventuress in a new sable coat, who scorned all paltry artifice of fashion and did her own hair, would be awaiting his return. Outwitting the evil machinations of Dr. Yang had been merely one more spot of bother at the end of a long and grueling ordeal by paprikash. Getting Lady Ychs to pay a bill had been a genuine triumph, something that no other man had ever yet accomplished.

And there she was, flinging wide the portal, stretching out eager arms. His own true Sarah.

"Darling," she cried, "whatever kept you? Your luggage arrived an hour ago. I was so overcome with joy, I tipped the messenger a dollar."

"Wastrel!" He clasped her fondly to him, but his loving hands encountered only voluminous folds of crepe de Chine smelling faintly of moth flakes. "Where the hell are you?"

"Oh sorry, darling. This is a dress Aunt Emma gave me and I haven't got around to taking it in yet. It's one she bought at Crawford Hollidge in 1947. Actually I'm a bit concerned, as the design appears to be coming back into fashion. You don't think it looks too awfully à la mode?"

"You could fray the sleeves a little. How about some breakfast, darling?" It had been a long time since that last plate of gulyas.

"Of course, darling. Go make yourself comfortable while I warm up the coffee."

Home at last! Bittersohn divested himself of the Savile Row suit that had served him so long and so faithfully, and draped it over a massive wooden hanger that had belonged to Sarah's great-uncle Nathan. There was still a lot of good wear to that suit. He took off his handmade shoes and inserted shoe trees, noting as he did so that the soles were wearing a bit thin from all that brisk striding. To the cobbler they should go. There was still plenty of stride in those shoes.

He took a quick shower, being careful not to waste the soap, put on a pair of faded but exquisitely darned pajamas, and reached for his bathrobe. It was one his mother's brother Hymie had bought off a pushcart on Blackstone Street back in 1926. Truth to tell, Uncle Hymie had never worn it much, but Max's mother had artfully frayed the sleeves to impart the proper aura of aristocratic penury. Smiling a bit at the endearing foibles of womankind, his kind of womankind, Max Bittersohn sauntered out to get his breakfast.

Monique

I never quite understood why I kept on going to Monique. The first time was simple enough. I was desperately tired and in considerable pain, and looking for relief.

I am one of those thin-skinned, small-boned little women who are almost indestructible, actually, but always well provided with alarming symptoms of one sort or another. Often these vary from day to day, but at this particular period in my life, I'd developed an ache in my back and legs that was sometimes bad and sometimes worse but never let up, day or night. For months I'd dragged around in misery, trying to cope with all the things that never seemed to get finished, no matter how hard I worked. I don't know what made me think of massage, but anyway I did, one raw January afternoon when the pain was even worse than usual. This was before all the scandals about topless massage parlors, of course.

Not knowing what else to do, I looked in the yellow pages. There was one name listed under "Massage" that I recognized. Truth to tell, I'd never been inside the shop and had never realized it was anything but a hairdresser's. However, I'd seen the sign often enough back when I was living in that part of city, and I suppose the place appealed to me simply because I could find it without effort. I phoned for an appointment and went that night, directly after work.

From then on, I began to go faithfully every Thursday at

half-past five, even though the so-called treatments were costing me more than I could conveniently spare and not really doing any good. I think I was getting a perverse enjoyment out of wasting money on myself for a change, instead of forking it over into one of the hands that were eternally stretched out toward me.

It was a tacky little place, I found, strictly a one-woman operation. Monique, she called herself, though I doubt if that was her real name. She came from somewhere in Europe and looked as though she had been modeled out of piecrust dough that had been made with too much shortening and baked until not quite done. She wore elderly white nylon uniforms that strained at the buttonholes and white nurses' shoes that were clean enough but sadly run over at the heels. She talked nonstop in a mixture of street slang and incongruously erudite expressions that I suppose she picked up from some of the intellectuals who lived around that rarefied neighborhood. She knew what the words meant but pronounced them wrong, with a heavy accent in a loud, insistent voice.

Monique had a knack of creating a sort of blowsy comfort. First she would lead me to a minuscule back room, hand me a clean sheet, and leave me to take my clothes off. After I'd undressed and was struggling to swathe myself decently in the sheet, she'd come back, whip away the sheet, and settle me into a queer kind of chair that was in fact a steam bath. This had a heavy plastic cover she'd zip tight around my neck once she'd got me settled to her satisfaction.

Here was a situation ready-made for claustrophobia. Once zipped in, I was a prisoner. I couldn't have stood it, I don't suppose, except that on my first visit I'd happened to see her open a door behind the chair that was normally kept bolted, and set out a bag of trash in the back alley. Perhaps a back entry was an odd sort of place to pass off as a steam room and perhaps I ought to have had qualms about sitting there naked virtually cheek to jowl with the trash cans, but I was familiar with city ways and knew one didn't waste expensive space, however dark, cramped, and unattractive.

Besides, I wasn't supposed to look at the dingy walls. I was supposed to shut my eyes, relax, and enjoy the steam. The chair would heat up fast and I'd begin to perspire under that heavy plastic. Monique would be doing somebody else's hair in the next room. Every so often she'd poke her head in to make sure I hadn't come up to the boil and tell me how much better I was feeling.

Extreme heat usually makes me sick, but I have to admit the chair never did. Monique used to put a spoonful of sulphur into the water that made the steam. This may have had some of the beneficial properties she ascribed to it, though I couldn't understand why it should.

I would suffer agonies of discomfort in other ways, though, for what seemed like ages but was probably just a few minutes, then gradually adjust to the heat and sink into a pleasant stupor. I suppose the chair reached a certain temperature, then leveled off like an electric iron. Just about the time I was really beginning to enjoy myself, Monique would come to unzip me. She'd help me out of the chair, lead me around a corner into another poky apology for a room, and tell me to get up on the massage table, which she had covered with my sheet. She always emphasized that the sheet was particularly mine. I found this rather appealing and at the same time disturbing, as though my being singled out for this favor was putting an extra strain on her laundry bill.

It was usually about this time that a man with a young-sounding voice popped into the outer room. Monique would dart out and say something to him, then she'd come back and start washing me bit by bit with a loofah that looked like a piece of tripe and dripped chilly trickles down my sides. I felt these keenly and resented her not stopping to wipe them away, but never had the gumption to tell her so for fear the man outside would come to see what the fuss was about.

As soon as she'd washed a small portion of me, Monique would massage the area in a halfhearted sort of way. I always wished she'd rub harder but again I didn't complain because she'd be talking incessantly about how hard she was working and all the good she was doing me.

There was always a draft around the massage table, no doubt from the ill-fitting back door behind the steam chair. What with being moistened in sections, inadequately dried, then lying there naked while Monique finished off the massage by rubbing me with scented hand lotion and flicking a huge, fuzzy powder puff all over me—she appeared to enjoy this and evidently thought I did, too—I was always shivering by the time she got through and longing to get back into my clothes. However, she would produce a second clean sheet, cover me with it, and instruct me to lie on the table as long as I liked.

Having been made to feel so guilty over the laundry bills, I felt I had to get as much good as possible of this fresh sheet, so I stayed. She would suggest a nice nap and tiptoe away to chat with her hairdressing customer or that young man—his name was David, I learned—who was always popping in and out but never stayed.

In those days I was barely sleeping at all, let alone on a hard table with only a sheet between me and that constant draft, and nothing at all to shield my ears from Monique's unstoppable voice. I'd lie there until I couldn't stand the discomfort any longer, which didn't take long, then got up and put on one of the huge terry toweling robes she kept hanging ready to hand.

I sometimes wondered if the robes got washed along with the sheets and if not, who'd worn them before me, but not to the extent of making a fuss over the matter. The magical sulphur fumes would no doubt have killed anybody's germs. Besides, I loved those robes. As I mentioned, I am a small woman. The robes came in a size that had to fit all comers, which meant one would envelop me from ears to toes and feel wonderfully snug after all that clamminess and chilling.

Monique would have let me wear them forever, I think. She never wanted her customers to leave. She always got annoyed with me because I left the table so soon, and scolded me for rushing the massage. Once properly chastised, I'd be thrust into a wooden chair with my head tilted over a sort of dripping pan that sawed at the back of my neck, and have my hair shampooed. One week, Monique might go through an elaborate routine with scented lathers and creme rinses she claimed she'd got from Paris. Next time, she might grab a cake of brown laundry soap in her doughy fist and rub it all over my head as if she were delousing me. After an inadequate rinsing, she'd pin up my hair without asking how I wanted it done.

I always accepted these impromptu coiffings meekly since she claimed to be doing them out of the goodness of her heart, even though they'd been rendered necessary by the sulphurous steam from the dryer, not to mention the sloshings from the loofah, and were more than covered by her fees. She might or might not set me under the dryer, depending on her mood and whether she had any other entertainment at hand. As I was apt to be the last customer of the day, she'd often keep me sitting to air-dry while she talked at me in that loud, belligerent voice of hers.

Monique was earthy as a parsnip. I got the impression, despite her hit-or-miss profundities, that she never thought at all, but lived wholly through her senses. She liked being massaged by a man, she told me. She liked food and riding in taxis, and she liked plants. Her little, sunless rooms were crammed with them: huge, coarse-leaved things in old plastic buckets or anything else that would hold water. No dirt, they all seemed to be amphibians.

She said when she heard a mounted policeman riding down the street, she'd run and watch out the front window. If the horse relieved itself, she'd go out with one of the plastic buckets and scrape up the manure for her plants. In spite of this amazing solicitude, the plants never looked thrifty. I always found something yellowish and unwholesome about them, like the jungle plants I used to scare myself by imagining when I was a child.

During these drying sessions, I got to know the young fellow who popped in and out. David was Monique's errand boy, I found, though he hardly qualified as a boy, being in his early twenties from the look of him. Monique didn't like to shop, she told me, even though the grocer was just across the street and the bakery next door, so David did it for her. One night while I was sitting in my robe and hairpins, she sent him out for a barbecued chicken. She spent the entire period of his absence telling me what a lovely boy he was and how much he enjoyed doing her favors. When he got back with the chicken, she tipped him about twice what the chicken had cost. I remember thinking he must get a good deal out of her, one way and another.

Not chicken, however. She did invite him to share it, but he said he had other plans. She invited me too, but I pretended I had to rush home and cook dinner for the husband I did not in fact have. So she went upstairs alone—she lived in a flat over the shop—to put the chicken away, leaving me feeling silly in nothing but that toweling robe and a headful of

237

pins, and David trying to look suave and poised.

"I only do it out of pity," he blurted when she'd gone. "I'd turn down the money, but I'm too much of a gentleman to hurt her feelings."

I made some hypocritical noise and he left quickly because we could hear her coming back. That night I insisted on leaving the shop before my hair was properly dry; but I kept my appointment the following week.

After that, I saw David a few more times. He was always neatly, even foppishly dressed, and he always went out of his way to impress me with his gentlemanly manners, managing each time to convey the assurance that he only tolerated the gross, middle-aged masseuse out of pity. I began to wonder why I myself tolerated her, but still I went.

It was along toward the middle of March I decided I'd had enough. I was in the chair with the sulphur fumes just beginning to rise around me. Monique was out in the other room, puttering around with her plants. David had come in. I could hear her complaining to him that they weren't looking so good as if she'd only just noticed what should have been obvious all along.

Suddenly I felt a blast of cold air on my face. The traffic noises that had been muffled became louder, and over them came the unmistakable clop-clop-clop of shod hooves on asphalt. So it had happened. A mounted policeman was riding down the street. Monique had thrown open a window and stuck out her head to see whether the horse was going to perform.

It must have. I heard Monique shout, "Here's de bucket an' shovel. Go kvick."

"Go where?" said David.

"Out dere. Scrape it up before it gets all skvashed in by de cars."

"Are you crazy? You expect a gentleman to—"

"What shentleman? You nuttin' but a young punk wit' pig ideas. My plants is wort' more dan you."

I don't know what he hit her with. I only heard the thud, and the crash when she must have fallen against the hairdressing table. I only heard him dragging the body through the doorway to the massage table around the corner from where I sat. I only heard him grunting, sobbing, cursing as he boosted his late patroness up on the table. And then I heard a lot more that I wish I could forget.

I knew what he'd got hold of, a big kitchen cleaver Monique had brought downstairs to show me when I'd rung the bell for my appointment. She'd been using it to cut up meat for a stir-fry, which was her latest culinary enthusiasm. She'd laughed and shouted about how she sliced the meat thin like the chef at Benihana. Quick as lightning. Whack! Whack! Whack! She loved doing that, she'd said. She'd whacked the air viciously a little too close to my nose, to show me how.

He was doing it now—whack, whack, whack, cursing and sobbing, yelling at her. "My plants wort' more dan you. Fuckin' old bitch! I'm a gentleman!" And then a small splash, like something being dropped into a bucket of water. More whacks, more splashes. God in heaven, he was feeding her to the plants!

And there was I, zipped up to my neck in heavy-duty brown plastic, a helpless prisoner in that accursed chair. There was not one God-blessed thing I could do but sit with the sweat pouring off me, listening to him whack and sob and curse and splash. The smell of blood was overcoming the smell of sulphur. What must that table look like by now?

Monique had taken away my sheet, the way she always did, to put under me when I'd finished steaming and was supposed to lie on the table and be dripped on with the loofah. He was cutting her up on my sheet.

I must have been getting feverish by then. I found myself worrying about how the laundry was going to get the bloodstains out. Don't ask me how long I sat in that scalding trap. One doesn't think of a nightmare in terms of how long it lasts. I could feel the blood pounding in my head, harder and harder, as if it was going to burst out and mingle with all that other blood. It was either the chair or the cleaver. I started to scream.

"Monique! Monique, where are you?"

I heard the cleaver clatter to the floor. Poor David, I thought quite unreasonably. He must have got the shock of his life. Then I thought, "Now he'll have to come and kill me."

But all he did was stammer, "M-Monique isn't here."

"Oh, David!" I put everything I had into hailing my rescuer. "Thank goodness it's you. Monique left me here and I fainted from the heat. I've been unconscious a long time, I think. I can't remember anything. Where is she?"

"A horse went down the street."

"You mean she ran out with that silly bucket and left me here? Doesn't she know how to treat a lady?"

"Sh-she wanted me to go." His voice was all to pieces.

"A gentleman like you?" I cried. "She must be out of her mind. Look, David, could you possibly come in here and unzip me? I know it's an embarrassing thing to ask a gentleman, but I'll keep my eyes shut so you won't be embarrassed. On my word of honor."

I'd keep the promise. I had no desire to see the blood-stained cleaver swinging down at me, though in fact I was almost past caring. Anything, anything to get out of this ghastly chair. I was in hell already. At least the grave would be cool.

"I'm a gentleman," he said.

"I know you are, or I wouldn't ask. My eyes are closed. Truly."

I heard him dithering around the doorway. Then, incredibly, the zipper was moving.

"Thank you, David," I said. "You've saved my life."

He started laughing, crazily, hysterically. So did I. I suspect he was high on something. I know I was. Finally I got myself under control.

"I know I don't have to ask a gentleman like you to please step out into the other room while I get my clothes on. Would you mind just shutting the door as you leave?"

It worked, feeble as it was. He did exactly what I'd prayed he would, slammed the door and locked it from the other side, forgetting about that back exit to the alleyway. I put on what few clothes I had. The rest were still in the other room, but thank God I'd brought my pocketbook with me into the steam room. One doesn't leave one's pocketbook anywhere, not in the city.

The shock didn't really hit me until I got outside. Then I had to hold on to the trashcans to keep from collapsing. A bitter wind had come up and perhaps that saved my life. I don't know. Anyway, it prodded me to grope my way to the curb and flag a taxi.

Somehow or other, I managed to give the right address and remain conscious until we got there. I believe I grossly overpaid the driver, because he was willing to leave his cab and help me up the stairs. I told him I was just out of the hospital after an operation and must have overdone. He would have come in, but I said my husband would be there to help me, and shut the door in his face. Then I flopped down on the rug in the foyer and passed out. After a while, I suppose I must have roused myself enough to crawl into bed.

Anyway, there I was and there I stayed. It did occur to me in flashes that I ought to telephone the police, but I couldn't hold on to the thought long enough to do anything about it. It wasn't until the following evening that one of my co-workers, disturbed because I hadn't called the office, stopped by the apartment. He took one look at me and sent for an ambulance.

I was in the hospital for several days before any visitors were allowed. I'd developed a rather spectacular case of pneumonia, it appeared, from the alternate steaming and chilling. During all this time, I wondered off and on about telling the police, but then somebody would come along to adjust my oxygen or pump some more antibiotic into me and I'd drop off to sleep again.

Finally they let my co-worker in to see me. I thanked him for his efforts on my behalf and for the strong, healthy, blooming plant the office staff had sent. I couldn't very well say I wished they hadn't because it made me think of unwholesome yellow leaves and doughy white fingers dropping into buckets. He said that was okay, they all missed me.

"I was worried sick when you didn't show up on Friday. I thought you'd been hurt in the fire."

"What fire?" I asked him.

"Oh, didn't you know? That place where you got your hair done."

"My hair?" I had to stop and think. Then I remembered he'd dropped me off once on his way home. I'd forgotten Monique's sign read HAIRDRESSING.

"Yes, it was a bad one," he said. "The whole shop was gutted. It started from overheated wiring, I believe, a dryer left on too long or something like that."

The chair. I hadn't thought to switch off the steam. Neither, of course, had David.

"Why didn't you tell me you weren't feeling well Thursday?" he was asking in a somewhat injured tone. "I'd have been glad to run you home. Anyway, you sure picked the right time to skip your appointment. One of the hairdressers . . . hey, probably I shouldn't be telling you this."

"No, tell me," I said. "I want to know."

"Well, they found a body. The remains of one, anyway. A young fellow who worked there."

"David?"

"I guess so. Did you know him?"

"I'd seen him a few times. He just came in to do . . . odd jobs. Was he the only one?"

"Yes, and the police are wondering why the woman who owned the place seems to have disappeared."

I started to say, "Did they look in the buckets?" Then I didn't. What was the point, now?

"It turns out she didn't have a very good record." He was trying to be delicate, I noticed. Prostitution or pandering, I guessed, thinking of those coarse white hands, the restaurants and taxicabs, the fluffy powder puff, and the way she hadn't liked to walk the streets anymore. "They think she may have torched the building for the insurance, then got scared when the man was trapped in the fire, and took off."

"That's as reasonable an explanation as any," I said.

It was, you know.

Counterfeit Christmas

"Deck the halls with boughs of holly,
    "Fa, la la la la, la la la la."
Professor Peter Shandy of Balaclava Agricultural College
found the carolers' injunction as superfluous as that inane
string of meaningless syllables tacked on after it. Every house
on the Crescent was already as bedizened as it could get, for
Yuletide was rife and the annual Grand Illumination was not
only heard all over campus and down in the village but could
also be seen, smelled, touched, and even tasted, if you got
close enough.

During most of the year, the open space encircled by eight
faculty dwellings, including Peter's, was placid enough;
merely a grassy sward kept in seemly order by the trusty men
of Buildings & Grounds and appropriately bedded out here
and there with flowers of spring, summer, or fall, depending.
Came the holiday season, however, and the usually by then
snow-covered Crescent erupted into a festive welter of illumi-
nated Christmas trees and quaint gingerbread houses cut
from plywood and assembled by the trusty screwdrivers of
brawny students, who then donned oversized elf suits and
flung themselves joyously into the time-honored Yankee
pastime of turning an honest buck.

From some of the gingerbread houses, bonny lasses in
frilly mobcaps and brave lads in stovepipe hats and home-

grown chin whiskers purveyed artifacts ranging from apple-head dolls to woolens woven from fleece donated by the college sheep. Others hawked mulled cider, hot coffee, hot chocolate, and hot peppermint tea. Cold switchel had been tried one year but hadn't caught on. Homemade doughnuts kept warm in imitation stoneware crockpots whose electric cords were cunningly hidden from the customers' view were a big item, though. So were hot dogs with festive garnishes of red-and-green piccalilli from the college kitchens.

Popcorn balls and taffy apples never failed to sell, as did more exotic comestibles. Foremost among these latter was a sort of antic sweetmeat made of shredded coconut, molasses, melted chocolate, and a number of other things that Professor Peter Shandy, the Crescent's least Yule-minded resident, preferred not to think about. Years ago, some coarse-minded wag had noticed the resemblance between these biggish, flattish, brownish, whiskerish confections and a certain bovine by-product familiar to every animal-husbandry student. Coconut cowpats he'd dubbed them, and coconut cowpats they'd remained. They sold even faster than hotcakes, and Peter Shandy thought them obscene.

But then, Peter thought most things about the Illumination obscene. For the first eighteen years of his residence on the Crescent, he'd been the self-appointed faculty Scrooge. Despite endless nagging by the Illumination Committee, he'd allowed not so much as a Styrofoam candy cane or a wreath of lollipops to sully the simple dignity of his small old rosy brick house. Then one year, goaded to fury by the Illumination chairperson's attempt to foist off on him a poinsettia fashioned from pieces of red detergent bottles, he'd gone hog-wild.

In a burst of uncontrollable fury, Peter had hired decorators to transform his premises into a veritable Walpurgisnacht scene of garish blinking light bulbs, life-size plastic reindeer, and hideous Santa Claus masks that lit up and leered. Then, fleeing the ire of his neighbors, he'd gone off on a cruise, got shipwrecked as he well deserved to be, and slunk home to find the Illumination chairperson's body stiff and stark behind his living-room sofa.

Oddly enough, Peter had emerged from this deplorable incident not only with a whole skin but with a wife. Under the benign influence of his delightful Helen, the renegade bachelor had been transformed into a relatively civilized husband. Even his next-door neighbor said so in her mellower moments, of which it must also be admitted she didn't have many. By now, Peter had gentled down to the point where he didn't even put up much of a squawk when Helen gently but firmly insisted on doing in Balaclava as the Balaclavans did.

Fortunately, Helen's instincts were for the tastefully simple as opposed to the more-is-better. There had been one unfortunate experiment with topiary trees made from fresh-cut boxwood that stunk the place up like a houseful of tom-cats, but on the whole she'd done fine. This year, Helen's decorations were particularly charming.

Eschewing the excesses of her neighbors, she'd made low arrangements of evergreen twigs for all the front windows upstairs and down, and trimmed them with a few small rose-colored baubles and velvet bows to complement the aged brick walls. In the middle of each arrangement she'd set a real candle, protected by a glass hurricane-lamp chimney so that it could be lighted after dark without setting fire to the house. On the front door she'd hung a fat balsam wreath tied with a larger bow of the same rosy velvet. To the wreath was fastened an old brass cornet that Peter had tooted in his high school marching band, salvaged from the attic and shined up till it dazzled the eyeballs. Peter had pretended to scoff but been secretly tickled. He'd even taken pains to wire the cornet to the door, lest it be pinched by some souvenir hunter among the multitudes.

For multitudes there were. Balaclava's Grand Illumination had been going on ever since the bleak Depression years of the early 1930s. Photographed and written up in newspapers and magazines, talked about on the radio and even shown now and then on television, the event had become a New England tradition, attracting visitors from far and wide to this rural Massachusetts community.

Fairly far, anyway, and reasonably wide. Wide enough to keep Police Chief Fred Ottermole and his force, which consisted mostly of Officer Budge Dorkin, oftentimes hard-put to keep the traffic unsnarled.

Fortunately the college had its own larger and better-equipped security force, so there was seldom any trouble about maintaining law and order.

The college, of course, was squarely behind the Illumination, and with good reason. Its student body was not rich; most of the kids were working their way, and here was a welcome source of tuition money. A fair number of students willingly forwent part or all of their Christmas holidays for the greater good of hustling the tourists. Peter could admire their self sacrifice and respect their motives; he just didn't see why in Sam Hill they couldn't maintain their blasted tradition someplace else.

Out beyond the pigpens, for instance. At this very moment, a disgusting youth in a just-purchased Viking helmet with plush moose horns on it was unwrapping a coconut cowpat and throwing the paper on the trodden snow. Peter was glaring balefully down at him through the upstairs front window and wishing it were the second week of January when he heard a thump at the door.

Some keen-eyed visitor must have managed to sort out the knocker from the balsam, or else a miscreant tourist was trying to swipe his cornet. Normally Peter would have flung open the window and stuck out his head to settle the matter with a lusty bellow, but he was loath to disarrange Helen's artistically disposed greenery and even loather to smash the hurricane lamp. There was no use even trying to bellow, he'd never be able to make himself heard over the general hulla-baloo. He bowed to the inevitable and went downstairs. It might be his old friend and neighbor Professor Ames, at loose ends between semesters, looking for a game of cribbage.

No, by George, it was about the third from the last person he'd have expected. Moira Haskins, the college comptroller, was a pleasant woman and a neighbor on the Crescent, but not one with whom he and Helen were on dropping-in terms. Peter had an ominous foreboding that Moira was after some-thing.

As so often happened, Peter was right. When he indicated a readiness to divest her of her storm coat and call Helen down from the den where she was wrapping presents, the comptroller shook her head.

"Thanks, Peter, but I can't stay. I just wanted to show you this and see what you make of it."

Moira's "this" was a twenty-dollar bill. It looked to Peter like all the other twenty-dollar bills he'd been shelling out with unaccustomed abandon during this expensive season, until he put on his reading glasses and studied it closely. Then he began to chuckle. Where he'd have expected the grim and lowering portrait of President Andrew Jackson, he saw instead the even grimmer and far more lowering visage of President Thorkjeld Svenson.

"My God! Where the flaming perdition did this come from?"

"One of the gingerbread houses, I assume. It was in with the rest when Silvester Lomax brought me last night's cash pickup. I was sitting at my desk just now, counting the money for this morning's deposit, when I did a double take and almost freaked out. What do you think, Peter? You don't suppose somebody got to doodling around on the bill with a drawing pen or something and—"

"Not on your life. Jackson's head is long and skinny. It might have been managed with Ulysses S. Grant, I suppose, if they could have got the beard off. Just a second, I think I've—" He fished in his wallet and pulled out a fifty, marveling that he did in fact still have one. "See, Grant had a heavy, squarish face like the president's. Rather as if he'd been hacked out of Mount Rushmore."

"Yes, I see," said Moira. "Then why didn't they use a fifty instead of a twenty?"

"Probably because fifties are less common and therefore more apt to be given close scrutiny. Is this the only such bill you've found?"

"So far. The only one that's been caught, anyway. We're into the fifth day of the Illumination, you know, and we've taken in an awful lot of money. There's no telling how many may have slipped through."

"Not all that many, I shouldn't think. This is a remarkably good likeness."

"Frighteningly good." Moira shuddered slightly despite the storm coat she hadn't taken off. "But President Svenson's so much more presidential than most presidents. If those kids in the booths did happen to notice, they'd take it for granted he belonged there. Most of them have probably never heard of Andrew Jackson anyway. I wonder what Dr. Svenson son's going to think of this."

"He'll think it's funny, provided we don't get stuck with a

whole flock of them. As for this one—" Peter kept hold of the startling counterfeit and handed Moira a genuine twenty taken from his wallet. "Fair swap?"

"No, really, Peter. Why should you stand the loss?"

"What loss? This bill's a collector's item, it's worth far more than the alleged face value. I'm probably gypping the college worse than the counterfeiter did. Drat it, Moira, this is a fantastically expert job. Look at the workmanship. Can you tell me why anybody with the talent to pull off such a magnificent fake would waste his time on a practical joke that could send him to jail?"

"Well, no, I hadn't thought of that. It doesn't make sense, does it?"

"It might, I suppose, though I can't think how. Look, Moira, let's keep this between ourselves for the time being. There could be something more than meets the eye here. I'd like to check around a bit before we spread the word. Let me know if you get any others, will you?"

"All right, Peter. I certainly don't want to involve the college in anything shady, especially at Illumination time. You know how stories get blown up and stretched out of proportion. You're quite sure I shouldn't go to the president?"

"You can't right now, he's gone off skiing. I tell you what, Moira: I'll have the security guards pass on to the students a general warning about being on the alert for funny money. A big event like this, run by young amateurs, creates an ideal situation for the passing of counterfeit bills. I'm surprised the Illumination's never been hit sooner, now that I think of it. Anyway, we'll cope. Thank you for coming, Moira."

"Thank you for listening, Peter. I'm sorry to be dumping on you, but then everybody does, don't they?"

That was true enough. Peter had been Balaclava's unofficial private detective ever since that great debacle at the earlier Illumination, when President Svenson had confronted him with the dire consequences of his ill-judged prank and saddled him with the job of catching the murderer.

Peter knew he'd get stuck again anyhow, so he might as well get to work right away, not that he had the remotest idea where to start. He let the comptroller out and went back upstairs with the aberrant twenty-dollar bill in his hand.

"Helen, what do you make of this?"

"Of what?" his wife replied somewhat testily. "Stick your finger on this knot, will you? I don't see why it's always the woman who gets landed with wrapping the parcels. I'll bet Margaret Thatcher doesn't wrap presents."

"Couldn't you have had them gift-wrapped at the stores?"

"Of course not. You have to stand in line till your feet kill you, then they charge you an extra dollar for a piece of fancy paper and a stupid little bow. You can take your finger out now."

"No, I can't, you've lashed it down."

"Oh, Peter!" Sighing, Helen freed the captive digit and yanked tight the knot. "All right, now what am I supposed to look at?"

"Behold."

Peter handed her the note. She stared blankly for about a quarter of a second, then burst out laughing.

"Where in heaven's name did you get that?"

"From Moira Haskins. She was here just now."

"Why didn't you call me?"

"I offered to, but she said she couldn't stay."

"Then why did she come? It's not like Moira to be showing silly jokes around."

"She wasn't joking. This thing turned up in last night's Illumination takings."

251

"Are you saying somebody actually succeeded in passing Thorkjeld's picture off as legal tender?"

"That appears to have been the case. Unless some student worker stuck it in as a joke. Which, I must say, seems a bit subtle for purveyors of coconut cowpats."

"I see what you mean." Helen picked up the magnifying glass she used for studying ancient documents from the college's historic Buggins Collection, of which she was curator. "You know, Peter, this likeness to Thorkjeld is quite a piece of work. I think it's actually a pen-and-ink drawing, but it reproduces the steel-engraving technique so expertly that I can't tell for sure. As a guess I'd say the artist, and I'm not using the word loosely, may have photocopied a real twenty, cut out the medallion on the front, inserted his drawing of Thorkjeld Svenson in place of Andrew Jackson, and run it off again. You could do that easily enough if you had access to a copier that does color work."

"Having made his own paper?"

"I expect this is simply a very-good quality rag content bond that's been dipped in tea or something and wrinkled up to make it look more authentic. It doesn't have quite the feel of real currency, but I can see where an inexperienced student clerk with cold hands and fourteen more customers clamoring to be served might not notice, especially at night with all those colored lights around. It would have been simply a matter of picking the right time and place. But why Thorkjeld?"

"Moira suggested it could be because the students would assume he belonged there."

"She's probably right. How many of these have been turned in?"

"Just this one so far, that Moira knows of. She's going to let me know if she gets any more. I'm wondering whether I ought to take this along to the state police, in case the bills are being passed elsewhere."

Helen shook her head. "That seems hardly likely, don't you think? To me, this looks more like somebody having a quiet little snicker at the college's expense."

"It also looks like one hell of a lot of work for a secret snicker," Peter replied, "but I have to admit that's how it strikes me, too. Can you think of anybody on the faculty who knows how to draw and goes in for being inscrutable?"

"Dr. Porble enjoys a private joke"—Porble was the college librarian and Helen's alleged boss—"but he can't draw for beans. He can't even doodle. He simply writes down the Dewey Decimal Code for whatever he happens to be thinking about but isn't going to tell you; then he smiles that sneaky little smile of his and scratches it out."

"You don't happen by any chance to have a pen-and-ink portrait of the president in the library files that Porble might have used?"

"We have a few mildly scurrilous caricatures, but nothing that could even remotely pass for a steel engraving. You know what, Peter? I'll bet you a nickel this was copied from the photograph on that program the art department got up to celebrate Thorkjeld's twenty-fifth anniversary as president of the college."

"The one Shirley Wrenne took, that makes him look like Zeus hunting for a likely target to hurl his thunderbolt at? By George, Helen, I think you're right. What happened to that program? We had a copy of it around here somewhere, didn't we?"

"Yes, but I took ours over to the library. The one we had in the files disappeared."

"How long ago?"

"I couldn't say. That particular file doesn't get much

attention as a rule. If the program had been a bunch of hog statistics, Dr. Porble would have been on it like a hawk. Want me to go over and get our copy back?"

"No, don't bother, I have to go out anyway. I promised Moira I'd speak to Security about issuing a general ukase on keeping an eye out for counterfeit money, for whatever good that may do. Are we dining at home, or would you like some handsome and dashing he-man to sweep you off your feet and take you out for a pizza?"

"La, sir, I'm just the bundle-wrapper; you'll have to ask the butler's permission. Let's see how we feel when the time comes."

Helen didn't abominate the Illumination the way Peter did, she couldn't be feeling the same frantic urge as he to get away from the crowd and the racket. Well, what couldn't be cured must be endured. There was always the faculty dining room to fall back on, provided its staffers weren't all off catering a marshmallow roast or some other unspeakable orgy. Peter gritted his teeth, put on his old mackinaw and his rubber-soled boots, and went forth to brave the surging tide of festivity.

The security office was up toward the back of the campus; Peter would have enjoyed the stroll if he hadn't been constantly beset by husky students in those infernally whimsical elf suits, giving rides to bundled-up tourists on bright-red hand sleds with curlicues on their front runners. He managed to find both sanctuary and Silvester Lomax inside the small brick building, showed Moira's find, and explained his errand. Silvester permitted himself one quick snort of glee, then buckled down to composing a stern memorandum.

In the face of such efficiency, Peter didn't feel disposed to loiter making small talk; so he went back to the library and satisfied himself that the portrait on the bill could in fact have been drawn from the photograph on the program. There'd only been about five hundred of them printed, he supposed, and not more than half of those taken home and tucked away wherever people were wont to keep their useless junk. That would limit the field, but not by much.

He fiddled around the library for a while, dropped in at the greenhouse to check on some experimental seedlings, then moseyed back to the Crescent. He found some gratification in the sight of Purvis Mink, one of Silvester's henchmen, passing out memos to the kids in the gingerbread houses; but little consolation at watching the harried kids give them cursory glances and stick them back among the piccalilli jars. He might as well go home and see if Helen had any more knots to be tied.

The next morning, Moira Haskins was on his doorstep betimes, looking fussed and bothered. "It's happened again, Peter."

"You've found another?"

"No, two. You did speak to Security?"

"I did, and Purvis Mink passed out notices. Whether the guards came around again later to warn the kids on the evening shift, I couldn't say, but I expect they did. There was an awful mob last night, though, as usual. Short of setting a guard at each booth to examine every bill as it comes over the counter, I don't see how in Sam Hill we're going to catch the passer."

"It does look like just one person, doesn't it? I don't know whether that makes the job easier or harder. Talk about needles in haystacks! Well, I must get down to the bank. Do you think I should speak to the manager?"

"I don't know, Moira. I'll talk with the guards and get back to you."

"Thanks, Peter. It's good of you to help. Oh, your cat's going out."

"That's all right, she won't go far; Jane's not one for getting her feet wet. Besides, she hates the crowds even worse than I do."

No visitors were about this early. Students were still picking up yesterday's litter, resanding the iced-over paths, replacing burned-out light bulbs on the overworked Christmas trees, taking care of the myriad details that must be seen to before the onslaught began anew. It was oddly peaceful. Peter stood for a moment watching the small tiger cat pick her dainty way down the front walk, stopping every few steps to give each white-stockinged paw an angry shake. She wouldn't stay out long. She never did. He went into his tiny first-floor office and began correcting exam papers.

Helen had gone up to the library; the phone didn't ring once; the sounds from outside hadn't started to build. Working alone in semi-silence, Peter found his task only mildly tedious. He must have been at it for upward of an hour before it occurred to him that tourists were arriving, but that Jane was not. Where in tunket had she got to? Surely he'd have heard if she'd asked to come in, Jane had her family well-trained. In some perturbation, he got up and went to the door.

Jane was not on the stoop, nor yet on the walk. She, the dedicated house cat, was over on the green. She, the snob who shunned all lesser felines, the timid soul who wouldn't even go back across the Crescent to visit her own mother at the Enderbles', was leading a squad of raucous felines in a concerted attack on the third gingerbread house.

Oddly enough, this wasn't the stand that sold the hot dogs and hamburgers, which might have made some sense. It was the one that dispensed the gingerbread men, the taffy apples, the popcorn balls, and the coconut cowpats. Even as Peter watched, nonplussed by the cats' frantic clawing and scrambling, a grandmotherly-looking woman picked her way among them and purchased three coconut cowpats, one for each of the two moppets who clung to her coat, and one that she stowed in her capacious handbag, perhaps to take home to Grandpa. The little girl slipped hers out of its waxed-paper wrapping, took an experimental nibble, rewrapped it, and stowed it carefully in the pocket of her snowsuit. The little boy ripped the paper off his and took a large bite.

Peter shuddered. So, oddly enough, did the boy. He made a terrible face and dumped the rest of the cowpat on the ground. Immediately the cats pounced on it, gentle Jane the first to spring. This was too much for Peter. Hatless and coatless, he dashed across to sort out his own cherished pet from the yowling, scratching heap, getting himself rather lavishly lacerated in the process, but managing to secure a fragment of what the little boy had thrown away. The fragile flower of felinity did not take rescue kindly, she wanted that cowpat.

Jane fussed all the way home, but quieted down once she got in the house and went off in a corner to sulk. Peter took his so painfully obtained fragment into the kitchen, laid it out on the saucer, pulled it apart with a couple of toothpicks, and studied it carefully. The texture was fibrous, as he'd expected, and not all the fiber was coconut.

He worked loose a fragment of the alien substance, sniffed at it, tasted it with utmost caution. He was not surprised by what he discovered. He applied healing ointment to his more spectacular wounds, tried to placate Jane, who only spat and growled, and went back to the third gingerbread house. The other cats were still fighting over the crumbs, a few were trying to climb up on the counter and being shooed down. The few early visitors were gawking in wonder, the workers were looking nonplussed.

"I don't know what's got into them," stammered the youngest student, a young woman whose eyes were wide and whose mobcap was sadly awry. "They've never acted like this before."

"I expect they've never had occasion to," said Peter. "Who brought in the latest batch of cowpats?"

The girl stared at the pile on the counter, her two workmates stared at her. Peter looked at all three. Balaclava was not a large college. Faculty and students got to know each other pretty quickly; if not by name, at least by sight.

The chap in the stovepipe hat was one of Peter's own seniors. He came from Maine, lived in the dorms, and worked in the greenhouses when he wasn't in class or peddling cowpats. The other young woman, also a senior, was majoring in botany. She also lived in the dorms, her botanical notebooks were works of art. She was possessed of a comfortable trust fund and she was engaged to the chap in the stovepipe hat. According to Mrs. Mouzouka of culinary arts, she was congenitally unable to boil water. She must be here because she'd wanted to stay with her fiancé or because she didn't want to go home, or both. She might have done the drawing of Dr. Svenson. She could easily have supplied the plant material. She could never in God's world have baked the cowpats.

All Peter knew about the girl with the big round eyes was that she was a freshman, she was studying culinary arts, and she didn't live in the dorms. Since there were very few rental apartments around town, and those few all grabbed up by faculty, she must either be living with her own family or boarding with somebody else's. Peter's face grew as stern as he could make it with one of the Enderbles' half-grown kittens crawling up his pant leg.

"All right, you three, come clean. Whose idea was it to bake those cowpats?"

"C-cowpats?" stammered the freshman. "I don't know what you're talking about."

"This critter does." Peter set the young cat on the counter; it headed straight for the oversized compote that held the cowpats. "You might as well give him one. You can't sell them, you know."

The male senior reached for one of the cowpats, smelled it and took a gingerly nibble. "It does taste—Kathy, this isn't funny! You could get us all pinched and the Illumination shut down."

"Gerry, what are you talking about?" snapped his fiancée. She grabbed the cowpat, nibbled, made a face, and burst into laughter. "You idiot, don't you know cannabis from catnip? Clarice, have you any thoughts on the matter?"

Clarice had no thought but burst into tears. Peter reached over and touched her arm.

"I think you'd better come along with me, Miss—"

"S-s-s-sissler. Am I under arrest?"

"Not at all. I have no authority to arrest anybody, we just need to talk. Miss Bunce"—he'd finally remembered the senior woman's name—"perhaps you'd be good enough to come with us. Can you manage alone for a few minutes, Pascoe?"

"I guess so, Professor," the male member of the group replied. "If you wouldn't mind impounding the evidence, maybe those cats would go away. I think this kitten's about to throw up on the counter."

"An excellent suggestion, Pascoe. I assume you have something to put the cowpats in. Come on, kitty, I'd better take you home. Are you ladies ready to go?"

"K-kathy doesn't need to c-come," sniffled the wretched

Miss Sissler. "Sh-she didn't do anything."

"That's all right, Clarice," said Miss Bunce. "I don't mind."

"Well, I d-do."

"All right then, if that's how you feel."

With a toss of her mobcap, Miss Bunce began rearranging the counter. Followed by a number of disappointed cats, Peter delivered the kitten to Mrs. Enderble, then led his weeping semi-captive away to the nearest dumpster and thence to the faculty dining room. He wasn't about to take a young female student into his own house now that she'd refused a chaperone, not with Helen gone. He'd assumed the dining room would be all but deserted at this hour, and it was. Nobody was around, except a student waiter who came somewhat reluctantly out to take their order.

"Now then, Miss Sissler," said Peter, "what would you like? Tea? Coffee? Hot chocolate?"

"S-strychnine, please."

"Come now, it's not that bad. Two coffees, please, and a couple of muffins. Just plain ones, not your holiday specials." Peter didn't feel up to snippets of red and green candied cherries this morning.

Neither of them said anything more until after the waiter had brought their coffee and corn muffins and gone back to whatever culinary beguilements awaited him in the kitchen. Peter waited until the lachrymose freshman had creamed and sugared her coffee and taken a timid sip.

"Now then, Miss Sissler, would you care to explain?"

She shook her head frantically. Tears welled again in the big round eyes. "I can't, Professor Shandy. Truly I can't."

"Young woman, are you by any chance trying to be a heroine? Here, have a muffin and tell me whom you're covering up for. Is it your boyfriend?"

"No!"

"Is somebody blackmailing you into trying to wreck the Illumination?"

"No."

"Then can you tell me why in Sam Hill you pulled such a stupid stunt? Did you think it was marijuana you were putting in those infernal objects?"

"Y-yes."

"Where did it come from?"

"I f-found it."

"Where?"

"Hanging up."

"Hanging up where?"

"In the k-kitchen."

"Whose kitchen? Not the college's?"

"Of course not! Mrs. Mouzouka wouldn't—"

"No, I don't suppose she would. Come on, Miss Sissler, let's get this over with. I have exams to correct. And you have a fresh batch of cowpats to bake, strictly according to the standard recipe, disgusting though it may be. The college is counting on you, drat it. Where do you do your cooking? You don't live in the dorms, do you? Where are your people?"

"In F-florida. I'm staying with my great-aunt, here in Balaclava Junction."

"She being—?"

"Miss Viola Harp. You know her. She calligraphs the college diplomas."

"Does she indeed? I'm afraid I can't quite place her."

"Nobody can! Nobody cares. That's why she—"

Miss Sissler essayed another sip of her coffee, and choked on it. As Peter watched her coughing into her napkin, a great light dawned. He took the three bogus twenties out of his

261

wallet and spread them on the table.

"That's why she got sore enough at the college to do this?"

Yet once more, Miss Sissler fell to sobbing.

"All right, Miss Sissler. Would you kindly explain why your aunt's venture into counterfeiting inspired you to perpetrate an even more harebrained machination? What did she do it for, anyway? Is she desperately hard up?"

"She has enough to get by on. Just about. But that's not why. She did it because nobody pays any attention to her. Nobody ever has. She's been calligraphing the college diplomas for twenty-seven years, and not once, not one single time, has anybody ever come up to her and told her what a lovely job she did. She drew that little picture of the administration building for the college stationery, and nobody even said how nice it was. And it is nice! It's just lovely! And I think you're a bunch of old pigs and I don't blame her one bit, and it serves you right. And I was on the booth last night when she came up, and I stood right there when Kathy took the money from her and didn't notice it wasn't real, and I didn't say one word. And I'd do it again! Again, do you hear me!"

"I hear you, Miss Sissler. Is Miss Harp planning an again?"

"S-she said she'd go on till somebody noticed, no matter what. Aunt Viola's determined to get some recognition for her work, even if she has to go to jail for it. And I don't blame her! I'll go with her. Go ahead, Professor Shandy, arrest me!"

"Sorry, Miss Sissler, I've already explained that I'm not a campus cop. To repeat my question, what made you decide on the catnip cowpats? And what made you think your aunt would have marijuana in the house? Does she smoke it?"

"Of course not, she'd rather die. I just thought—oh, I don't know what I thought. A kid in Florida had some pot once and I thought maybe Aunt Viola had picked some by accident. She likes to pick things and hang them up to dry; she thinks it looks picturesque. The stuff was there and I used it. All right, so I flunked botany. It's the college's fault, not mine. I never wanted to take botany in the first place. You and your dumb old curriculum!"

"Very well, Miss Sissler, I'll accept full culpability on behalf of the college if you'll tell me what gave you the bright idea of hurling yourself into the breach."

"It was that notice they sent around yesterday from Security, about watching out for counterfeit money. I knew then that Aunt Viola's work had been noticed, and they were out to get her. And it was all very well for her to say she wouldn't mind going to jail, but she'd hate it really. Aunt Viola's not young, you know, and she—well, she likes things nice. She'd miss her canary and her goldfish and I just think she'd die! And I do love her so. So I thought if I put marijuana in the cowpats it would make a stink and take Security's mind off the counterfeit bills."

"It never occurred to you that you yourself might get caught? Or that your being arrested might be even harder on your aunt?"

"Oh, no, why would they have arrested me? I mean, lots of people bake for the Illumination, they're always bringing stuff. It could have been anybody. Well, maybe not just anybody. Anyway, I was going to make up this story about this mysterious stranger wearing a ski mask who—I guess I wasn't very smart, was I? So what are you going to do, Professor Shandy?"

"I'm going to finish my coffee and pay the check."

"And then what?"

"Trust me, Miss Sissler. You may wish to do something about your face before we go. Your aunt will be at home this time of day, will she?"

"No! Oh my God, I forgot! She'll be coming up here to pass another bill. She said she was going to try it in broad daylight this time, because nobody's noticed the last two times and she thought it might be on account of the dark and all those crazy colored lights. Come on, we've got to head her off!"

Pausing only long enough for Miss Sissler to dip her napkin in her water glass and mop the tear streaks off her face and for Peter to leave some money on the table, they rushed forth into the by now fairly thickly touristed Illumination area. The cats were all gone, but a small, slight figure in an outmoded dark-green winter coat with a black astrakhan collar and a black felt hat that Peter vaguely recalled having seen around the village off and on for the past couple of decades was just coming up the walkway, her eye fixed grimly on the third gingerbread house.

"There she is!" cried Miss Sissler. "Hurry!"

He travels fastest who travels alone. Peter left the mobcapped freshman to struggle through as best she might, and plunged straight through the mob, abandoning gentility in the interests of alacrity. He reached the small, slight figure about two elbows' lengths before she'd got to the fateful counter.

"Miss Harp?" Peter was again the gentleman, his hat raised, his countenance affable. "My name is Shandy. I was on my way to call on you, on behalf of the college. I expect this is a bad time to come asking a favor, but I'd be very grateful if you could spare me a moment. Ah, here's your niece. Miss Sissler, would you join us? I wonder if you'd both do me the honor of stepping over to my house? It's that little red brick one over there. I'm not sure whether my wife's at home, but I know she's been wanting to meet you. She's a great admirer of your work, as are we all."

"Really?" Miss Harp wasn't too dumbfounded to forget her grievance so easily. "I don't recall anyone's ever having said so."

"M'well, Miss Harp, if the college's having depended on you for twenty-seven years in a row to calligraph its diplomas doesn't demonstrate our appreciation of your talents, I'd like to know what does. Which brings me to my purpose in seeking you out. Mind the step here, it may be a bit slippery. Would you care to remove your coat?"

"Why, I . . ."

Peter didn't press her. Miss Harp was like a canary herself, he thought, tiny and fragile and easily fluttered. When she unbent far enough to loosen her top button, he wasn't at all surprised to see that she wore an old-fashioned lace collar, pinned with a small gold locket-brooch that had a pressed violet inside. Of course a frail creature like this couldn't go to jail, he'd better get down to business before she started beating her wings at the windows.

"Perhaps we'll go into the dining room, if you don't mind. It will be easier for you to write at the table. I'm going to ask for your autograph."

"My-my autograph?"

"If you'll be so kind." Peter took the three twenties from his wallet and laid them out in front of her.

"As I'm sure you realize, Miss Harp, these three bills are going to be valuable collectors' items. We do appreciate your kindness in contributing them to the Illumination, but we'd have been ever happier if you'd signed them first. Could I prevail upon you to do it now? One will be for the college archives, one a Christmas gift for President Svenson, and the third, I must confess, will go into my own private collection. If you wouldn't mind? Perhaps here, above the 'Treasurer of the United States'? I hope I have a suitable pen."

Miss Harp was not too flustered to start digging in her handbag. "Oh, that's quite all right, Professor Shandy. I have my own."

It was a slim mother-of-pearl fountain pen with a gold tip, dating probably from the nineteen twenties, like its owner. With sure, deliberate strokes, Miss Viola Harp added her own tiny, perfect signature to those of the Treasurer of the United States and the Secretary of the Treasury.

"There you are, Professor Shandy. Is that what you want?"

"That's exactly what I want, Miss Harp. And now for the big one. What we're particularly hoping is that you'll sell us your master drawing, which is indeed masterful. We want to have it framed, in gold if that can be managed in time, and present it to the president and his wife at a reception which will be held on"—he sneaked a quick glance through the door toward the kitchen calendar—"the eighteenth of February. We'd want the drawing signed, of course, and we further hope that you yourself might consent to attend the reception and make the presentation as a tribute to your artistry and your long association with the college. We—er—don't know what price you've put on the drawing. Would a thousand dollars be—er—adequate?"

Miss Harp was sitting up very straight now, happy as a canary with a brand-new cuttlebone. "A thousand dollars would indeed be adequate, Professor, but I should prefer to donate the portrait. This will be my return to the college for its faith and trust in me down through the years. And, yes," she added with a proud toss of her head, "I shall be pleased to attend the reception. After so many years of having seen my work presented to others by others, it will be a refreshing change to make the presentation myself. I shall deliver the portrait to you as soon as I have it properly signed and mounted."

"How remarkably good of you, Miss Harp. The committee will be delighted. We'll be getting back to you, then, with full particulars about the reception and presentation."

As soon as he and Helen had managed to think up a reasonable excuse to hold the event, settle the details, and whomp up a suitably impressive guest list. The actual reason need never be told, except of course to the president, his wife, and maybe Moira Haskins. Surprisingly, the increasing volume of revelry from the Crescent was no longer jarring on Peter's ear.

"Thank you again, Miss Harp, and a very merry Christmas to you. Miss Sissler, I expect you'd like to see your aunt safely home. I'll drop over and explain to Miss Bunce and Mr. Pascoe that you've gone home to finish your baking."

"But they won't understand!"

"They'll understand. Merry Christmas, Miss Sissler."

After one last sniffle, the freshman managed a watery smile. "Merry Christmas, Professor Shandy."

Arm in arm, the great-aunt and the great-niece went down the walkway toward the village. As Peter watched them thread their way among the merrymakers, a repentant tiger lady came to rub against his pant leg. He picked her up and tickled her behind her ears.

"Merry Christmas, Jane. If you mend your rowdy ways, maybe we'll ask Mrs. Santa Claus to bake you a nice fresh catnip cowpat."